ONE

AMERICA READS

Rediscovered Fiction and Nonfiction from Key Periods in American History

THE GREAT DEPRESSION

Little Napoleons and Dummy Directors (1933)
Being the Narrative of the Bank of United States

The Barter Lady (1934)
A Woman Farmer Sees It Through

The House of Dawn (1935)
A Novel

WORLD WAR II

The Island (1944)
A History of the First Marine Division on Guadalcanal

Robinson Crusoe, USN (1945)
The Adventures of George R. Tweed Rm1c on Japanese-Held Guam

The Bismarck Episode (1948)

THE 1950s: VISIONS OF THE FUTURE

The Flying Saucer (1950)

Limbo (1952)

One (1953)

ONE

a novel by david karp

WESTHOLME
Yardley

Westholme Publishing, LLC
904 Edgewood Road
Yardley, Pennsylvania 19067
Visit our Web site at www.westholmepublishing.com

First Printing: September 2010
10 9 8 7 6 5 4 3 2 1

ISBN: 978-1-59416-128-5

Printed in the United States of America.

for my son
ethan ross karp

ONE

1

The faculty dining hall was built in the ancient collegiate
tradition, with high, oak-paneled walls and thin, cleresto-
ried windows providing the major source of light. In the
renovating period of the last president of the college fluorescent lamps had been built into the high ceilings to
make the room brighter, but time and dust and the death
of a thousand insects whose bodies were trapped between
the lamps and the diffusing glass had brought the dining
hall back to its original gloom and dimness. Because of
that, Burden had to look twice before he could be sure
who had made the remark.

The remark had been made by someone at the art table. Of that much he was certain. He had not been listening and because he hadn't, he felt a sense of guilt. His
mind had been taken up with other matters—softer,
quieter, more important matters. And yet it was important that he listen. It was most important. He had been
told where to sit in the dining hall to take full advantage of the room's peculiar acoustics. He was expected to

hear everything, and yet he had missed the identity of the speaker who had made the remark. It was unfortunate. He was being negligent in his duty and it was not the first time it had happened. His own negligence disturbed and puzzled him. He must make the effort to discover who, at the art table, had made the remark. Of what use were all his instruction and training if he did not remain alert? Even the talent he possessed, so carefully developed and practiced, was useless unless he remained alert.

It was an odd talent for a professor of English. If his colleagues had been told about it some might have smiled, others would have frowned, and some would have been frightened. None, however, would ever forget that Burden could read lips and all would act accordingly.

Burden was a slight man in his early forties. He stooped slightly so that people generally mistook him for a short man, which he was not. In his youth his nickname had been "Red" and even now there were some who still called him that. But the years had thinned and faded the reddish-blond hair, faded the freckles on his face, bleached the fine blond hair on his hands and in his beard. He wore rimless glasses for reading, but reading so much and so often led him into the habit of leaving his glasses on all the time. They gave him a mild, detached look. Added to his gentle, deliberate, and calm manner of speaking you were led, almost inevitably, to guess correctly his occupation. He had been a teacher almost all of his adult life and was considered a success by both his colleagues and his students. There were a few who thought he was more than a success, that he was both gifted and brilliant. While he had never done any original work in his field, he had published three books of criticism on contemporary letters which were considered definitive. His life, his work, his home in faculty row, his vividly dark wife and two sturdy sons were all familiar and known. There were some who were tempted to say there was no more to be known of Professor Burden. There were others who were uncertain; still others kept their own counsel. None, however, knew that Professor Burden read lips.

While he daintily drank his soup, his calm blue eyes regarded the plate of crackers in front of him and his ears remained sharply alert to all that was said in the room. The remark, he decided again, came from the art table. It had been spoken by a woman. The voice, too, had been unfamiliar. By the simplest elimination it meant that the girl with the rich chestnut hair and heavy, sensuous lips had made the remark. Burden reached for a cracker and in the process took a careful look at the girl. She wore a clean smock but even under its obliterative lines Burden could tell that she had a full, rich, young body. Her skin was clear and glowing even in the poor light of the hall, and when she spoke she showed large, white, faintly irregular teeth. They gave her long, square face a rather interesting cast. The light in the room placed shadows on her cheeks so that her face seemed to have a slightly caved-in look of hunger or mystery or sensuality. The rest of the art staff seated with her at the table was composed of rather delicate young men who sat up with self-conscious straightness and ate their food with gestures and deliberation that suggested the well-bred public manners of young women. By contrast to the men of her own age around the table the girl seemed earthy, perhaps even coarse.

"I'm sick to death of literal transcription . . ." Burden read the girl's lips as saying to the rest of the table. "For once in my life I want to do something that isn't photographic. You know, art wasn't always a line-for-line representation of things as they seem to be. There used to be—"

11

Burden missed the word, "—men like Picasso and Mondrian and . . ." Burden recognized none of the names except that of Picasso. Early- and middle-twentieth century painter, Burden decided. But he knew little about him. Someone crossed between Burden and the diners at the art table and he missed more of what the girl said. When again he could see her she was not speaking. Burden turned to Doctor Middleton, a colleague in the English department, and asked, "Who's that striking girl over there with the art people?"

"I didn't think you'd notice," Middleton said with a smile.

"Very interesting face," Burden said calmly. "Is she new?"

"Oh, yes. Came on staff at mid-term, I think. Damned good-looking wench, isn't she? Too bad she won't find much personal outlet with that crew." Middleton smiled. Burden turned slightly away from his colleague with a faint sense of distaste.

"You don't happen to know her name?"

"Drake." Middleton regarded Burden with a mischievous smile. "Would you like an introduction?"

"No, no, no," Burden said, ill at ease and somewhat hurriedly. Middleton laughed richly at having annoyed Burden.

"Wouldn't you even care for one quick roll in the hay?" Middleton asked, his eyes aglint with an oblique look of pleasure. Burden shook his head impatiently and rose before Middleton could speak again. He didn't quite understand the meaning of the expression, which he knew was archaic English, but Middleton's tone and glance were unmistakably smutty.

Burden made his way through the dining hall, nodding here and there to colleagues, friends, and acquaintances.

At the cashier's desk he signed the charge book for his meal and went out into the long hall. A chill seized him the moment he left the dining room. The halls were never properly heated or ventilated and complaints to the administrative offices were always followed by severe notices posted in the common rooms that began, "*The present heating plants of the college are sufficient to provide, during the months of September through March, an average mean indoor temperature of 68.5 degrees F . . .*" Members of the physics department had taken over a thousand different temperature readings in all parts of the college at one time or another in order to prove that nowhere was the temperature an average mean of 68.5 degrees during school hours. But the school custodian chewed his toothpick, narrowed his eyes, and insisted that it was. What followed then was the notice in the common rooms. It was an exasperating and sometimes silly business that led one physics department lecturer to complain bitterly. Burden had occasion to remember the remark verbatim.

"In God's name," the instructor had said, "who are they going to believe about the temperature—a group of scientists or that ignorant, thick-witted Mallon? Don't we qualify as authorities against that vegetable?" Burden had remembered the remark as a major heresy. For one thing, the custodian was called "a vegetable"—an unconscious revelation of that physics instructor's thinking and social attitudes. If the custodian represented something less than human to the instructor then it meant that the instructor harbored a sizable resentment against members of the custodian's class. It was the official attitude of the State that all labor was dignified and that there was no distinction between the work the custodian did and the work instructors of the physics department performed. To

13

draw the distinction between "scientists" and that "ignorant, thick-witted . . . vegetable" was to assume that the scientists were superior. Heresy, Burden noted gravely. Heresy of the first rank, since it smelled of intellectual superiority, of pretensions beyond the right of any man. This information was made part of a daily report that Burden wrote and it was quite in keeping with his job. Not as professor of English in the college but as a State spy—a job that Burden had held for nearly ten years.

2

Burden's progress across the campus was marked with salutes from the students dressed in the freshmen cloaks of gray with the distinguishing orange piping on their gowns. Burden nodded pleasantly and was careful to return the salute, since he knew an omission to do so would be noted. He knew that he was not the only police spy in the college. There were others, but he did not know who they were. It sometimes amused him to think that others were solemnly filling long daily reports on his remarks as he filled reports on theirs. Well, Burden decided cheerfully, all in a good cause.

He had few classes for the rest of the day and was glad of it because a smoky, chill fall rain was coming down— precisely the sort of weather he enjoyed at home in his room with the fireplace going and his books about him. Mrs. Burden would have a good, hot meal for him and for his sons at dinner and then he would retire to his room to make out his report. Following the report he could settle down with some of the tattered copies of special books he kept locked in a special drawer. They were books no longer available for general use and the only copies in mint condition were in a locked display at the capital. He, along with Mrs. Burden and the boys, had seen them four years ago on a visit during a summer holiday. The books were part of an exhibit group called "Minor Political Thinkers XIXth & XXth Centuries." Burden recognized many things in the books as mild heresies. But they were coated with the patina of dated quaintness and could no longer be taken seriously. He felt only slightly guilty when he read them.

Burden finished his classes and then went to his conference cubicle to await students. Nothing of importance was being said in class these days. Students seemed so unwilling to do any original thinking, Burden thought a little sadly. He got back in discussion precisely what he had given them. It recalled to his mind something Doctor Middleton had said, about college being the place where knowledge was uttered by the teacher and heard by the student without going through the minds of either. It was a typical Middleton remark and Burden felt that it was probably not originally Middleton's at all. He felt annoyed with Middleton and for an instant wished that Middleton would utter a heretical remark so that he would have occasion to put him in the report. Burden suddenly caught himself up short and his blue eyes grew worried as he unconsciously glanced about the cubicle. It was a foolish thing to even think. The report was not intended to be a punitive weapon. Burden's superiors had made their feelings particularly clear on that point. The report was precisely what it meant—a significant record of the attitudes, thoughts, and expressions of students and faculty of the college. It had nothing to do with the punishment of heresy. *Punishment.* Burden shook his head again at his own stupidity. There was no punishment. Punishment, punitive—odd the way the concept kept cropping up in his thinking. That was all done with. It no longer existed as a socially accepted concept. Odd, Burden thought, and felt a vague uneasiness that he did not understand.

The first of the students came in to interrupt his train of thought. Mr. Fulver, freshman English. Bad spelling, stilted construction, a fairly sterile young man. Burden looked at Fulver.

"We seem to be having difficulties, Mr. Fulver," he said to the pupil. The young man nodded and Burden noticed that the boy's eyes were slightly out of alignment. He had a weak chin, a nest of blackheads around his nose and under his eyes like lines of fatigue. His legs were twisted awkwardly around the supports of the chair and his heavy, foolish lips were partially opened. Adenoidal breathing, too. Poor devil, Burden thought. Probably miserable at college. Burden's eyes fell on the boy's class card. A quota student. It partly explained the bad spelling. The local schools weren't strong on the academic techniques. They stressed co-operation and obedience. Fine things in themselves, but they didn't add up to good spelling. "Happy here, Mr. Fulver?" Burden asked with a faint, kindly smile.

"Yes, sir," Fulver replied, somewhat guarded.

"Find the work difficult, Mr. Fulver?"

The uncertain eyes moved uncertainly and Burden thought they seemed more out of alignment than ever.

"Fulver'll catch it, sir," Fulver finally managed.

"No doubt about that, Fulver. No doubt about that at all," Burden said with a heartiness he did not feel. He looked again at Fulver's paper and a silence fell between student and instructor, a silence that seemed deeper be-

17

cause of the cramped space of the chamber and the gloom that the desk lamp failed to dispel.

"Bad, isn't it, sir?" Fulver asked unexpectedly, looking at his paper.

"Oh, no, not at all," Burden assured the boy. "I've seen worse. Much worse. You mustn't lose confidence in yourself. Your spelling's a little—er—uneven and there could be a little more freedom in the way you write, but your ideas are clearly presented, in a logical and orderly manner and er—" Burden cast about for some more encouraging words and suddenly said, "and you have a very pleasant handwriting." He was instantly sorry he had said it and almost bit off his tongue for the inanity of his remark. But Fulver seemed deeply pleased and smiled a ragged, toothy smile.

"Penmanship was Fulver's best subject, sir," Fulver said with a pride that was unmistakable.

"Was it?" Burden asked, pleased, leaning forward with interest. Odd, the way you struck a chord in a boy quite without intention.

"Oh, yes, sir. Teachers used to say that there was no one who wrote a prettier hand than Mr. Fulver," he said.

"Ah," Burden said, nodding, smiling, finding something obliquely charming in the way the boy referred to himself in the third person. He was probably of a Church of State family. It was a mark of that group. They all spoke of themselves in the third person as if they did not exist by themselves but only as part of a third group. *Me, my, I, mine* did not exist in the language of the Church of State families. They were very highly thought of in official circles. Some of the top administrators of the nation, as well as most of the convicted criminals, were members of the Church of State. Burden knew few State Churchers. There were none on the faculty and only about a fifth of the students were of that persuasion, although he had heard somewhere that the freshman class for the following year was composed almost entirely of them.

"If it were just penmanship, sir, Mr. Fulver wouldn't be too scared," he said.

"There's nothing to be scared of, Fulver," Burden said. "You won't be asked to do more than you can."

"Yes, sir, that's understood."

"The aim of education in the colleges is not to burden you with any arbitrary goals, Fulver. You understand that, don't you? You learn the best you can and I'll be satisfied."

"Yes, sir."

"You'll try, won't you?"

"Oh, yes, sir."

"Good lad," Burden said, clipping together the pages of Fulver's theme. He knew the boy was telling the truth. They were reliable, State Churchers. It was one of their great virtues. "Study the words you've misspelled. I've noted them with their correct spellings. Read what you've written aloud and see if it is difficult to read. The mark of good writing is that it can be read aloud easily. All right, Fulver?"

"Yes, sir," Fulver said, rising and accepting his theme from Burden. As soon as Fulver left the cubicle, Doctor Middleton poked his head in. He was smoking one of those small, black cigars he affected so much.

"Hello, Burden—about done for the day?"

"About," Burden said, tidying up the papers on his desk.

"That was a grisly specimen that just left," Middleton said, indicating the departing Fulver with a nod.

"Quota boy," Burden said calmly.

"Ugh," Middleton said and Burden checked his feeling

of distaste. "Sluggish little vermin. You can't get things into their heads without pounding. When I was a student things were quite different. You didn't get to college unless you had the mental capacity to absorb the instruction."

"We're all born with the same mental capacities," Burden said flatly.

"What?" Middleton asked with great surprise, taking the cigar out of his mouth.

"I thought it was a scientifically accepted fact that all men were born equal," Burden went on, eyeing Middleton with a look of severity. Doctor Middleton surveyed his colleague for a moment, started to speak, but then thought better of it and put his cigar back into his mouth.

"Oh, well, yes," Middleton finally said through the cigar, "I suppose practically speaking you're right. We're all made much the same way, livers to brains. It's the development that counts." Middleton chewed on his cigar thoughtfully. "Still, these quota kids don't seem to be as sharp and up to snuff the way the others are." Middleton looked at Burden again as if to judge the effect of his words and then went on, in a softer tone. "But, of course, as I said—it's all a matter of development. These quota kids generally come from substandard local schools. They don't get the chances."

"Yes," Burden said, nodding his head. Unfortunately, Middleton had uttered an important heresy. It would have to be reported.

Conferences over for the day, Burden stuffed his brief case full and came out of the building into the foggy, smoky rain that was coming down, coating the needles of the pine trees planted along the walks. The college buildings huddled wet in the gloom and darkness of the fall evening, occasionally glistening in response to a touch of light from a window, a door opened for a moment. Burden was going home with a feeling of satisfaction, a day completed, a productive evening ahead. His coat was buttoned against the cold and his hat was well down over his forehead, but fog still misted over his glasses so that from time to time he had to stop to wipe them clear.

When he got to his house he found it as well lit, warm, and inviting as he had recalled it during the day. Mrs. Burden smilingly helped him out of his coat.

"Weather like this is going to bother your arm," she said, touching his elbow.

"Oh, no, it mustn't. I've got a lot of work to do tonight, Emma," Burden said.

"Never mind," she patted him fondly, "I'll rub some of that ointment on it before you go to bed. That is, if you come to bed at a reasonable hour. I'm not going to wait up the night."

"I promise," Burden patted her cheek, "a reasonable hour. Or, as my Mr. Fulver would say—Burden promises a reasonable hour."

"Fulver?" Emma Burden asked as she hung up her husband's coat, hat, and muffler.

"A freshman student of mine. State Churcher."

Emma looked at her husband uneasily for a moment and then asked, "We're getting an awful lot of State Churchers into the school, aren't we, dear?"

"Not particularly, Emma," Burden said, looking at his wife's face. When she started to speak again Burden had a presentiment of danger and hurriedly interrupted, "I'll wash up a bit before dinner. The boys are ready for theirs, I suppose?"

"Oh, yes," she smiled, "they've been growling about food for hours now. You know."

"Well, nothing gets as hungry as a fifteen-year-old boy,"

Burden said with a smile. "I'll go and wash now." Burden hurried off to the bathroom with fear dogging at his mind. In the privacy of the bathroom he looked at himself in the mirror. Why hadn't he let Emma go on with what she wanted to say? Was it because he knew she was going to utter a heresy? Burden looked at himself more closely in the mirror. Her heresies could not interest the administration. She was not an intellectual, not a maker of the culture, not a manager, not a contributor to the informed climate of opinion. She was just a woman—a mother, a wife, a gentle, loving person who had nothing to do with the affairs of the country.

Burden sat down on the edge of the tub, his mind troubled. He could keep Emma safe as long as he lived. It was the boys. How many heresies had the boys heard from her? How many had they repeated?

He shook his head against the thoughts that crowded into it. Even if heresies had been reported against them nothing would be done to harm them. Harm? Hurt? Punish, punishment, punitive—again and again during the day the words came to mind. What could he be thinking even to let such words enter his thoughts? There was no punishment. Burden's face tightened. How often did it have to be explained? There was no punishment. It had been abolished as a social and official concept nearly three decades ago, when he was just a boy. No one was punished—not for anything. People whose thinking was antisocial, heretical, were adjusted—by therapy, psychoanalysis, instruction, and understanding. In time the roots of their heresy, their antisocial thinking were torn up, exposed to the light, and withered. That was the concept of the State—no man was outside the fold of mankind. Wrongdoing stemmed from wrong precepts. You did not whip a flower for growing crookedly toward the sun.

You tied it to a stick gently for guidance upward. Punishment was dead, gone and forgotten in the civilization of free men. Sin no longer existed—merely error. And errors could be, *must* be corrected. It was the benevolent age in which they lived. He understood that. He believed it. Then what was there to fear? No one would hurt the boys. Burden got up from the tub's edge, annoyed with himself. Again the word *hurt*.

At dinner Burden kept a sharp eye on his two sons. Mark, the younger, bubbled with laughter; more than once Burden found himself smiling at the boy.

"I wish I were let in on the joke," Burden said.

"Don't ask him, Dad," Paul said disgustedly. "It's idiotic."

"Oh, p-p-please ask me, Dad," Mark said, stammering with laughter.

"Shut up!" Paul exploded angrily.

"Paul," Emma Burden remonstrated with a frown.

"That isn't a polite way to speak, Paul," Burden said calmly. Paul seemed upset, so Burden signaled Mark to stop. The younger boy finally did, choking on his food several times. The rest of the meal was eaten in silence and Mark, cautioned against bolting his food, did so anyway and hurried from the table. He made some remark to his brother as he hurried off and Paul sprang up, knocking over the chair to chase him.

"Paul!" Burden cried after his eldest son, but it was too late. Paul streaked after Mark and the cries of the two boys were carried upstairs and out of hearing.

"If you ask me, Mark deserves the thrashing he's going to get," Emma said, beginning to clear the dishes away.

"What's it all about?"

"Why, a girl," Emma said, faintly surprised that he didn't know.

"A girl?"

"Paul's been rather sweet on a girl named Erna—"
Burden frowned thoughtfully.

"Erna Fellowes," Emma said when she saw the name meant nothing to her husband, "Dr. Fellowes' daughter. You've seen her. She's all pink and white and *lithps*," Emma said, exaggerating the lisp.

"Oh, yes."

"Paul is love-sick over that little nitwit and wrote some poems to her. Mark, unfortunately, found them. You know what savages twelve-year-old boys can be. The poems are painted on rocks scattered all over the place."

"Paul painted the poems on the rocks?" Burden asked with astonishment.

"Heavens, no! Mark and his friends did."

"Oh," Burden said with an understanding smile. "I suppose they're the usual love poems?"

"The usual—sticky, silly, and oh, so sentimental."

"How awful for Paul," Burden said with a grin. "I hope he doesn't kill his brother." There were several loud thumps on the ceiling above and Emma nodded.

"That's Mark calling for help. Well, he won't get it from me. Not for a while. Let him learn what it means to betray the secrets of others. It's time he learned that there are still some sacred things left in the world."

Burden's eyebrows knit. The remark smacked uncomfortably of heresy. "Emma, if Paul is in love with this Erna he shouldn't hide it. He should be proud of it. There's nothing wrong in writing love poetry to a girl you admire."

"Good grief, you're not suggesting that Mark was right?"

"No," Burden said deliberately, "I am merely saying that you are wrong." Emma Burden looked at her husband for a long moment.

24

"Darling—" Emma began, and again Burden felt the prickle of danger and interrupted.

"The meal was delicious, Emma. I think I'll go up and separate the mortal combatants so that I can get to work in peace."

"That's the second time this evening you've kept me from saying something," Emma Burden said calmly.

"Forgive me, dear," Burden said gently, "I didn't mean to be rude. If you'll excuse me—" and he left before she could speak again.

There was no need to separate Mark and his brother. They were both resting on the floor exhausted, flushed, and breathing hard. Mark had his shirt collar torn and there was a scratch on Paul's cheek. Burden told them to stop their rowdyism and apologize to one another. Both boys, flat on their backs, nodded breathlessly and said it was all settled. Burden retired to his room with a smile.

3

A tidy man, Burden sat down to his report at precisely
eight o'clock. He was generally able to finish the report in
an hour, which gave him time to read it again leisurely
and then take it down to the letter box in time for the
last pickup at ten thirty. That meant that the report would
be in his reader's hands at nine in the morning. Burden
had often wondered which of the dozens of girls who sat
in the small, glassed-in booths read his reports. He had
only once seen the reading rooms and their quiet had impressed him. There were perhaps fifty young girls reading reports constantly. Occasionally he would see a pencil
note made, or a girl referring to a thick bound volume, but
aside from that the activity was entirely devoted to the
reports. Surely the girl who read his report must know a
great deal about him, Burden thought. For nearly ten
years he had made daily reports of a thousand words or
more. They represented a staggering total of words—
nearly four million of them, describing the lives and activities of his college and all who lived and worked in it.

Combine those with the reports of a hundred, a thousand, ten thousand, a hundred thousand other informers like himself, and the accumulated picture of the intellectuals of the nation would be overwhelming. Burden shook his head in awe. The Department of Internal Examination was a huge organization. And yet this ponderous body, with its thousands of employees and hundreds of buildings and acres of vaults and files and libraries, turned on two small jeweled pivots—justice and benevolence. It held four to six trials for heresy a year and its court had never been known to condemn a defendant. It was a remarkably pure and fair organ of government. While scandal and corruption might be breathed against other bodies of the government, the Department of Internal Examination had always held a spotless reputation—detached from politics, incorruptible, the greatest bastion of intellectual liberty and individual freedom in the world. And his reports formed part of that organization's immense libraries. He was a tiny contributor to the huge block of pure, scientific benevolence of the Department. Burden smiled faintly. It was quite a role.

He smoothed out the official report form in front of him, filled in the heading with his name, his address, his professional position, his age, the day, month, and year. The report form was typical of the Department—it eschewed all mysterious coding symbols and numbers. Directly beneath the heading was a heavy line and the single printed sentence that read: "Begin your report here." As simple as that.

"Today, in the faculty dining room, I had occasion to overhear—" Burden paused, trying to select from the conversations he had overheard the most significant details. There had been Professor Kloetter's remark concerning the tendency of professional journals to "popularize" and

27

"vulgarize" scholarly reports. Yes, Burden decided, that would do well for a beginning. He started to write again.

Burden's pen moved slowly and deliberately. Only now and then did he hesitate over the proper word. When he came to the discussion around the art table Burden stopped. There was Miss Drake's remark. Was it worth reporting? Burden put down his pen and looked at his report. He had more important things to deal with than Miss Drake's complaint against literal art. There was all that Doctor Middleton had to say about quota students and State Churchers. Those were far more important heresies. And then Miss Drake was young, newly admitted to the faculty. Would it be fair for him to place her remark on the report? After all, the remark had been made casually, without heat, without great conviction. It seemed unfair to give the same stress both to Miss Drake's minor heresy and to Doctor Middleton's far more serious heresies. Did he not have a certain obligation to be selective? He was asked to report significant detail—not every detail. Burden thought again of her rich chestnut hair and the heavy, sensuous mouth. She was young and exuberant and the remark could very well have been innocent. Middleton, however, was a far different case. He was a mature man in a high place, and his heresies were of greater importance to the nation and to the Department. And then, too, he had forgiven minor heresies in Middleton's remarks before. Middleton had gone on his report only four times in the past ten years. Burden decided in Miss Drake's favor and turned back to the sentence that read, *"At the art table a remark was made concerning the doubt of the speaker as to the desirability of literal art as opposed to the art of men like Picasso or Mondrian. By this I presume the speaker meant symbolic or expressionistic art as opposed to literal art. How-*

ever, no discussion resulted from the expression of this deliberately provocative question." Burden looked at what he had written with a faint smile of pleasure. Yes, he had managed that neatly. He hadn't failed to report Miss Drake's remark and yet she could not be pointed out as the speaker. If for any reason they decided to investigate further—well, he would have to name her. But she could always argue that she did not hold the opinion herself but merely put it forth to provoke discussion on it. The phrase, *"deliberately provocative question,"* provided Miss Drake with a neat out. Pleased with himself for this touch of gallantry, Burden turned to the subject of Doctor Middleton. *"A most serious expression of heresy was made in my presence today by Doctor Alexander Middleton. I was having a conference with one of my students— an earnest, hard-working State Churcher named Fulver. Doctor Middleton came into my office just as Fulver was leaving—"*

The report was completed by a few minutes past ten. Because he was anxious to get to the tattered, carefully hidden books he had been reading, Burden forwent the ritual of rereading what he had written. He placed his report into the thick, plain envelope, addressed it to the central office of the Department of Internal Examination, and then went downstairs. Emma was reading by the fire in the living room. She took off her glasses as she saw him go into the hall.

"Are you going out for your walk, dear?" she asked.

"Yes," Burden said, struggling into his coat. He wrapped the muffler around his neck and reached up for his hat. Emma came into the hall, carrying her book with her, her glasses in her other hand.

"It's so miserable and raw outside. Couldn't you skip your walk this once?"

"Emma, my darling, I'm a creature of habit, and creatures of habit have no more sense about their habits than do the habits themselves. I don't go out to enjoy the weather. I go out because, mysteriously enough, I get restless at this time of the night and I have to walk a little while, fair weather or foul."

Emma came forward to pull his coat more tightly about his muffler. "You're getting to act more and more like a professor every day."

"Is it so dull for you?" Burden asked kindly.

"It would be if I didn't play a little game of the mind with myself. I pretend you're going out to do something I know nothing about. Sometimes I pretend it's another woman, and sometimes I pretend it's something magical or forbidden." Emma's smile disappeared as she looked at Burden. "It's only a game, dear."

"Emma," Burden said gently, taking her into his arms, "I would never do anything wrong. You know that."

"Of course," she said warmly, "but it would be dull if I couldn't pretend that you might."

"My darling Emma," Burden said quietly, "I'm nothing more or less than the man you've known since he was nineteen."

"Are you?" she asked in a tone that Burden didn't understand. Did she suspect that he was an informer? There had never been any notes needed in his work but the mental ones. He was too well-adjusted and too healthy to talk in his sleep and he knew Emma never disturbed the papers on his desk. Then could she suspect anything? Had he been acting differently? Any differently than he had acted for ten years? Burden kissed his wife, opened the door, and stepped out into the dark, damp street. Smoke and fog curled sensually along the lampposts. A fine rain was falling, its drops so light that they floated in front of his face. He suddenly felt curiously frightened and alone, as if he were a tiny bit of aquatic life caught in a dark and cold current. There was something about him that had changed, something that Emma had noticed. But what? Burden finally came up to the mailbox. It bore a coat of rain on its official gray paint. The envelope with its report gave a thick, satisfyingly heavy crackle under his fingers as he pinched it. He hesitated before the box. Some instinct made him wonder about the report. It revealed much of the life that went on about him in the college. It reported the heresies of others. But what did it tell the reader about *him?*

With a swift, guilty gesture he pulled open the chute, inserted the letter, and closed the chute. The letter fell inside without a sound. Burden turned back toward the house, walking quickly, like a man who is not certain that he has not heard a strange and sinister sound behind him.

4

Burden's letter came in with the truckload of mail sacks and was dumped unceremoniously on the unloading platform of the Department of Internal Examination's outer perimeter building. The Department's great physical plant was built in the shape of an immense honeycomb, great circles of buildings shrinking back in against themselves like a gigantic target on the landscape. The complex and efficient sorting system routed Burden's report finally into a box labeled simply "Miss Hennessey."

At a quarter of nine in the morning a slender girl with glasses, flat heels, mousy brown hair, and a thin mouth came into the sorting room and presented her identification badge to a uniformed officer. The officer then went along the row of boxes filled with reports, selected Miss Hennessey's box, and brought it back to her.

Miss Hennessey walked to her glassed-in cubicle on flat rubber heels, her face expressionless. Once inside with the door closed she placed the reports box on her desk. After seating herself comfortably and adjusting her chair, she took all the reports out of the box and quickly, professionally stripped them flat, crimping her fingernail against the creases that their senders had put in them. She thumbed them for a moment with the deftness that a professional gambler uses on a deck of cards and began to count them. When she reached ten she pulled out the tenth report and tossed it aside without glancing at the name of the sender. It was Burden's.

Carefully she aligned the remaining reports. Satisfied with their alignment, she turned her cold, blue-eyed attention to Burden's report, but only long enough to attach to it a small red plastic tab. Then she placed it in a long envelope large enough to accommodate it in its freshly flattened state.

The envelope containing Burden's report was placed on her desk, comfortably apart from all else. The legend on the envelope read "Special Service." There the envelope remained until ten o'clock in the morning when a bright, handsome young man wearing a long linen duster came in after ceremoniously rapping on the door. Miss Hennessey favored the young man with a brief, mechanical smile. The young man picked up the envelope for Special Service and left.

At Building Four of the Department's concentric rings of buildings, the young man with the linen duster got off the intrabuilding shuttle and took an elevator to the sixth floor. He stepped smartly out into the long corridor and headed without hesitation to his right. At an ordinary frosted glass door he paused for a moment to adjust his tie and went in. Here three girls worked constantly at electric typewriters and one sat in front of a teletype machine, sipping coffee and smoking a cigarette. A receptionist got up with a smile and took the reports that the young man handed her.

"Looks like it might snow," the young man said to the receptionist as he turned and left.

"Oh, it's too early for snow. It's only the middle of October!" she called after him. Then she turned with the reports to a row of small, partitioned offices at the end of the room. She knocked at the first, poked her head in, and then handed over an envelope. She did the same at each of the offices until she had given out all four envelopes. The envelope containing Burden's report was given to a man named Conger. Conger accepted the envelope from the receptionist with a smile and a nod and tossed it negligently on his desk.

Conger was a great mountain of a man with full, rosy cheeks, a rather small mouth, and a generous bulb of a nose. His eyes were shrewd but not unkindly. He fussed trying to light an ancient, fat-bowled pipe with an exceedingly well-bitten and short stem. Finally having lit it and drawing upon it heavily so that clouds of gray smoke filled the small, crowded room and drifted over the top of the partition wall, he pulled over the envelope containing Burden's report. He opened the clasp that held the flap down and shook the envelope gently so that the top portion of the report came out, bearing Burden's name, profession, age, address, and the date on which the report had been made.

Conger dropped the report with its envelope back onto his desk and, still nursing the light in his pipe, reached out a heavy foot, hooked it around a leg of the dictation machine, and pulled the machine on its casters closer to him. Conger's cheeks puffed and shrank as he worked to keep the pipe drawing. With his free hand he groped for the small hand speaker on the machine. Finally he nodded with satisfaction about the pipe's drawing power and propped it comfortably into a corner of his mouth.

Consulting the name on the heading of the report, Conger dictated into the softly humming machine his first letter of the day.

"To Professor Burden, Templar College, Templar. Sir. You are instructed to report to the Special Service Detail Office, Building Four, sixth floor, on Monday, October 12, at 10 A.M. Transportation costs borne by you in connection with travel requested by the Department will be reimbursed to you upon application. Signed, Frank Conger, Special Service Detail Officer." Conger shook the envelope so that the report fell back into it. He marked the envelope with the date and time of Burden's appointment in his office and then pulled over his large day book, thumbed forward a few pages, and marked Burden's name and the time of the appointment on the page headed Monday, October 12. That done, he placed the envelope inside a drawer and closed the drawer with his knee. There the envelope containing Burden's report rested, unmarked, unread, untouched until a few moments before Burden appeared to meet Mr. Frank Conger on Monday, the twelfth of October.

5

The twelfth of October was one of those hard, bright fall mornings that wakes the senses, sharpens the appetite, and makes one voluptuously pleased to be alive. Burden had left the house in fine spirits, mysteriously tickled to be away from the routine of the college for a day, like a schoolboy who has been suddenly presented with a holiday. The letter had said nothing about secrecy but Burden had decided not to tell Emma about the letter. He told her, instead, that his trip had to do with a meeting to discuss an intercollegiate seminar to be held during the spring semester. However, to the chairman of the department, Burden had to be more truthful. He showed Doctor Corning the letter and the chairman at once granted him the day off.

The trip to the Department was a pleasant three-hour ride by train that Burden would have enjoyed more had not the coach he was riding in been so overheated and overcrowded with commuters to the intermediate stops. By the time Burden reached his destination he was partially put out by the pushing and hauling and crowding. But the moment he stepped off the train his good humor returned with the rush of crisp, sunlit air that came up from the station. He inquired about a taxi but was told he could walk to the Department's buildings if he was not too much in a hurry.

The walk was delightful, through winding, carefully kept streets with neat, small homes, their long, rolling lawns raked clean of leaves. Here and there he caught the smell of burning leaves and the comforting sounds of dogs and children. The sight of the outer perimeter building of the Department was completely out of keeping with the pleasant, quiet view of the town. Its marble and glass walls rose sheer and tall out of an enormous tract of land that had been completely cleared of trees. Surrounding the immense outer ring of steel, marble, and glass were grassed areas as huge as football fields. There seemed to be literally miles of paved walks repeating the concentric circle motif. The sight was quite overwhelming.

Burden's trip to Building Four, sixth floor, took only a few moments but it seemed so complex, so bewildering, so filled with long, gleaming corridors and doors and lights and people that he began to worry that he would ever be able to find his way out again.

The Special Service Detail office looked small and disappointingly plain once he was inside it. He had rather imagined that it would be a huge room filled with all sorts of complicated mechanical things, swarming with people doing mysterious and purposeful jobs, jammed to the ceilings with walls of steel files. But it was, of course, nothing of the sort.

The four tiny partitioned cubicles at one end of the room looked flimsy, and the three girls at the electric typewriters wore small, plastic ear sets with which they listened to records of dictation. The girl at the teletype machine seemed to have nothing to do but file her nails, and the receptionist was having a difficult time keeping her interest on a magazine she was reading.

Burden rested against the plain oak bench, waiting for Mr. Conger to see him although it was already ten o'clock on the electric clock on the wall opposite the bench. Ever since he had received the letter Burden had speculated upon the reason for his order to appear. He had told himself that very probably he was being called in for a routine matter. Actually, it was the first time in ten years that the Department had ever taken special and official notice of him. Burden had rejected the notion, but it still clung to the fringes of his mind, that he was being selected for a decoration of a sort—some minor, official award for ten years of service. He smiled to himself. It was the sort of thing that a bureaucratic mind might decide to do. A gold star for attendance, for good conduct, for faithful performance of duty. For some people such attention might be enormously flattering and stimulating. Burden knew that not all the Department's agents were as sophisticated as he was and might find such an award an immense honor. Well, he thought, no harm done. He would act properly appreciative and pleased and take the medal or the citation or whatever it was home and put it away in a safe place. Burden looked again at the clock. It was seven minutes past the hour for his appointment.

In one respect Burden was quite right about the reason for his visit. It was routine. His report had been the tenth received by Miss Hennessey on that morning. In twenty other cubicles twenty other readers had counted off the tenth report and the young man with the linen duster had collected twenty other envelopes marked Special Service and in twenty other small cubicles like Conger's letters had been dictated to twenty other agents instructing them to report. It was routine. But it had nothing to do with medals or citations or decorations.

Conger reached into his desk drawer and took out the envelope containing Burden's report. Again he unfastened the clasp, shook the report down so that he could read the name, the profession, the age of the correspondent. He made a few notes on a pad of paper and then took the report out of its envelope completely. For the first time he read it very quickly and made a few other notes. He flipped the appended pages of the report with a heavy hand and placed his palm flatly and lightly on its face. A long-winded man, this one, Conger decided, and rose with a sigh. He walked around his desk and pushed his door open slightly. That done, he returned to his desk, opened a drawer, and took out his pipe. He was stuffing it with tobacco when the door was opened and Burden stepped in. Conger nodded pleasantly, indicating that Burden was to take the chair opposite the desk. Burden sat down, his hat in his lap, his blue eyes watching Conger.

The lighting of the pipe and the adjustment of the draw were part of a ritual that Conger went through every morning and he skipped none of the steps. He seemed disinterested in Burden but he didn't miss the slightly condescending smile on his face, nor did he miss the relaxed manner in which he sat, his legs crossed at the ankles. This one, Conger decided, was not afraid. He was very much at ease. A little too much at ease, probably. Self-satisfied. Well, he would have to be jolted out of that.

Finally satisfied with his pipe, Conger picked up the

report and tossed it forward on his desk toward Burden.

"This is your report, Professor Burden?"

Burden picked up the report and examined it. Conger waited, watching the small details. Burden looked at the first page closely, turned the page and looked at the next and then at the next, and then at the fourth and final page. Finally he nodded with a smile and laid the report back on Conger's desk.

"Yes, sir, that's my report."

Conger grunted. Burden had touched the small red plastic tab while reading. That was significant. Sometimes the tab terrified them. Sometimes they ignored it. Those who were terrified at the sight of the tab might be anything from heretics to hysterics. Those who ignored the tab were generally too stupid to speculate upon its significance. But Burden had touched the tab. It was a faintly nervous reaction. The close examination of the pages of his own report was significant. A truly cautious man might have read the report word for word. A frightened man would have hardly glanced at it. A timid man might have acknowledged it at once. Burden, evidently, was not any of these. He was sure of himself. But not quite as sure as he was at the moment he had entered the office. The tab had thrown him off slightly. If there had been no tab he might not have examined the report so closely. Perhaps he was now beginning to suspect that there was something wrong with this report. Good, Conger decided.

Conger picked up the report and weighed it in his hand and then turned his eyes on it. Slowly, deliberately, he turned its pages. It was an old, probing trick. Conger was not reading the report. He was listening for any slight changes of position Burden might make in his chair. There were several creaks and a slur of shoes on the floor. Conger was satisfied. The trick had worked. He had made Burden uncomfortable, faintly uneasy. That was better. You could not work well with a man who was too sure of himself.

"Professor Burden," Conger said quietly as he put down the report, "have you any idea why we should call you here?"

"Why, no."

"Really?"

"No, of course not. Your letter didn't say why I was to report."

"Haven't you had some thoughts as to the reason you were asked to report?"

"Well, yes, of course, I have had some thoughts."

"Such as what thoughts?"

"Well, I don't know."

"Don't you want to tell me?"

"Of course I want to tell you. I mean, if you really want to hear them. I was probably wrong, anyway."

"What were those thoughts?"

"I—" Burden shifted slightly in his chair, "I had the rather naive idea that I was going to be—complimented, officially, for my work."

"Now, that's interesting. How complimented?"

"Well, you know what I mean—a medal or a certificate," Burden said, flushing now that he had said it outright. It sounded so juvenile, so much like a schoolboy.

"I'm interested in knowing why you should think the idea was—what did you call it? Naive?"

"What I meant was—that after all, I can't expect to be decorated for doing my job."

"Why not? Don't you think the Department has occasion to decorate people for performing their duties?"

"Well, of course *some* people might merit awards for their work."

"But you would not?"

"Well, no, not especially."

"Why not?"

"What I meant was—a decoration by the very nature of its definition means recognition for something above and beyond the ordinary call of duty."

"Yes, of course. And isn't your work above and beyond the call of duty, Professor Burden?"

"I'd hardly say that," Burden said uncomfortably, shifting in his chair. It seemed so presumptuous the way the fat Mr. Conger was putting it.

"And yet you said you came here with the expectation of being decorated?"

"Well, ye-ssss, I guess I did. But as I said, it was naive of me to think that."

"In other words, when you view your own work realistically you come to the conclusion that you don't merit an award. Is that what you're saying?"

"Yes, I suppose that's what I mean. After all, one can hope for awards and recognition. I mean, it's just the usual vanity that every man has."

"You consider yourself a vain man, Professor Burden?"

"Why, no, not at all," Burden said with some alarm. It was odd the way this fat, seemingly lethargic man intellectually seized the unexpected meaning from a remark. Perhaps it was because he was so literal. That was a fault quite common with government people and bureaucrats.

"And yet you said everyone has some vanity, Professor Burden," Conger went on calmly. "I presume you, too, have some vanity?"

"Yes, of course I have. Everyone has. It's part of the

nature of every human being to cherish some belief about himself, whether it's accurate or not. One man thinks he's handsome—" Burden paused. He didn't want to offend Conger and very probably he had done just that with that remark. Conger was certainly not handsome. He was a gross-looking man. "And, well, another man might think he's got a particularly keen sense of humor, and still another might feel that he has a flair for writing. I mean, there you are. All minor vanities."

"And your vanity is that you feel that you're a superior correspondent of the Department?"

"Well, I like to think that my reports were a little above the average."

Conger looked at Burden for a long moment. It was time to jolt this man a little, to confuse him some more, to mix him up. "Your reports have been well below the average, Professor Burden," Conger said dryly.

"I beg your pardon," Burden said, almost rising from his chair.

"I said your reports are well below the average in judgment, perception, accuracy, and completeness."

"I challenge that," Burden said, now rising from his seat. "You can't determine that on the basis of one report. I demand that Mr. Young be brought here to testify as to my reports."

"Who is Mr. Young?" Conger asked blandly.

"Mr. Young happens to be my superior. The gentleman to whom I have been writing reports for nearly four years. Before that my superior was Mr. Teller. He's read my reports for nearly six years. Ask either of those gentlemen about my reports!"

"There are no such people," Conger said calmly and truthfully. Burden looked shocked. For a moment he did not know whether to smile or to look pained. He did, however, sit down. Conger was pleased with the reaction.

"But, surely, I've written thousands of reports to Mr. Young and to Mr. Teller," Burden said in a small, uncertain voice.

"Nevertheless, there are no such people," Conger insisted evenly. And there were not. Both Young and Teller were code names for the readers. It was part of a simple system devised for the use of the routing personnel and it effectively kept correspondents from finding out who their readers were.

Burden had been called up for a routine examination. It was the first time in ten years that his report had fallen into the statistical sampling that went on continuously. Conger had seen thousands of agents in that time. Now it was Burden's turn.

Burden had exhibited, to Conger's thinking, some normal reactions, but he had also exhibited some abnormal ones. Conger smelled intellectual pretension in the man. That was a bad sign. It meant that a normally perfunctory interview would have to take longer, that Conger would have to probe deeper.

"But if there are no such people," Burden said, "then who's been reading my reports?"

"Your reports have been read very closely, Professor Burden. That's the reason you've been called here. It is the opinion of the Department that your reports have been slipshod, that you have deliberately concealed and distorted certain conversations." Conger tamped down the charred tobacco in his pipe. The Department held no such opinion at all. It was merely the secondary stage of Conger's line of questioning. Burden had exhibited belligerence. Conger was testing that belligerence for density. Was he really angry and outraged, or was he merely confused and worried and covering his apprehensions with anger?

"I can't understand that," Burden said, feeling his hands grow cold with guilt, "I simply can't understand that. I've been both judicious and accurate in my reports. I've tried to include significant data and yet not over-burden my superior with unimportant details."

"Then you admit you've suppressed details?" Conger asked, lighting his pipe.

"Not *suppressed*," Burden protested, "that's hardly the word for what I did. I—*selected* what I considered significant matters."

Conger nodded as he drew on his pipe. Burden's tone had changed. The anger was synthetic. Underneath was a heavy layer of fear. That was normal. Now Conger had to determine the depth of that fear. "Are you absolutely certain that you could judge what details to select?"

"Well, yes, I mean, after all, I can't be expected to report *everything*, can I?"

"Can't you?"

"Well, of course, I *could*. But it would entail practically a stenographic report of everything I saw and heard each day. As it is, I spend a full hour on my report."

"Do you feel that an hour is too much time?"

"No, no, no, not at all," Burden said hastily. "Look here, Mr. Conger, I'm afraid you're getting the impression that I begrudge the time I spend on my job as a correspondent for this Department. I don't. I look forward to the work, to the reports. I'll be perfectly honest with you—I enjoy writing the report."

"Why do you enjoy it? Do you enjoy it because it gives you a special power over your colleagues and friends?"

"Well, no, not that."

"Do you enjoy the idea that you're doing something no one around you suspects you're doing?"

"Well, there is an element of that in it," Burden said with a faint smile.

"It makes you feel mysterious, does it?"

"No, not exactly mysterious. I don't know what the word for it might be. Like a conspirator, if you know what I mean."

"Conspirator?"

"Yes, you know. When you were a child—didn't you play at games in which you had a secret role that none knew about? Not your parents or your friends or anyone?"

"You mean a game in which you share a secret with a few pals and no one else?"

"Exactly, that's it," Burden said, pleased now that he was getting through to Conger. "Well, being a correspondent for the Department is, in a way, like that. I'm in on a secret that others can't guess."

"In other words, you enjoy a privileged position among the people with whom you live?"

"Well, yes, if you want to put it that way. I know something they don't know."

"And it gives you a certain sense of importance, of superiority to others, this knowledge that is privately yours?"

"Well," Burden hesitated, uncertain as to Conger's tone. The wording seemed faintly sinister, as if a trap were being laid. The remark contained a highly charged word, *superiority*. It wasn't a word lightly used and Burden distrusted it. For the first time he began to wonder about this fat investigator's purposes. "I wouldn't say that," Burden finally said guardedly.

"You wouldn't say that," Conger echoed. "Then what would you say about this private, inner feeling that you're apart from others?"

"Now, look here, I suppose every correspondent feels exactly the way I do—the need for secrecy, the daily reports, the position of trust. After all, one would have to be less than human if he didn't feel a slight sense of being different from other people—people who aren't agents of the Department."

"Is this feeling of being different from others a pleasant feeling? Or do you dislike the idea that you're different from others?"

Burden paused. That question was weighted unfairly. No matter how it was answered it showed him in a bad light. "Now, wait a minute. I don't say it's pleasant being different from others—having to be secretive, reporting them for their least little transgression. But at the same time it isn't unpleasant. I don't dislike my work."

"It seems to me that between liking something and disliking something the only choice left is indifference. Are you indifferent about your status as a correspondent?"

"Now you are being unfair," Burden said, on firmer ground. It was simple sophistry he was dealing with here. Conger might be an experienced investigator, but Burden now felt competent to handle him. "I don't admit that the only three states of emotion are love, indifference, and hate. That's primitive thinking. One can love and hate a thing and one can love and be indifferent to a thing at the same time. I'm fond of my work but I dislike the need for secrecy. I hate the idea of giving up time writing a report at the same time that I derive a pleasure from doing the report well. You see, it isn't as simple as you're trying to make it."

"Your feelings, then, are mingled," Conger said.

"All feelings are mingled," Burden insisted.

"It might interest you to know that mine aren't," Conger said flatly. "Good day, Professor Burden."

"What?"

"I said, good day."

"Is this all?"

"Yes."

"But, I mean—was this what I was called in about?"

"Yes."

"I haven't yet cleared up the matter of my reports. I don't think they've been below average. I'd like to have that matter thrashed out."

"It has been thrashed out, Professor Burden."

"I don't understand."

"Good day, Professor Burden."

"Now, wait a minute. You must be fair about this. I've been a correspondent for this Department for ten years. As far as I knew I had been doing satisfactory work. I mean, after all, no one's called me in during ten years. Now I am called in and told my work is unsatisfactory. I'm given no explanation. After a rather inconclusive discussion of my feelings concerning my work I'm dismissed. What am I supposed to think?"

"Think what you please, Professor Burden."

"That tells me nothing. Am I to continue writing my reports? Am I dismissed? Will I be given an opportunity to discover in what instances my reports have been lacking in perception and accuracy and completeness? I mean, after all, you must be fair about this. You can't very well damn me for being remiss and not give me the chance to answer specific charges."

"Do you feel that you're being treated arbitrarily?" Conger asked blandly.

"I certainly feel that I haven't been given any real opportunity to answer whatever grievances the Department feels it has against me—my work."

"Are you seriously interested in finding out the exact feelings of the Department?"

"Why, yes, of course."

Conger did not fail to note the hesitation, the softening of the voice, the slight retreating motion of the eyes. It was curious, he thought, how often you tested these people and what looked firm and definite was actually mushy, without substance. Burden was rattled now, badly rattled, and perhaps he was even regretting that he had been so insistent, so professorial. "You'll be given a hearing and an examination at the Department's earliest convenience. Is that what you want?"

"Yes, of course," Burden said, uncertain whether he should have pursued the matter so far.

"Very well. We'll get in touch with you, Professor Burden. Good day," Conger said.

Burden hesitated for a moment, put on his hat, and murmured "Good day," as he went out, softly closing the door behind him.

Conger regarded the closed door for a long moment and then tapped the pencil in his hand against Burden's report. He pulled over the dictation machine with his foot, pressed the switch, and picked up the mouthpiece. Carefully, slowly, he dictated.

"To Chief of Agents Section. From Frank Conger, Special Service Detail Officer. Subject, Professor Burden, collegiate correspondent, Templar College." Conger paused. Stooping slightly in his chair, he reached under his desk and snapped a switch that stopped the recording machine he had started when Professor Burden had first come into the office. Then he turned back to the machine, picked up his pipe, clamped his teeth on the stem, and resumed dictation. "First examination in ten years. Burden's initial reactions were uncharacteristic. Unsatisfactory reaction to primary questioning. Unsatisfactory reaction to secondary questioning. Further questioning recommended. Suspect major heresy of deep, subconscious level. Burden is not a stupid man. Heresy is probably deeply integrated and profoundly felt although he has masked it from himself as he has from the Department. Signed, Frank Conger." Conger snapped the switch on the machine, took the pipe out of his mouth, and rapped out its dottle on the ash tray.

6

On Friday, the sixteenth of October, Burden's hearing and examination were held in a room on the third floor of Building Four.

For this trip to the Department Burden had to receive special permission from the dean of the School of Liberal Arts. It was given without question once he showed the letter. Emma, however, was not so easily put off the second time with the story of an intercollegiate seminar. Burden did not want to tell her the truth and asked her not to worry. But the very look in his eyes and the sound of his voice did worry Emma.

"Won't you tell me where you're going?"

"Not far, Emma," Burden said tenderly, his mind troubled. He was sure that he would acquit himself well at the hearing, but deep down an indefinable sense of apprehension tracked its cold and ghostly feet across his soul.

"You won't be gone overnight, will you?"

"I may," Burden said, although he did not expect that he would.

"Surely you won't be gone more than two days?"

"I hope not, dear," Burden said, and Emma looked at him closely, her eyes frightened. "Now, now," Burden said gently, taking her into his arms, "don't act that way. I've been away from home before. I'm not going far. It's just a three-hour trip by train from here."

"Can't I go with you? Or join you there tomorrow?" she insisted when Burden shook his head to the first question.

"Emma, Emma, what is this? Suspicion? Not at this late stage of our marriage!"

"I'm afraid," she said, nestling closely against him, her cheek against his.

"Of what, for heaven's sake?"

"I don't know," she finally admitted. "Why won't you tell me where you're going?"

"All right," Burden said, finally deciding that it would be silly to keep her in the dark. "I've been asked to appear at the Department of Internal Examination." His wife's reaction alarmed him. She let go of him and gasped, her eyes wide and dark and filled with terror. "Good heavens, Emma," Burden said, alarmed now, feeling his own fear gathering momentum from Emma's reaction and growing inside of him.

"They'll hurt you," Emma said, putting her hand up to her mouth, trembling.

"Now where on earth did you get such a wild idea? The Department's got a world-wide reputation for fairness, for justice, for benevolence."

"I've heard things," Emma said, biting her lips, "people they've driven out of their minds, things they've done in those buildings that no one knows about."

"Emma, stop that!" Burden felt his own breath coming short now. These were heresies of the worst sort. Of course such goblin rumors had always floated about, no one willing to vouch for them. But he hadn't heard them in years, not since he was a boy. Not in thirty years had he heard a whisper against the Department. Not since the abolition of punishment as a social concept. "Now, Emma," Burden took his wife's hands and was shocked to discover how cold and trembling they were, "those are things you heard as a child—years and years ago. They're no longer true, if they ever were. No intelligent person believes those ghost stories any more. I've been inside the Department's buildings. No torture racks, no dungeons, no keepers, no men with whips. It's just an enormous group of office buildings. Nothing at all sinister about them. Believe me. I've been there and I've seen them already. In fact, I wouldn't be going back at all this time if I hadn't requested it."

"Then call them and say you've changed your mind." Emma was upon him, clutching, dragging, holding him back.

"Emma, that's out of the question," Burden said, wondering now if he could possibly revoke his request. He had the uncomfortable feeling that perhaps he couldn't, that now the die was cast and he had no choice in the matter but to go through with the hearing. Now, quite suddenly, he wished that he could change his mind. But that wish was checked by another fear—the fear that he would be told that he couldn't. Somehow it seemed more desirable if he could retain the feeling that the hearing was being held at his own request. It seemed safer. Safe from what? The thought caught at his throat, but he did his best not to communicate that sudden, wild scratch of terror to Emma.

When he was able to calm her he left the house and took the train. This time the small, calm suburban houses didn't look quite so innocent. It seemed to him that the blinds were closely drawn in all the houses and that he actually saw no one in the streets. True, it was cold and gray and bleak, but still, not to see *anyone* appeared improbable, sinister, as if all the people had remained discreetly indoors, perhaps fearing to go out. Fearing what? Again the word and the emotion. Of what was he afraid? What could the hearing possibly turn up but that he had done the best job he possibly could? What else was there to turn up? Surely he had omitted nothing from his reports, distorted no facts. He had taken the job voluntarily and the worst that could happen would be that he would lose the job of correspondent. Well, what harm in that? He had never been paid any money for the job, nor had he received an ounce of extra privilege for his work. It seemed to him that he had been entirely on the giving end of the relationship and that he had never asked for or received any benefit from his work. It was entirely too one-sided.

The hearing room, like the Special Service Office, was disappointingly small. At a small, simply painted rostrum three men in ordinary business suits were seated, papers in front of them. A stenographer sat between Burden and the three examiners. Burden took no oath; he did not, in fact, move from the chair which he was given when he entered the room. There were no spectators and the plain monk's cloth curtains were drawn over the windows. The only sound came from the stenography machine the girl used and the occasional rattle of paper or a cough from one of the examiners. Behind the examiners was a long mirror in which Burden could watch himself. He thought he looked well when he spoke.

The questioning seemed, to Burden, to be flat and uninspired. No one seized on his remarks the way Conger had done in the first interview. In fact Burden found the examiners extremely fair. They allowed him to develop his points at great length, only occasionally interrupting to ask him to elaborate or to clarify a statement.

"My own feeling in the matter," Burden said, aware that he was doing extremely well thus far, "is that my relationship with the Department has been a good one— although one-sided."

"How, one-sided, Professor Burden?" the center examiner asked. Although none of the examiners seemed to take the lead in questioning, Burden had the feeling that the center examiner was the one of greatest authority. He also had seemed the most sympathetic.

"Well, I've done work for the Department for ten years now. It has been, to the best of my knowledge, conscientious and honest work. I have turned in complete reports, reports that have been selective, balanced, judicious." The center examiner nodded understandingly. "I have had no one to guide me in my work for those ten years. In the absence of criticism or suggestion I have applied my own standards to my reports, constantly seeking to improve my work for the Department. If I have taken the wrong direction somewhere along the line during those years, it seems to me that my superiors should have pointed it out to me. If I had been doing so badly for ten years why wasn't I directed correctly sooner than this?" Burden paused but the examiners offered no answer although the center examiner smiled encouragingly.

"Will you explain further what you mean by your description of your relationship with the Department as being one-sided, Mr. Burden?" the examiner with the fair mustache on the left said. He glanced at his papers as if something had occurred to him. "I beg your pardon. Did I say Mr. Burden? Of course, I meant Professor Burden."

"That's quite all right," Burden said, smiling back. "Yes, I'll explain what I mean. In the relationship between servant and master, if I may use that analogy, the servant has his obligations but the master, too, has his obligations to his servant. And one of the obligations of the master is to praise or correct the work of his servant. In ten years I have received neither. I have been completely in the dark as to the feelings of my superiors. My only conclusion was that I was doing well. Perhaps not superlatively well, but adequately. At least that much." The examiner with the fair mustache nodded in agreement. "And to have this charge thrown at me for the first time—a general charge—without specific point I mean— it's unfair. It's uncharitable. It's worse than that—it's downright ungrateful."

"Ungrateful?" the center examiner asked quizzically.

"Yes," Burden said, wondering if perhaps the word had been too strong. Well, never mind. It was time he stood up and spoke back. He *had* been treated shabbily. "After all, I have assumed a burden working for the Department. I have devoted time and energy and some personal expense. I don't begrudge these things. I give them freely and willingly, without sense of reservation about them. But a man does want appreciation for what he has done. A man deserves the feeling that his efforts aren't wasted, that his work is vital." Burden kept one eye on his image in the mirror and thought he struck a particularly effective pose several times. "After all," he went on, "the essential dignity of man is the sense of worth, of purpose, of meaning that his life gives him. I am a modest man and I have lived a modest life, but this does not mean that I consider myself worthless or what I have done as trivial. These reports have been an important part of my life and of my work," Burden's voice was quite clear and strong in the hearing room. It was equally clear and strong in the adjoining room, but only because his voice was coming through the amplified tones of speakers set into the ceiling. His gestures, his words, and his person had been under careful scrutiny all morning by four men who sat at a long table or lounged in easy chairs looking through the mirror that was on the wall behind the examiners. It was a trick mirror which reflected on one side, the side Burden saw, and was transparent when looked through on the other—the side which the four men faced.

"Remarkably well-buried heresy," one of the four men said as he watched and listened.

"Conger was right," another said. "Completely integrated. He doesn't even know he's a heretic."

"Remarkable how they can live separate lives," the first man said.

"Well, there are such things as completely schizoid personalities," the fourth man said. He was thin and lanky, with large, pale eyes and hair that was almost too long for a man, thin and silky and disordered. His slender, pale fingers were plunged into his hair in a thoughtful posture as he slumped in his easy chair. His lips were heavy and drooping and slightly parted. His eyes were faintly luminous in their paleness and they seemed oddly possessed as he watched Burden. Now and then his lips moved very faintly as if he were repeating Burden's words silently, or as if he were praying to himself. His name was Lark and of the four men in the room he was the most important, the most poised.

"Do you notice how he keeps harping on the gratitude theme?" one of the two men at the table asked Lark. The slender, abstracted young man seemed to be lost in his own thought and did not answer.

"As though it were of primary concern to him," the other man at the table said.

"The question is—how important is gratitude to him and how much of what he calls gratitude is really a bid for recognition as an individual? Don't you agree, Lark?"

Lark remained silent, his eyes fixed on Burden, his long pale face pressed against the bony, long fingers.

"I don't think there's any doubt but that what he calls gratitude is a bid for individual recognition," one of the men at the table said.

His neighbor nodded. "Absolutely. He's constantly under pressure to assert himself as an individual as opposed to what he considers the anonymous mass of correspondents."

"I wonder if he's indulged in the reverie of identification?" the man in the other easy chair asked.

"No doubt about it," the man at the table said. "I'm sure he's told himself that his reports are eagerly looked forward to, that he's considered quite an ace of a correspondent. I'm also certain that he thinks his superior thinks he's one devil of a fellow."

"Odd, the way they want personal attention from their superiors," the man in the armchair said thoughtfully. "Do you remember Chapman?"

"They fall in love with the internal images," one of the men at the table said, nodding.

"Chapman was a fascinating subject," the man in the armchair continued. "Toward the end he started making indecent proposals in his reports and drawing pictures in them. His reader was quite shocked."

"What was astonishing was that Chapman knew his superior would report him for it," the man at the table said.

"That's precisely why he did it, don't you see? He thought if he could meet his superior he could seduce him, and what better way to meet him than to lay himself open to investigation?" the man in the armchair said.

"Fantastic, what lengths they'll go to for love," one of the men at the table said.

"Had enough of this?" Lark asked unexpectedly, turning to the three other men.

The three men nodded quickly. Lark stretched out an incredibly long and lean leg and pressed down on a pearl button with the heel of his shoe. In the hearing room a small light came on under the desk where the examiners sat. It was the signal to conclude the hearing.

"Thank you very much, Professor Burden," the center examiner said with a smile.

"I want to thank *you*," Burden repeated to the three examiners, "for your patience, your kindness, for your gentlemanliness in allowing me to say the things I felt must be said—not in my own defense so much but in protest against such treatment. I'm sure you'll render a just and compassionate verdict."

"That is our desire always, Professor Burden," the youngest examiner with the blond mustache said softly.

"Thank you—" the rest of Burden's words were lost as the speakers went dead in the adjoining room. The four men had risen and Lark, leaning negligently against the wall, his long legs crossed, had his hands sunk deep in his pockets. Now, straight on, the long, pale face seemed dwarfed by the enormous light eyes, the thick lips, the delicately pointed chin. There was something primitive and dedicated in the face.

"Well?" Lark asked the three men who faced him in a rough semicircle.

"I consider him a heretic with profound compulsions," one of the men said. The other two nodded their agreement.

"And?" Lark asked, his eyes traveling restlessly among the three men.

"Your chances of obtaining social conformity are practically nil," another of the three said. The other two stared at Lark gravely.

"Then in your opinion we shouldn't try for conformity?" Lark asked.

"No," the man who spoke last said. The other two shook their heads negatively.

"Then we'll have to kill Professor Burden."

"That's my opinion," the spokesman said and looked at his two companions who agreed, nodding thoughtfully.

"Thank you very much," Lark said with a queer smile, and then turned and pulled open the door and stepped through. The three men followed him out of the room but by the time the last man closed the door behind him Lark was gone somewhere down a long, empty corridor.

In the hearing room Burden was shaking hands with the examiners and thanking them again.

"You may have to wait around awhile, Professor Burden," the center examiner said, "there may be some more questions. But the formal hearings are over."

"Do you know if I will have to be back tomorrow?"

"Oh, I don't think so," the examiner said with a doubtful look. "But this afternoon—"

"I'm completely prepared to spend the day here," Burden said with a smile. It had, after all, turned out well. Of course there was no verdict handed down, but he couldn't help feeling that he had made a good impression. A very good impression.

7

On the first floor of the building in which he found himself Burden ate in a large, well-lighted restaurant. The atmosphere was quiet and unhurried and the food was excellent and quite cheap. It was apparently a restaurant designed solely for the personnel of the Department working in Building Four.

After the meal, somewhat at a loss what to do next, Burden sat at the table and watched the people about him. Most of them were young and the proportion of men to women seemed fairly equal—far more equal, in fact, than would be found in the student dining halls at the college or in the faculty dining hall. Everyone seemed cheerful and talkative despite the bleak weather outdoors. Burden read lips here and there among the diners about him. But most of the conversations were either overly cryptic with official language or trivial and dull. That struck him as strange. Despite the animated expressions in their faces and the intensity of their conversations, none of the people in the room whose conversations he could follow seemed to be saying anything that sounded remotely interesting or faintly provocative. At one table they were discussing summer vacations with a vivacity and a zest that suggested that all the people had just returned from their holidays just a few days before. But by the calendar that couldn't possibly be true. Those same people must have eaten together for months since their vacations ended and yet they were apparently pursuing a topic of table talk that must have been exhausted and stale long before this. Still, they showed no lack of interest. Their eyes sparkled, they listened eagerly. At another table, out of boredom, Burden had followed a long and banal discussion on food preferences. The young men and women of that group must have known each other well and yet the discussion had all the air of people baring their inner souls for the first time in their lives. Burden's eyes swept across the room. Suddenly a thought struck him. To be certain, he looked over the room more slowly, more carefully. Odd, he thought. There was no table in the room, barring his own, where fewer than four people were seated. Indeed, there were no groups of twos or threes. It was always four or more at a table. And yet the restaurant was by no means crowded. Two people could easily find a quiet, softly lit corner for themselves. And yet no two people did. The groups of four and more sat in the center of the restaurant under the brightest lights. What was still more curious, there were no tables where more men than women were seated, nor were there any tables where the opposite condition obtained. Burden's brows knit with puzzlement. Now, that *was* odd.

His interest aroused, he counted the number of tables occupied in the restaurant, checking at each table to see the distribution of men to women. It was almost always exactly equal. When he had finished surveying the entire restaurant he was faintly perplexed to discover that the ratio of men to women was exactly equal, one to one. Nowhere was there a table devoted exclusively to men or a table devoted exclusively to women.

Burden leaned back in the chair, awakened by this statistical accident. Perhaps it was common. Perhaps he was being perplexed by something that was not at all unusual. And yet there was something off key about the restaurant. People left while he ate and he noticed that whole parties left at once. Well, that certainly wasn't uncommon. Their lunch hour over, most of them working in the same offices or departments, groups left together. That was reasonable enough. And yet—Burden chewed his lower lip. No one did any "table-hopping," as Middleton called it. There was a great deal of that in the faculty dining hall. Burden had found it objectionable because it frequently blocked his view and he could never read the lips of a table hopper who was leaning down to whisper something to a friend or a colleague who was seated. Yet here there was no table hopping. No whispering, in fact. Of course, it was considered impolite to whisper. But still, people did whisper. Not here. Not as far as he could tell.

Burden stirred slightly in his seat. The more closely he examined these people who worked in the Department the more he discovered. For one thing, at no table were there two two-way conversations. At every table the four people conducted a single conversation. All were included in the conversation and all listened attentively. Now, that *was* odd. It might be the very height of social politeness, but it seemed strained. Burden snapped his fingers. That was the word he had subconsciously been groping for. There was an intense underlying sense of strain in the restaurant. The attention was too pointed, too bright, the politeness too rigid, the balances too equal, the air of conviviality too strenuously maintained. It was as though they felt compelled to act the way they did, to seat themselves like the animals of Noah's Ark, two by two.

How extremely odd, Burden thought. They acted almost as if they were—Burden checked himself. Then, looking about the restaurant with new eyes he examined the diners again. They acted like badly frightened people.

II

Lark was not a man and not a boy. He was not a scientist nor was he a mystic. Lark was something infinitely subtler, enormously wiser—part woman, part serpent, part magician, part seer, part lunatic. The Department had its specialists, its investigators, its clinical technicians, its psychologists, its policy makers, its administrators, and had them all by the scores. But it had just one true inquisitor. Lark was its inquisitor. Lark was the core of the Department—a fact that virtually no one understood. He certainly did not have the title, or the salary, or the prestige. He had only the soul, the brain, and the intuitive grasp of the real inquisitor. In Burden he saw the worst, the very worst of all heresy. In Burden, Lark saw the destruction of an empire, the dissolution of a way of life, the lever by which a world could be torn loose from its moorings. In Burden Lark saw the gleaming, terrible essence that wakes the true inquisitor as a lion might be roused from sleep by the tantalizing scent of warm, living flesh. As he watched Burden and listened to him, Lark felt his skin crawl, the roots of his long, silky hair stiffen. There was within him the sudden frantic scramble of his heart, the sense of blood thinning and rushing with enormous speed through his body. Burden was the ultimate heretic. Burden was the pure and living embodiment of all that an inquisitor hates and fears and desires. No one understood it as well as Lark. Conger did not smell anything but difficulty. Lark's assistants sensed nothing but complexity and the chance of eventual failure. The examiners in the hearing room were amiable props who understood nothing. Only Lark knew the danger, the hideously exciting peril that Burden represented. He had to have Burden. Lark had sworn to himself that Burden must be given to him. But he would have to act slowly, cautiously, feeding his superiors a bit at a time. To gobble down at one swallow all that Lark knew of Burden would be too much for his superiors. They would gag, rebel, spit the professor out. They would miss the perfection of the heretic.

"Will you please tell me why you don't want Burden destroyed?" the Commissioner asked Lark finally.

"For one thing, it would put us over last year's figure," Lark said calmly. Slowly, slowly, he told himself.

"Oh, I don't think so. We've got at least six cases to play with until the end of the year."

"Six aren't many, sir. That's why I feel we ought to work with Burden as much as we can."

"But a totally integrated heretic has always been automatically marked for destruction. That is our policy, Lark. You'll correct me if I'm wrong?" The Commissioner's eyes remained calm.

"But by doing that we'll never be able to find out whether or not we can do anything with those people."

"It seems to me that we have tried in the past."

"Our techniques keep getting better, sir. There's been a great deal of work done since the last time we tried. It seems to me that there's been a tendency to skirt the difficult cases by at once declaring them totally integrated when, quite possibly, that may not be true at all."

"Well, does it matter very much, Lark? After all, how many cases warrant execution?"

"I know there aren't many, sir. But we have reason to believe that heretics are increasing in number."

"Oh, the mild, delusory cases," the Commissioner said, looking at his nails, trying to hide the interest he always felt when he watched Lark maneuver.

"Yes, sir. And we've been successful with them. It's no trick to do the easy cases. Our problem has been to increase the scope of our abilities to salvage heretics. If we keep our standards at their present levels there will always be twelve to fifteen heretics a year who must be destroyed. It's my feeling that the number should be brought down."

"Do you propose that we waste time and effort on those twelve or fifteen integrated heretics?" the Commissioner asked blandly.

"I'd hardly call time and effort wasted in bringing our results up to the highest standards," Lark said innocently.

The Commissioner laughed. "Right from the book. What's that ancient fencing term for a good stroke?"

"*Touché?*"

"Yes, that's what I'd call a *touché*. Well," the Commissioner leaned back in his chair, folding his hands across his stomach, "you've got me on the defensive. Continue with your attack."

"I wouldn't dream of suggesting that what I'm saying constitutes an attack, sir," Lark said evenly, soberly.

"No, you wouldn't. But continue."

"I think I understand what you mean when you say it might be a waste of time. But something may be efficient but not sufficient, if you will excuse the play on words. I don't say that we haven't worked the greatest good for the greatest number. But when a society can comfortably provide for the bulk of its members, it turns its attention to the small groups which have been neglected for the sake of the majority. My feeling is that now is the time we started to work with the cases we have always had to dismiss."

"You're right," the Commissioner said, smiling, "and I only interrupt at this point to remind you that there is such a concept in human endeavor known as the sub-marginal return."

Lark paused. The Commissioner was a difficult man to understand. Sometimes he played with a subject as an idle man toys with a bit of thread and then, with a startling speed that suggested he gave the matter no thought, made up his mind one way or the other. Lark didn't believe that the Commissioner was a capricious person, but he didn't want to run the risk of losing the professor. Lark wanted Burden because he was a rarity. Another such heretic might not come along in Lark's lifetime. Lark decided to try boldness.

"It is my understanding that our branch of the Department is devoted to the resolution of heresies and the purging of heretics. It is also my understanding that if the resolution of heresy and the reclamation of the heretic cannot be successfully accomplished, our society is doomed."

"I didn't realize the situation was quite so dramatic," the Commissioner said softly, smiling.

Lark pressed on, ignoring the smile. "I would put it even more dramatically, sir. Heresy breeds rebellion in the presence of suppression. Heresy, in a free society, is meaningless and feeble. But in a society that is rigidly joined, heresy is an explosive force. The benevolent state has a long way to go, whole areas of supervision ahead of it. Our society is slowly being poured into the mold. If we cannot successfully remove heresy at this stage of the game, then we may as well give up any idea of continuing the creation of a new society."

"You think heretics are as important as all that?"

Lark could not decide just what lay behind the Commissioner's eyes, the tone of his voice. It might be amusement, or mockery, or thoughtfulness. "I know they are," Lark said flatly. "The history of earth is filled with examples. The Judean heresy of one God put the first crack in the pagan world. From the Judean heresy arose the Christian heresy that split the Roman world. The Protestant heresy split the world that was Catholic. Heresies have shattered empires—the Russian, the English, the Dutch. The heresy of self-determination broke the empire concept. And the heresy of democratic representation in the affairs of government sent royalty out of power forever. It always begins in the mind, sir. There the seed of heresy flourishes. From thought to attitude, from attitude to action.

"This state of ours is going to extend its powers upon the behalf of the people. It's going to insist that the individual good is completely and utterly identified with the national good. Eventually we must erase the concept of individuality. Ultimately we must come to the stage where no man bears a separate, private identity. The final stage of our society calls for conformity both from within and from without by each of its members. You may breed them eugenically to be equals, and school them to feel equal, but the closer you come to the last stage the tighter the vise is going to close. And when that happens, the heretics will come springing out of the ground like mushrooms after a heavy rain. You will be forcing up into the light all the buried egos, all the hidden heresies. And then you will have to deal with thousands of heretics. Are you going to kill them all? Violence breeds violence, and with each heretic you kill you create two others. It gets completely out of hand. If we cannot now reclaim Burden, then we'll fail seventy-five years from now—and our society will crack down the middle because of the intolerable task of ridding ourselves of the last, desperate heresies of the individual."

Lark's eyes were large and intense, and his face so pale that it seemed almost translucent, betraying the delicate blue tracery of veins in his throat. There was about him the air of a man possessed. He had said a dozen dangerous things, predicted several doubtful conclusions, and made at least three serious charges against the State. It had been a desperate and dangerous thrust. In the past the Commissioner had encouraged him to speak freely but Lark had always moved carefully, cautiously, tentatively, testing his way for firmness. This time he had been rash, and now had exposed himself to the Commissioner's considerable power and intellect.

"You make out a strong case, Lark," the Commissioner said. "Not a valid case on all its points, but a strong one." The Commissioner looked at Lark with eyes that appeared to twinkle with caprice. "You have a gift for rhetoric, Lark. That's something I've noted before."

"Thank you, sir. But I hope I've done more than exercise my talent."

"You've also a gift for sharpness," the Commissioner said dryly. Lark flushed, accepting the rebuke and reminding himself to curb his impatience the next time. "Well," the Commissioner said, leaning forward, putting his elbows on his desk, "you've touched on so many points that I hardly know where to begin."

"Yes, sir," Lark said politely, knowing that it was a lie.

"As you say, heretics are our primary concern—wherever they are, of whatever degree of heresy they possess. They are sick people, Lark—desperately sick people. For their own good, for the good of the State, they must be healed, they must be reclaimed. My orders now, as they always have been in the past, are these: Go as deep as necessary—root out heresies, cleanse the heretics, make them useful citizens of the State."

"I would like to start with Professor Burden, sir," Lark said, an incipient sense of triumph making him feel light and alive, as he hadn't in years of dully tracking the puny, defenseless, and stupid delusory heretics.

"Professor Burden." The Commissioner mused for a moment. "He hardly seems to be a very difficult case, Lark."

"With your indulgence, sir, I think he is."

"My dear Lark, I may be as indulgent as your own father, but that still does not convince me that he would be worth expending a great deal of effort upon." The Commissioner paused, watching Lark carefully.

"May I suggest, sir, that there are a number of reasons why Burden should be a logical first choice?"

"Suggest as much as you please, Lark," the older man said, "but that still tells me nothing."

"Very well, then." Lark steeled himself not to flush or reply sharply. Evidently the Commissioner was in a mood to be difficult. He would have to be handled carefully. "Very briefly, sir, here are the reasons I feel Burden is unique." Lark detailed them carefully and at length, but as he spoke he knew that none of the reasons proved Burden to be a unique or even an exceptional heretic. And Lark could not advance as a sane consideration that Burden raised wild, shrilling, psychic alarms within him. It was not a reason Lark could put into words. He had already exposed himself to the Commissioner, but he did not intend to make the exposure complete.

The Commissioner listened and nodded occasionally, watching Lark closely, admiring the young man's drive, and his ability to quarter and tack intellectually with a finesse that would have done tribute to a mind of twice the age, cultivation, and experience. "And that's the basis on which you think we should work on Burden?"

"Yes, sir," Lark said, his throat dry, a sense of failure already chilling the triumph he had known a short time ago.

The Commissioner turned a hand in an oddly helpless gesture. "I'm baffled, Lark. I'm truly baffled. I've always thought you a genuinely perceptive and acute investigator. I've thought highly of you and spoken highly of you. In fact, I've bragged about you in official circles. But this demonstration—" the Commissioner shrugged his shoulders. "It's most disappointing. You've gathered together a seedy grab bag of phrases and words that mean nothing. You've told me nothing I could not read in the summary of the report—a summary that makes Burden look like every integrated heretic who has gone before him. Frankly, I'm at a loss to understand this fixation of yours."

Lark's face rose in color as he listened to the Commissioner. He knew he had failed, but he did not expect the Commissioner to point it up so cruelly. It was another facet of his superior that he must file away for future reference.

"I'm sorry, sir," Lark said. "Those were my thoughts."

"Perhaps," the Commissioner said, deciding now he would ease Lark out of the situation gracefully, "but

I have the feeling that the most important thought you've had on the subject you've somewhat selfishly refused to share with me."

"Sir?"

"Or perhaps you think I don't appreciate intuition?"

Lark regarded the older man carefully. He had never thought the Commissioner a fool, but he was unprepared for this brilliant divination. "I wasn't sure, sir," Lark admitted.

"Raises the hair on your scalp, doesn't he?"

"Yes, sir," Lark said, his eyes fixed on his superior.

"It isn't something you can put into a report. But that's no reason to ignore it, Lark," the Commissioner smiled. "You know, we were animals long before we were rational human beings, and there are some who think that we're more animalistic than rationalistic. I appreciate the instincts that make a man's scalp crawl. I appreciate them—and I trust them just as you do."

"Then Burden will be acceptable?"

"You're the one who will have to work on him, Lark. Will he be acceptable to you?"

"Yes, sir, eminently so."

"Well, then, we'll have to let you have your heart's desire, Lark." The Commissioner smiled.

Lark felt his blood leap in his body.

"However," the Commissioner held up a warning forefinger, "I still hold to the belief that there is such a thing as sub-marginal return. And I am inclined to think that we will get less back from Burden than we are entitled to by way of balancing work done against results achieved. More than anyone else in this Department, you know the enormous amount of work we must do day in and day out. You also know that we can't indefinitely tie up the resources, the personnel, and the equipment of this Department for the sake of one heretic."

"But it isn't just one heretic, sir. It's the pattern of the future we'll be developing."

"Possibly," the Commissioner went on, still cautioning with his finger. "But after all, this is something that proceeds from your somewhat dubious evaluations on the growth of heresy and your sheer instinct with regard to this one man." Lark's lips tightened impatiently, a movement that did not escape the Commissioner. "I know, we old men move damnably slow. But someday you'll be sitting here and you'll have a deputy breathing fire into your face, and you'll tell him to calm down, to reconsider, to wait. Then you'll be the damned old man, and when you are remember that compromise is the heart of government, and if you keep dividing your money before you bet it you'll never be completely out of the game." The Commissioner smiled warmly. "I'm sure you'll forgive my tendency to homily. It's a prerogative that comes with the office."

Lark wanted to ease himself enough to smile, but he was too keyed, too intent on what conditions the Commissioner would place upon the project.

"Very well," the Commissioner said, realizing that he could not hope to cool Lark down at this point. "Let's do this. Take Burden. Take him for, let's say, two weeks. Do as much as you can during that time, and at the end of the two weeks—whether you fail or succeed in reclaiming him—the project is ended. What we'll do with him then depends upon what success you've had with him. If you fail, he goes through as an integrated heretic to execution. If you succeed—well, we'll see. Now, is that fair enough?"

"Yes, sir," Lark said, without pausing to evaluate the limitation, "that will be enough time."

"All right. Today's the 16th of October," the Commissioner said, consulting his calendar. "I'll set the target date for Saturday, October 31st. That gives you a little over two weeks in which to do what you can with Burden. Fourteen days and twelve hours to be exact."

Lark nodded his head. They would have to be enough. He would see to it that they would be.

"I hate to place the element of a race into this, Lark," the Commissioner said, "but you know I do have the rest of the Department's work to consider." The Commissioner began to wonder if he had set the time limit too arbitrarily. After all, Lark was attempting an enormous job. The Commissioner knew its possible importance, but he also knew that Lark worked best under pressure. There were men who might take years to refine a job, but who would do the same job in a week if forced to that limit.

"Don't worry, sir," Lark said beginning to feel his body throb, "I'll reclaim him. I'll break his heresies one by one, I'll dig out his soul and squeeze it between my fingers. Give me the fourteen days and twelve hours and all the resources of the Department and I won't fail with Burden." His voice rose with excitement and anticipation. "I'll reclaim him, I'll heal him, I'll cleanse him. I'll make him fit for a Paradise."

"Yes, I think you will, Lark." The Commissioner, caught up with Lark's fervor, watched his deputy with frankly admiring eyes, certain now that one day he would recommend Lark for his own position.

Lark, beyond caring or hearing what the Commissioner said, knew that something crucial in his own being clung to his success with Burden. He had Burden—for fourteen days and twelve hours—only until the 31st of October. But he had Burden.

8

They were, Burden observed, quite polite but equally firm.

"But I don't need any medical examination," Burden protested.

"I'm very sorry, but it's part of our routine," the clerk said, and he accompanied a severe-looking nurse to the elevator. They got off at the eighth floor where the corridors seemed a little quieter, the paint a little brighter, and there was the faint but unmistakable blend of medicinal and antiseptic odors.

The clerk and the nurse took him into a small room which contained a bed, a night stand, and a small couch with a low table in front of it. It was quite a pleasant room, with a small glass vase filled with thick, creamy-looking chrysanthemums and fall leaves. Cheap prints were neatly hung on the walls and the floor was carpeted with an unusually thick and springy monotone gray rug. A small window facing the brick wall of the next building in the ring was the only depressing note.

"Please take all your clothes off and put these on," the nurse said, going to a closet that Burden hadn't noticed and bringing out a pair of wrinkled and faded blue pajamas. Burden saw at a glance that they would be much too large on him. He hesitated for a moment, but the clerk sat down on the bed with his clip board in front of him and the nurse waited pointedly for him to undress.

"I don't understand the purpose of this medical examination," Burden said once again.

"It's part of our routine, Professor Burden," the clerk said. He produced a large manila envelope. "This is for your valuables. You'll get a receipt for them."

"I only have a wallet, a wrist watch, my wedding band, my fountain pen, and some loose change—can't I keep that with me?"

"You may keep your wedding band but I'm afraid you'll have to give up the other things, Professor," the clerk said patiently.

"You happen to realize that this is very pointless, I hope?"

"Routine," the clerk said with a half apologetic smile.

"It's ridiculous routine," Burden grumbled, putting his wallet, pen, change, and watch into the envelope. "I didn't come here for a medical examination. I was here for a hearing. I was told to keep myself ready for further questions. No one suggested that I would be medically examined. Are you sure you have the right person?"

"Professor Burden of Templar College, a correspondent for the Department," the clerk repeated calmly. "You're not suggesting that there are two such people, Professor, are you?"

"No, I guess not," Burden finally sighed, and then began to undress. The nurse would not budge from the room so Burden had to remove his underwear in the closet. It was cramped and smelled strongly of camphor and cedar and Burden came out with his eyes stinging. The pajamas were ludicrously large and he felt as if the trousers would slip off his hips with the slightest motion so he came out of the closet holding them bunched safely with one hand.

"Thank you," the nurse said dryly, and stuffed Burden's underwear into a pillow slip with the rest of his clothes.

"Your receipt, Professor Burden," the clerk said efficiently, handing him a printed slip of paper. While Burden was looking at it both the nurse and the clerk went out of the room. Burden put the slip on the top of the night stand and realized that he was barefooted. He was tempted to open the door and call after the nurse but decided to look under the bed for a pair of slippers. There were no slippers under the bed, or in the closet, or in the drawers of the night stand—not, in fact, in the entire room. Burden was annoyed and looked about for a bell or a push button with which to call the nurse but there was none.

The whole situation, of course, was completely ridiculous. Somehow his name had become involved in red tape and he was being held for a medical examination. It was typical of large organizations—the misreading of a notation on a slip of paper, the misdirection of a memorandum. And he had always thought the Department was so efficient. Apparently, like all huge organizations, it had its moments of lunacy when its gears were thrown into improbable positions and things like this happened—the condemnation of his reports, his forthcoming medical examination. Obviously someone had made a mistake and it was now being compounded. Burden sighed as he sat down on the bed, letting his legs dangle. It would be as useless to protest now as it would be to complain later. He would simply have to wait until they discovered their error. That, he had no doubt, would not take too long. He was grateful that Emma was not expecting him back until the end of the week. It might frighten her if he did not call her and she was expecting him home the following day. Burden sighed again. Well, thanks were due for small comforts like that.

Bored with sitting on the bed, Burden began to explore the room. The view from the small window was bleak. Only if he craned his neck and stooped a bit could he see the sky, which was now deepening from a sullen gray to black. It must be nearly four-thirty now, Burden judged by the sky and by the elapsed time since he had last looked at his wrist watch. Ridiculous.

Curious about the last occupant of the room—a monster, if he were to judge by the size of the pajamas and the height to which the bed had been raised from the floor. Burden looked through the drawers of the night stand. They were empty. In his curiosity and boredom he even turned over the pillows of the couch and groped down between the arm rests and the ticking over the springs for something that might have been dropped there—a newspaper, a magazine, anything that might divert him for a few moments or satisfy his curiosity as to the last inhabitant. There was nothing but some stale wool ravelings, dust, and tobacco crumbs. Disgusted, Burden flopped down on the couch, propped his bare feet up on the low table, and sank his face against his cupped hand to wait.

His eyes traveled unhappily about the room. Plain, painted beige walls, a ceiling lined with squares of perforated cork or composition material, a chipped, brown, painted iron bed with adjustment arms and springs painted silver. The pictures on the wall were ordinary, cheap lithographed copies of idyllic country scenes—a hazy afternoon near a grist mill, a farmer leading a horse home from the fields after a day of plowing, with the sky hung between twilight and darkness. Perhaps they were chosen for their restful quality, Burden thought. The fall flowers and leaves attracted his attention. Whoever had last occupied the room had left the bouquet behind. Evidently he had had visitors. Deciding that perhaps there might be a card among the leaves and flowers, Burden pulled the vase toward him and began to grope between the leaves when he was struck by something strange. The leaves were too dry. Burden touched the chrysanthemums. A little oath of surprise came from him involuntarily. The bouquet was made of paper. The leaves, the flowers, the ferns were all paper or rubber. Burden looked at the fraud with indignant eyes. How could he have been taken in so badly? Well, perhaps it was the water in the vase. Now, why on earth should anyone want to put paper flowers and leaves in water? It made no sense. Unless, of course, they intended to fool others. Burden pushed away the vase angrily. It was such a petty, stupid thing to do— to put artificial flowers and leaves into a vase filled with water. His anger flared unreasonably. He had the uncomfortable feeling that he had been made a fool of. It was so unnecessarily cruel to cheat and defraud someone that way. For the first time Burden despised the Department. Of course, he thought, checking himself, it would be silly to blame the whole Department for this one minor deception. Probably some nitwitted supervising nurse thought flowers would cheer patients and some equally nitwitted budget director decided that paper flowers and rubber ferns would be cheaper in the long run. But why put water in the vase? That was the criminally deceptive thing. And fresh water at that. The water was clear and looked as if it had come from a tap no more than twenty minutes ago. What was more irritating, someone must have gone to all the trouble of changing the water and dusting the paper and rubber flowers, leaves, and ferns. They had time for that, but not time to leave fresh pajamas and slippers for the next occupant of the room. There was time for that silly, vain little trick, but no time for someone to check his records more carefully so that this whole silly medical examination could have been avoided. There was time to add touches to this little forgery and no time for anyone to read his reports carefully, or send him some helpful hints about his work. No, all that was ignored.

"By God," Burden said aloud, rising from the sofa angry, flushed, feeling bilked and humiliated, ready to vent his anger upon someone or something when the door opened and a young man with a short white coat and a stethoscope dangling from his neck entered.

"Are you in charge here?" Burden demanded loudly, realizing even as he spoke that this young man was nothing more than an interne.

"Why, what's wrong?" the young doctor asked.

"I resent the entire stupidity of this examination!"

"Don't you think a medical examination can be helpful?" the doctor said, putting down his long black leather case on the night stand.

"It can be helpful but it so happens I have not come to the Department for that reason. I came here for a hearing. In some typically stupid bureaucratic manner my name has been confused with another name and here I am, without slippers, wearing pajamas too large for me, about to take an examination which is not meant for me and which I do not want. Now, you march right out of here, young man, and bring in someone who has access to the records and we'll straighten this out."

"Suppose you march over here and take off the top of your pajamas," the doctor said calmly, indicating the door side of the bed.

"I'm telling you that you're examining the wrong person," Burden said loudly.

"Professor Burden, Templar College?" the doctor asked, reading from a slip he brought out of his pocket.

"Yes, I'm he. But the fact of the matter is, the error still exists and your slip has derived from that error. Now I want to see someone who has some authority around here."

"If you don't mind," the doctor said, putting the stethoscope to his ears, "the top of your pajamas, sir."

"I will *not*," Burden said stubbornly.

The doctor, who had not heard him, waited another moment. He flicked his finger impatiently. "The pajamas, Professor."

Burden folded his arms across his chest and shook his head stubbornly. He would insist upon his rights. He could not be forced to take a medical examination against his own wishes. After all, it was such a private, personal thing.

The young doctor looked at Burden for a moment and took the ear pieces out. "Don't you wish to be examined?"

"I am not the person whose examination you want," Burden said, trying to be patient. Evidently it was not the interne's fault. The stupidity arose somewhere else. Probably with that self-satisfied clerk. Or perhaps with the person who operated the public address system. Anyway, someone had made a mistake.

"Professor Burden, you are the person. The correct person. Now, will you allow me to examine you?"

"No," Burden said, although a quiet inner voice nagged

at him to give up fighting back, that it would be simpler to do what was asked of him.

The young doctor picked up the narrow black leather case and without a word walked to the door, opened it, and left. For an instant Burden felt the impulse to call him back. He didn't want to be difficult and he didn't want to hurt the young man's feelings, but all the same *they* had made the mistake, not he.

He chewed his lower lip thoughtfully, a sense of guilt nagging at him. He shouldn't have kicked up such a fuss. There was no need for it. After all, a medical examination was not a painful thing and perhaps, in the long run, it might be good for him. Certainly it would have cost him nothing but some good-natured forbearance. Burden was about to decide that if the doctor came back he would be willing to submit to examination when his eye fell on the false bouquet resting in the perfectly honest vase with its perfectly respectable clear water. That was intolerable. His anger came back. It was dishonest and cheap and sly and he resented it as an insult to his intelligence, his judgment. If he submitted now to any of their other mistaken orders he would be compromising his intelligence and personal integrity still further. No, there had to come a time when a man declared an error was an error and stood for the truth. They had made an error with his reports, had they not? Conger had made an error. True, the hearing examiners made up for Conger's obtuseness and stupidity. But now, this ridiculous error. Someone would make up for it. The Department had a reputation for scrupulous honesty and fairness. But he would certainly not permit it to go any farther. He had stood up to Conger and all indications were that he was right for standing up to the investigator and demanding a hearing. There are people who will try to intimidate others, Burden knew, and he also knew that the answer to intimidation was the refusal to flinch or to show fear. That was precisely what he would do. He sat down on the couch, his legs crossed, his arms folded, righteously waiting.

It was quite some time before the door opened again. Burden had lost track of the time entirely and he felt hungry and headachy. His bare feet had fallen asleep from chill and his back ached from his position on the couch. A few times he was tempted to rest on the bed but decided against it lest he fall asleep. He wanted to be awake if anyone should enter.

A stocky man in an ordinary business suit came into the room. He had thick, curly hair and a heavy-featured face that was a cross between a Botticelli cherub and a cheap gangster, pictures of which Burden had seen in history books of the middle-twentieth century.

"Are you the man in charge?" Burden asked uncertainly. He was too hungry and tired to quarrel.

"Yes, in a manner of speaking," the stocky man said, closing the door behind him and pulling over a chair in front of the low table. "My name is Richard," the man said with a brief smile as he sat down without offering his hand.

Burden straightened up a bit on the couch, doubting that Richard (was it his last name or his first?) had anything to do with the medical staff of the Department. "Well, I'm afraid that there's been an error made, Mr. Richard. I was asked here to attend a hearing and some damned fool has had me sent here mistakenly for a medical examination."

"I know, Professor Burden," Richard said calmly.

"Well," Burden straightened up still further, expectantly, "then you do understand an error has been made. I'd like to have my clothes back and hear the results of my hearing so that I can get home sometime this evening."

"Oh, but you must have the medical examination, Professor Burden," Richard said mildly. "That wasn't a mistake. That examination was as much for our protection as it was for yours."

"Protection?"

"Why, yes. Of course, it *is* an old ordinance of the Department and very probably one of these days it will be superseded. But for the present we have to observe it as long as it is in effect. You see, in the old days, oh, probably forty years ago when the Department was first founded, members of the Legislature feared that the Department might resort to physical violence in its investigations. Don't look so surprised. The police methods prevailing some fifty years ago were quite barbaric. A man might quite easily be beaten in order to make him speak. Well, as I said, members of the Legislature, being rather apprehensive of the broad powers of the Department, explicitly appended to the Department's codes the ordinance that all persons who shall be under investigation within the physical limits of the Department's buildings shall, before discharge, be given a physical examination by an officially approved medical officer to determine whether the suspect has been subjected to physical violence. As you may have guessed, I'm quoting the ordinance almost word for word. So, you see, before you leave you must be examined to satisfy that ordinance."

"How curious," Burden said, seeing at once how all the baffling events that went before now neatly and easily fitted into place. No mistake had been made after all. And he had kicked up such a fuss.

"Of course," Richard said, "someone should have told you this before. But sometimes our people get so absorbed in the routine of their jobs they quite forget that other people don't see the sense of what's being done."

"Now it certainly does make sense. It is an archaic ordinance, isn't it?"

"As I said, Professor, it's been on the Department's code since its founding. We've never appealed to the Legislature for its repeal because, frankly, we'd rather have it in force so that not the slightest question of doubt can be cast on the Department's methods."

"I didn't think you'd worry about that, Mr. Richard," Burden said with a smile, "not with the reputation the Department enjoys."

"Thank you, Professor Burden."

"Well, then, I assume that my hearing is over? I mean, no further questions?"

"Oh, just a few routine ones. I would have been here sooner if you had taken your physical examination. You see, the physical is almost the last thing. You can see why, I trust?"

"Oh, yes, yes, of course. Well, could I have the physical this evening?"

"Well, I'm afraid it's past the dinner hour now and it might be a little difficult. But let me see what I can do after I leave."

"Oh, yes," Burden said, remembering, "you did say you had a few questions to ask. Well, let's get on with them, Mr. Richard."

"Fine," Richard said, producing a small pad and a pencil. "Professor Burden, you said that you had never received any communication from your superior in your ten years?"

"That's right. That's what I told the hearing examiners and Mr. Conger."

Richard made a note on his pad. "And because of this you presumed that your reports were satisfactory?"

"Of course. Wouldn't you?"

"To tell you the truth, yes," Richard said with a sudden laugh. Burden nodded pleasantly. He was beginning to warm to this young man. He was certainly more human than the literal-minded Mr. Conger. "Would you like to continue in your capacity as correspondent for the Department, Professor?"

"Why, yes, I guess so."

"I can't blame you for being a little hesitant," Richard said understandingly. "You have been given a rather rough going-over."

"Oh, everyone's been very nice to me, Mr. Richard. The hearing examiners were particularly kind and thoughtful. The only one who's given me a 'rough going-over,' as you put it, was Mr. Conger. Frankly, I don't understand his attitude."

"Well, Conger is a rather suspicious cuss, Professor. He's a good man but a trifle officious and overbearing."

"That's exactly the way I felt. I'm glad you people know about him. I don't want to hurt the man's position or anything like that, you understand," Richard nodded quickly, understandingly, "but he treated me as if I were mentally deficient or trying to hide something. I mean, some of the things he suggested about me—well, they weren't true at all."

"Yes, of course we know that. You see, some of Conger's questions and assumptions were deliberately provocative. We wanted to find out what your reactions were."

"Oh?" Burden asked, interested. "You mean, some of the things he said to me weren't true at all?"

"Of course not," Richard smiled. "For instance—the remark about your reports. It was just a riser question.

You know, a question or a statement intended to get a rise out of you."

"He certainly got a rise out of me," Burden said with a chuckle, recalling the way he had felt and acted in Conger's office.

"The Department works in many different ways, Professor Burden, because we have many different sorts of people to deal with. You can understand, of course, why Conger should use the standard techniques on you."

"Yes, of course. I mean, it's his job. I know that. He has to do his job. But I just had the feeling that he wasn't discerning enough."

"Well, as I said, Conger is a fairly ordinary, unimaginative sort. Between the two of us, I've always disliked the man. I've had a few other cases like yours."

"Is that a fact?" Burden leaned forward intimately.

"I wouldn't want you to repeat this, Professor," Richard said with a quiet warning shake of his hand.

"Of course not," Burden said, interested.

"But frankly, I've had my fill of Frank Conger. I mean, some things are excusable in an investigator—but this is unfair. I mean, there would have been no need for a hearing or for a physical examination or for my visit if Conger had used simple common sense in your case."

"Yes, I suppose so," Burden said thoughtfully. "He's probably started a terrific chain of events in motion by his attitude toward me."

"Oh, Lord," Richard said with a shocked smile, "the paper work, the memoranda, the schedules, the reports, the assignments—you know, every hearing entails an enormous amount of preparation. Did you realize all of your reports for the past ten years had to be read and abstracted for the hearing?"

"Good grief," Burden said with a sense of shock and

awe. Evidently he hadn't the foggiest notion of the amount of time and effort the Department had to expend to give him his hearing. Burden's resentment against Conger mounted with the thought of all that might not have had to happen if Conger had been less zealous and more perceptive. "If I had realized what it meant I never would have asked for a hearing."

"Oh, you were perfectly within your rights, Professor. And frankly, I think you acted wisely in that respect. I mean, we owe you a debt of gratitude for showing up Conger. This whole mess goes into his rating file."

"Ummm," Burden said thoughtfully. It sounded serious for Conger and he was going to speak up at this point in Conger's defense but Richard went on, "But, after all, in an organization this size there's bound to be an enormous amount of official stupidity. That can't be helped. I don't know what breeds these blind spots in people in the Department. Maybe they're in their jobs too long without examining the purposes of their work with any real understanding. I mean, some of the minor things—so incredibly ridiculous."

"Ummm," Burden agreed quickly, "like that bouquet, for instance."

Richard stopped and looked bewildered for a moment.

"Those flowers in the vase," Burden said, "they're false. Paper flowers."

"Oh?" Richard said politely.

"Well, I mean, if you're going to use paper flowers and rubber ferns—why put them in fresh water?" Burden asked. Richard looked at the vase and turned back to Burden. He was smiling, but Burden saw that the agreeable Mr. Richard didn't understand. "Well, don't you see the fresh water?"

"Why, yes, of course," Richard said. To Burden it seemed as if Richard's eyes had narrowed slightly with puzzlement.

"But—the incongruity of it—using real water with false flowers. If you're going to use paper flowers, use them, but don't try to fool people into thinking they're real by placing them in real water."

"I'm afraid I don't follow you, Professor Burden," Richard said, genuinely puzzled.

"Isn't it obvious that it's an official stupidity to treat paper flowers as if they were real flowers?" Burden was slightly disturbed by Richard's failure to understand the point. It was really so simple—the dishonesty was so manifest.

"Well," Richard said with a bland smile, "people have their reasons for everything, don't they? But what Conger's reasons were for failing to understand that you're a cultured man—" Richard stopped when he saw Burden's face. "Professor Burden, what's wrong?"

Burden had been looking at Richard with a hard look. There was something about the man's failure to see the dishonesty of paper flowers in fresh water that upset him.

"You don't understand what's wrong with putting paper flowers in real water?" Burden asked, watching Richard narrowly.

"Well, really, Professor," Richard began with a smile that quite suddenly disappeared. Even his voice seemed to change subtly in tone when he spoke again, "After all, you use paper flowers as an illusion. If you can aid the illusion by adding real water to it—what's wrong with that?"

"But the paper flowers are obviously frauds—"

"Didn't they fool you?" Richard asked coldly.

"Yes," Burden said after a long moment, "they did."

"Then they obviously aren't as fraudulent in their appearance as you say they are."

Burden listened to the remark and fell silent. There was something very wrong with this pleasant young man who seemed, at first, so understanding, so genuinely warm and nonofficial.

"Well, anyway, flowers aside." Richard once again picked up the thread of intimate warmth and companionability he had been using, but even he sensed that something had gone wrong, for he stopped and waited.

"Have you any more questions?" Burden asked in a calm, cool voice.

"I guess not, Professor Burden," Richard said, rising now and closing his notebook, "as I said—this was just a routine visit."

"I hope you can arrange for my physical examination this evening—and oh, some dinner, if that's possible. I'm very hungry."

"Oh, yes, of course," Richard said, picking up the chair and replacing it neatly beside the bed, "dinner can be managed very well. About the physical—let me see what I can do. I hope it won't inconvenience you too much if it has to be put off until tomorrow morning? I mean, you do have a comfortable bed and room here."

"There's no bathroom," Burden pointed out.

"The first door on your left as you go out," Richard said with a smile.

"Yes," Burden replied, but the smile no longer pleased or satisfied him. There was something very wrong with Mr. Richard—almost as much wrong with him as with Mr. Frank Conger. "But I would appreciate being examined this evening so I can catch the late train home," Burden said as Richard was opening the door.

"I'll do my very best, Professor," Richard said as he stepped out and closed the door.

Burden regarded the door for a long time after Richard left. There was something struggling in his head. It flickered uneasily, stirring lightly. It had something to do with the Department—with the feeling that he was being deliberately manipulated and used. First Conger, who was deliberately hostile; then the hearing examiners, deliberately pleasant, noncommittal, understanding; and now this Richard. Why? Toward what end? What did they expect him to do or say? There was some purpose behind all the things that had happened, but what was it? Did they suspect him of something? But of what? Certainly not falsifying his reports, neglecting his duties. But what else? Heresy? Was that it? Did they suspect him of heresy?

Burden's dinner came within twenty minutes after Richard left. It was a good meal but a little sparing, the way hospital meals are apt to be, and the food was cold. But Burden was so hungry he was grateful for the tray. He asked the ward attendant who brought the tray to see if he could be brought a pair of slippers. The ward attendant said he would see about it. When he returned for the tray he brought Burden a pair of new felt slippers without heels. The slippers were so new and so filled with sizing they felt cold and slippery on his feet. Burden rested in bed, thinking odd thoughts, wondering if the door were really open. For a long time he rested in bed, his legs crossed, his new slippers on his feet, his back propped up against the pillow, speculating upon whether or not the door could be opened from his side. He had seen the doctor do it, seen Richard do it, seen the ward attendant do it. And yet he had the feeling that if he wanted to open the door he couldn't. Finally, when the heat had been turned off and the lights were out, he got out of bed, walked to the door, and tried the handle. He had been right. The door would not open.

Burden got back onto the bed, let his slippers drop to the floor, and got under the covers, certain that he wouldn't be called for an examination before the next day.

But he was wrong. At four o'clock in the morning they came to get him.

9

They couldn't have selected a better time for it. The instant Burden felt the firm, sharp hand on his shoulder shaking him he was aware of a terrific pain in his bladder. The room was dark and cold and it was only by the reflection of the moonlight on the starched white blouse of the man who woke him that Burden could make out a face. All he could tell was that it was a face.

"Your physical, Professor Burden," the face said in the soft, low-pitched voice of someone who does not want to disturb other sleepers.

"I have to go to the bathroom," Burden said, straightening up in bed.

"All right, but please don't waste time," the face said, and Burden felt himself helped out of bed by hands that were cold and bony. He groped for the slippers and shrank involuntarily at their clammy contact. The rug retained some warmth and he gratefully felt it beneath the stiff felt, the sizing, the chilled flesh of his feet. The door was opened on a corridor that seemed endless in length. At its extreme end burned a sickly yellow light. In that light, as if Burden were watching a perfect miniature, a figure worked on its hands and knees scrubbing the floor. Whether the figure was a man or a woman Burden could not tell, but he heard the distant, rhythmic slur and return of a brush. He turned in the wrong direction for the bathroom and felt the hand at his elbow correcting him.

Burden pushed open the door and found the bathroom in darkness. Its antiseptic smell struck his nostrils sharply and he was astonished at how cold the bathroom was. The windows were open wide to the night air. Burden barked his shins on a pail set in the middle of the floor and the pail clattered on the tiles. The pain so surprised and seized Burden that he stopped short—and then hurried on.

His head throbbed and he panted a bit from the intense relief. He hesitated a moment, feeling giddy, resting his hand on the cold enameled steel. Light struck the polished copper pipes and he saw the beads of wet condensation on them.

"All right?" the man with the white jacket called to Burden, who nodded his head in reply.

In the corridor Burden was able to get his first good look at his escort's face. He was no doctor. At least he didn't seem to be a doctor. He had a hard, flat, broken face like that of a professional prize fighter. He walked beside Burden, keeping pace with his painful steps on the cold floor. The man in the white coat said nothing during their long walk down the corridor toward the tiny figure with its brush. Burden could still not tell whether the figure was that of a man or a woman. There was something curiously shapeless and anonymous about it, as if it had no sex, as if it were a neuter in gray doomed forever and ever to wash and wax the long corridors during the dead of night. It seemed such a lonely fate. Perhaps if there had been two figures instead of that lonely one. If the figure were in the middle of the corridor instead of its distant end. But then, Burden thought, there was no end to the corridor. It circled back upon itself and for all he knew the figure progressed completely about the circle during the night and repeated the trip night after night.

"We're going to see the doctor?" Burden asked of his escort, just to shake the thought of the night cleaner from his mind.

"Yes," the man in the white jacket said.

"And will I get my clothes then?"

"After you see the doctor you'll get your clothes."

Then the man in the white jacket took Burden's arm and stopped him and steered him through heavy swinging doors with polished copper striker plates. It was some sort of a clinic or laboratory. It was not lit except for a small desk lamp at the far end of the room. Burden could make out cubicles with white cloth screens stretched on iron pipe frames. There were padded leather examining tables in the cubicles and on the wall opposite the cubicles was a row of porcelain and copper tubs. There was a network of piping on the wall with an elaborate system of valves and wheels and temperature gauges. Some sort of hydrotherapy equipment, Burden decided. All the equipment looked new and here and there gave off cold glints of surgical cleanliness, gold, silver, pale white. There was a padded leather examining table in the center of the room and Burden's escort steered him to it. His escort smacked the leather top with his hand. It made a sharp sound reminiscent of a hand striking bared flesh.

"Hop up on here, Professor. The doctor'll be with you in a minute."

Burden mounted the table, feeling the cold leather chill his buttocks through the thin pajamas. He faced the cubicles, the tubs at his back. He could see that long windows lined the wall, one for each of the cubicles. They, too, faced the brick wall of the neighboring ring building but moonlight filtered through faintly so that the white screens looked starched with terror.

Footsteps at the entrance to the room made Burden turn his head. A doctor came toward them. Not the same young man who had first come into Burden's room. This was an older man, heavier, who walked more slowly. He came up to Burden and put his hand on his knee. It was a heavy hand, warm and somehow reassuring.

"Good morning, Professor," the doctor said, and Burden nodded his head. The doctor seemed rather kindly, reminding Burden somewhat of a colleague on the staff at Templar. For some reason the colleague's name escaped him. The doctor, his hand still on Burden's knee, said something to the young man with the fighter's face and the young man nodded and walked to the opposite end of the room where the desk lamp was lit.

"Well, we've got a physical examination, haven't we?" The doctor tapped Burden's knee reassuringly. "Won't take long. Take off the top of your pajamas," the doctor said. The skin on his back prickled from the cold air in the room. The doctor fixed the horns of his stethoscope in his ears and placed the tube on Burden's chest. "Breathe in deeply, please—exhale—again, please—exhale—again, please—" The doctor plucked the stethoscope horns from his ears and smiled faintly at Burden. "You're a little excited, aren't you?"

"No," Burden said.

"Your heart's going a mile a minute," the doctor said calmly, taking Burden's wrist and looking at his watch.

Burden felt his pulse increase its beat under the pressure of the doctor's thumb. He also thought he felt his heart picking up in its rate. "Man, what are you so upset about?" the doctor asked, smiling. "I'll bet if I took your blood pressure now it would be over a hundred and eighty. Calm down. Do you normally have high blood pressure?"

"No, not normally," Burden said, wondering where the young man with the fighter's broken face had gone, wondering what the doctor had whispered to him.

"Have you been unusually upset the past few days?" the doctor asked, picking out a small black instrument from a drawer in a table near the examining couch.

"Well, not unusually," Burden said, feeling more fear now than he ever had in his life. There seemed to be something in the back of the doctor's mind that he sensed, something that frightened him. They were always talking, the people of the Department. They were always trying to lead him into something, admitting something, confessing something, agreeing to something. What? Why?

"You're very tense," the doctor said, snapping the switch on the small black hand instrument. A tiny beam of light came out. The doctor gestured at Burden's glasses. He removed them and the doctor used the small pinpoint of light on Burden's pupils. Finally satisfied, he snapped off the light and then turned Burden by the shoulders. "Mmm, no bruises, contusions, abrasions, or welts."

"Can you tell in this light?" Burden asked dryly.

"There never are any, Professor Burden," the doctor replied with weary good humor, "it's just routine. However, there is something about you that isn't quite routine."

"Yes?" Burden felt himself alerted, his pulse increasing.

"You're very tense and upset about something. I don't imagine you'll sleep well unless you get some sedation."

"I don't want to sleep at all," Burden said, "I want to get my clothes and get out of here. If I'm going to do any sleeping I'll do it at home, in my own bed. May I have my clothes now?"

"Good heavens, man, you don't think I have them, do you?"

"You can get them, though, can't you?"

"It's four o'clock in the morning, Professor. There isn't anyone around who could open the wardrobe room, much less select your clothes bundle. Anyway, there are half a hundred forms and releases and papers to be filled out and signed before you can go home. That'll all be taken care of in the morning."

"Red tape again?"

"Red tape," the doctor smiled. "Let me get you that sedative."

"I don't want any, Doctor."

"Professor Burden, as a qualified physician I feel that you ought to take some sedation. You're not exactly a young man and a day of some strain combined with a sleepless night isn't the best regimen for someone your age."

"I'll want to leave as soon as possible in the morning, Doctor, so I think I'll stay up the rest of the night, if you don't mind."

"My dear Professor, you don't imagine that you'll be processed at the crack of dawn, do you? Tomorrow's Saturday; that means only half the clerical force is on duty. It will be nearly noon by the time they get around to you. Thank your lucky stars I did Mr. Richard a special favor by taking you on now. Otherwise you'd have to wait hours for your examination and *then* begin your wait for the paper work. Now, be a good fellow, put your pajama jacket on, and lie down here for a few moments. I'll be right back. Some six hours of rest now would do you a world of good." The doctor turned then and walked down the length of the room toward the desk with the burning lamp. His footfalls were heavy and slow in the examining room.

Burden buttoned his jacket, his hands trembling. Perhaps the doctor was right after all. A good night's rest would do wonders for him. In a way, the doctor was being quite thoughtful and he shouldn't be so suspicious and contrary. And yet he could not shake off the sense of something sinister, something very wrong approaching him on silent feet.

The doctor returned with a warm woolen blanket that he spread carelessly over Burden. "Cover yourself up. The warmer you are the quicker the sedation will take effect. Once you're asleep we'll put you on one of the wheeled stretchers and take you back to your room."

When Burden saw the light glint off the barrel of a hypodermic he started to rise from the table. "I thought it would be a pill or a powder."

"Don't tell me you're afraid of the needle," the doctor said with a tired smile as he held the point of the hypodermic up and gently pressed the plunger to fill the hollow needle. "This is much quicker than any pill or powder. Now, keep covered up. You don't want to catch a chill." He reached under the blanket and drew Burden's arm out. He pushed up the pajama jacket sleeve and Burden felt the cold, alcohol-wet pad being briskly rubbed on his forearm. Then the slightest stab of pain and the weight of the needle pulling slightly at his flesh as the plunger was depressed. "That's all there is to it," the doctor said with a smile, pulling down the sleeve and putting Burden's arm back under the blanket. "You'll be asleep in a little while and I'll have the attendant take you back." He tucked the blanket around Burden much in the manner that he recalled his mother doing when he was a child. He stared up at the ceiling that seemed dizzyingly high, a long pale oblong with many recessed bars of light so that they looked like the ties in railroad tracks.

Burden felt a deep, suffusing flush as if his blood were being heated. He wanted to push the cover away from his chin but the doctor's hand pushed it back. His body felt warm and a sense of stifling overcame him. He put up his hand to push at the cover.

"You leave that alone," the doctor said softly, "you'll cool off in a few moments. You don't want to catch a chill now. Let yourself relax a little and you'll be asleep in no time." The doctor's voice seemed remote, as if he had retreated a few paces. But, of course, he hadn't. Burden could still see that. The doctor's face was close enough for him to see that he hadn't shaved too carefully under the rounded point of his chin, which bore a thin line of gray bristles like a minute fringe. Now his eyes began to sting and burn, his limbs grew heavier. Somehow he got the impression that the doctor was looking at his eyes. Not at his face, but only at his eyes. Desperately he wanted to tear off the cover. But when he tried with the tips of his fingers he couldn't. The doctor was holding it down against his chest, just under his chin. It shouldn't have been difficult to push the doctor's fingers aside, they seemed to be resting so lightly on the blanket. But Burden found it impossible to summon any strength in his fingers. He felt as if he were floating from the table, the warmth began to disappear, and a sense of chill began to settle in him. Almost at once an overpowering surge of nausea swept into his throat and he waited for the retching.

"Take it easy," the doctor said quietly, "that'll pass. In

a few moments you'll just feel lazy. Just relaxed and lazy."

The nausea disappeared and then, as the doctor had said, he began to feel lazy, luxurious, disassociated from himself; a wonderful feeling of passive pleasure began to seep through him and he wondered if he had ever rested so comfortably. It was like lying in bed of a Sunday morning after breakfast, with spring bright and promising outside the window, birds making their tender, high piping sounds on the grass of the front lawn, and the miraculous sensation of having nothing to do. The doctor's face grew indistinct and he began to forget where he was. He could almost swear that he was at home again, his father still alive, his brother Ralph humming as he shaved and showered, his mother working on the garden. They must have had breakfast already. Strange they hadn't called him, he thought. He was always being badgered to get out of bed on Sunday morning and have breakfast early so that they could all go to church. But there was no church this morning, no dull droning in a dark, cold building, no breakfast in the kitchen with the sense of hurrying. No one cared if he got out of bed at all. Perhaps it was a holiday from breakfast and church. A holiday, he decided delightedly. Well, what sort of holiday? Not Christmas, not anyone's birthday. But it was a holiday. Well, who cared which one? He was snug and cozy in bed, no one was bothering him, and he didn't have to have breakfast if he didn't want to. When Ralph came out of the shower he'd ask him to bring something up—if he should feel hungry. And he knew Ralph would smile and say, "Sure"—not that Ralph always did, but he would this time. He would because it was a holiday.

"The early recollections are typical," someone said and

he wondered who had said it. Was it Ralph? Not Ralph. He was still in the shower. But surely, that couldn't be right. Ralph was dead. He was crushed to death on that farm by a tractor. He had been sleeping on the ground and no one had noticed him.

"Ralph was important to you, wasn't he?"

Well, of course he was. He was my brother. Now who asked that?

"Was it because he was just your brother?"

What? What nonsense. He was my brother and I loved him. He was honest and strong and he hated a liar. He hated anything that was false or impure or wrong. Like my father. A thing that is wrong is like a thing that is sick or stunted.

"Then to be sick is to be wrong?"

No, no, not at all. You don't understand. Who is asking these foolish questions, anyway? Not that. My father never said that at all. You are reversing it. It doesn't mean that at all. It means that a thing that is wrong contains a sickness, a kind of malaise. A thing can be sick and not be wrong. A person might be sick and not be wrong or impure or a lie. Don't you see that? It's quite simple. No, I don't have to explain that. Why should it have to be explained? You can see it at once, like a nail that has been driven improperly. It's not too complex. It's quite simple.

"Go on."

Go on about what?

"Anything."

Now that's nonsense. Only a fool goes on and on. What shall I go on about?

"About the nail."

Don't be a fool.

102

"Is it easy to recognize something that is wrong or impure or a lie?"

Of course it is. My father said any man who can call his soul his own can tell about those things. There's no trick to it. All you have to do is to use your eyes and your ears and your soul.

"Is it a lie to report your friends and colleagues?"

Report them for what?

"Heresy."

Only a fool would ask that.

"Is it wrong?"

Don't be childish.

"Is it?"

Don't ask that.

"Why not?"

Don't ask it.

"But why?"

Don't.

"Why?"

No. Don't.

"Try something else."

Try what else? What should I try?

"It's concealment. Deep concealment. He won't tell you."

Who is concealed? What won't he tell you?

"Is there such a thing as heresy?"

Oh.

"Is there?"

They brought my brother's body back on the hottest day of the summer and I could smell him right through the coffin. It was awful. I wished that my nose had fallen off. I wished that I had been struck blind or crazy or dead. He stank and I didn't want to think that. It was wrong to think. He was my own brother. It was an awful thing to think of your own brother who was dead and would never talk or listen or laugh or read his books or go on to important things that everyone was so sure he would do. I wished I was blind or dead or something. I couldn't stand the idea that I could smell him and the smell was awful. Oh, God, it was a sin.

"Won't he answer that one, either?"

Answer what? If you want to know—ask. Ask and ye shall be given. Who are you?

"You'll hear more of his childhood if you ask questions like that. He won't answer them. Ask him things he's consciously thought out."

You are certainly impolite, whoever you are. I don't want to hear about anyone's goddamned childhood, least of all yours.

"He must have been in his teens when his brother died."

Did someone's brother die? That's an awful thing. It happened to my brother, you know. My brother, Ralph. He was going to be an artist. They had great hopes for him. I know how you feel about that. It happened to me. Such a horrible accident, too. So unnecessary in the way it happened. A tractor—

"Do you enjoy the reports?"

The reports?

"The reports you write for the Department."

Yes, I like to write them.

"Why?"

Oh.

"Is he going to start that again?"

Start what?

"Ask him again. The hesitation is sometimes only a momentary block."

Hesitation *is* a momentary thing. Hesitation by its very definition means a pause, an interruption in something that is in motion. I suppose you're a freshman student. That would explain the confusion over such a simple word.

"Why do you like the reports you do for the Department?"

Oh, they are pleasant. Like literary exercises. You show off so much.

"How, show off?"

To show off. It's an old English slang expression. It means to demonstrate one's powers with a sense of vanity or pride in one's own accomplishments.

"Then it is your vanity that is involved in your work?"

Yes, of course. Every man is vain about something.

"What do you hope to get from your reports?"

Nothing.

"What do you hope others will think of you?"

Oh, that I am a cultured, intelligent sort of person with a soul.

"Different from others?"

Different?

"Different in that you are intelligent and cultured?"

Well, yes, I mean that.

"Do you feel superior to others?"

Yes.

"Many others?"

Yes.

"To everyone?"

Don't be a fool. Of course not.

"But superior to most?"

Yes.

"Superior to Mr. Frank Conger?"

Absolutely. He's a fool, that man.

"Superior to Mr. Richard?"

Yes. He has no soul. He seems to have a soul but he doesn't. There's a quite a difference. He wouldn't understand the bent nail as a lie. He didn't understand how much of a lie the paper flowers were.

"What upset you about the paper flowers?"

They were false.

"But why should it upset you?"

False, wrong, a lie. Don't those things upset you, too?

"But they were only flowers."

They were like everything in the place.

"What place?"

The Department. They were all a lie.

"Who are 'they'?"

They, the people. The people in the restaurant. They seemed to be enjoying themselves but they weren't. They were frightened. Conger said I had done badly and he had lied, too. He was trying to frighten me. And Richard. He lied, too. He pretended to be my friend but he wasn't. He pretended he understood but he didn't. The flowers tripped him up. He was lying. He wasn't of our sort.

"Our sort?"

Yes, of course.

"What do you mean by our sort?"

I mean the people with souls, the people who understand what a lie means, what a soul means. People who understand how false it is to put paper flowers in fresh water.

"These people with souls, who understand about the falsity of things—are they friends of yours?"

Yes, of course. All of them.

"Are they all members of the college faculty?"

Don't be a fool.

"These people—our sort—what are their names?"

I can't tell you that.

"Why not? Are you forbidden?"

Of course not. What sort of question is that?

"Then tell their names."

There are too many of them. And so many of them are strangers to me.

"You know some of the names, don't you?"

Well, of course I do.

"Then tell the names you do know."

Oh, people like Emma.

"Emma who?"

My wife, Emma. You are dense. And Middleton. Doctor Middleton. He's a good sort even if he does have a foul mouth. I think deep down Middleton is one of our sort.

"A colleague of yours?"

Yes. On the staff of the English Department. Haven't you met Doctor Middleton?

"Are there other colleagues of—our sort?"

Oh, I don't know. Most of them are frightened. Middleton speaks out too much for his own good. He'll be caught for heresy someday. I wouldn't like that. I think Middleton's a man with honesty, with a soul, deep down.

"There must be others of—our sort. Who are they?"

Oh, I don't know. Probably that Drake girl in the art department. I'm glad I didn't put her on the report that time. She had spirit, that girl. A rare thing these days, spirit.

"Others?"

Oh, I don't know. Professor Kloetter, probably. He talks too much for his own good, too. Someday I will have to tell him to keep his opinions to himself. They're heretical. Minor heresies, to be sure. But I suspect that deep down he's our sort. I suppose it would shock him if I told him I had been reading his lips for ten years.

"These people—do you meet with them?"

Oh, occasionally. At lunch and between classes, things like that, you know. Only rarely a social evening at home. Emma doesn't care for Middleton's jokes. She thinks they're vulgar. They probably are, although I notice she laughs at them. They are funny sometimes.

"At these meetings—do you discuss plans?"

Plans? What sort of plans?

"Plans to spread your heresy further?"

What nonsense. Why should we spread heresy?

"Is it not a plan directed at the government?"

Oh, you must be out of your mind. We would never dream of a thing like that. You're speaking of conspiracy, are you not?

"Aren't you a conspirator?"

Of course not. I can see the semantic confusion. You must have come from an especially poor local school. They turn out some wretched products. It's unfair how much the children have to miss. Those local schools and that ridiculous, watered-down religion.

"You mean the Church of State religion?"

Hogwash. It's a religion without meaning. It teaches people to be obedient sheep, to ignore their individuality, their immortal souls. It substitutes some sort of mass soul of which everyone has a share. It's ridiculous. Don't they know that God gave each human a soul to call his own? Each of us is a separate miracle, one quite as miraculous as the other. We owe that debt to God to retain our separate, personal identities. Otherwise we behave like some segmented insect—a caterpillar, or a centipede, or a barnacle. Man is uniquely one.

"Then men owe allegiance to no one but God?"

No, I didn't say that. Allegiance is owed in a certain order. Above all a man owes allegiance to himself. To thine own self be true, and it must follow, as the night the day, thou canst not then be false to any man. That's one of the commonest quotes in ancient literature. True to one's self, to one's God, to one's loved ones, to one's fellow human creatures. That's all the allegiance any man owes.

"You put the State last."

I did not include the State at all. It doesn't belong except in so far as it is part of a man's self or his conviction, or part of his fellow men and their convictions. But, in any case, it comes last. A man gives up certain privileges of will to the State so that he may pursue his more important allegiances, but when the State interferes in those more important allegiances he has a right to ignore the State and the right to break off his contract.

"Tell more of that feeling about allegiance."

What else is there to tell? It's perfectly clear.

"Illustrate it."

Well, it's simple. A man owes an allegiance to his own sense of self-respect. No state has the right to order a man to betray his own sense of what is right by asking him to swear to one thing when he believes another.

"Be more explicit. How?"

No state has the right to ask a man to believe in heresy.

"The State does not ask you to do that."

But it does. The State says that heresy exists.

"But you admit that it does exist."

Nonsense. Heresy means that an opinion is held against established doctrine. There is no established doctrine permissible under the contract citizens sign with the State. Hence there can be no heresy.

"Are you saying that the State has no right to establish doctrine?"

Yes, that is precisely what I am saying.

"Are you a heretic?"

No. I told you there is no heresy and hence no heretics.

"Within the present meaning of the term—are you a heretic?"

The present meaning of the term is in error.

"Within the present erroneous meaning of the term—are you a heretic?"

Yes, of course.

There was a long silence, and Burden slept without dreams, without sounds, without words.

10

Burden awoke with a faint headache. He felt sick to his stomach. He was back in his small room on the high bed. The curtains were parted and he could see the bleak day outside, the windows streaked with rain. It looked as though it were still raining. He tried to move and found his bones and muscles ached. He must have slept for quite a long time after the doctor gave him the needle but he didn't feel at all rested. It took a great deal of effort for him to straighten up in bed but he knew he had to get down and see someone—a nurse or a doctor, someone. Surely his papers were ready to be processed now. He brought his legs out from under the covers and sat up in bed; his head swam and he had to put out his hand to steady himself.

The door opened and a nurse came in. "Oh, you're not trying to get out of bed, I hope?" she asked brightly.

"I—I'm leaving this morning," Burden said, feeling terribly weak. It must have been powerful sedation to have this sort of aftereffect, he thought. But if it were only a sedative, should it have left him as limp as this?

"Now you get right back under those covers and I'll bring you some broth and crackers," the nurse said, smiling professionally and gently forcing him back against the pillow.

"No, no, I'm all right. It's a sedative the doctor gave me early this morning. I haven't quite shaken it off. I'll be all right in a few moments."

"You'll be all right tomorrow morning," the nurse said, gently but steadily pressing against his chest.

"Tomorrow morning?" Burden asked, alarmed.

"You get a day's rest in bed and a good night's sleep, and tomorrow morning we'll let you off the bed. You've been a sick boy."

"Sick? I haven't been sick at all."

"Oh, no? Would you like to see your temperature chart?"

"Temperature?"

"I took it myself this morning while you were asleep. One hundred and two. It's down now. But not nearly enough for you to get out of that bed. Now, come on, be a good boy and I'll bring you some delicious broth and crackers."

"But I'm not sick," Burden protested feebly, feeling her strength and her youth pushing him back, watching her close the covers about him again.

"You are sick. Now, lie there and be a good boy and I'll be back in a few moments."

After she left Burden rested against the pillow, shocked and confused. She believed what she had said. But he wasn't sick. It was the effect of the sedation. It must have caused him to be feverish during the night. But that didn't mean he was sick. He hadn't been sick. Didn't these doctors understand the effects of their own drugs? Surely the doctor who had administered the needle had told the nurse what to expect. The doctor had warned him against catching a chill. Had he caught a chill, then? Was that what they meant when they said he was sick? But this was criminal. If he caught a chill it was because they were negligent. After all, he was under the influence of a sedative, he couldn't be responsible for keeping his covers about him. Burden's hands flapped helplessly with frustration. They kept making mistakes. Sick or not, he would have to insist upon being released this afternoon. He didn't know how he would manage the trip back home. Perhaps he could call Emma and have her borrow someone's car and drive down to pick him up. It would be the simplest thing to do but Burden didn't want to upset Emma. And now he felt so exhausted and shaky that perhaps it would be best for him to remain overnight. Errors, errors, and errors again. They seemed to have such a wicked, fiendish ability to reproduce themselves in larger, uglier images. The chain would have to break somewhere and he would be free of the Department. This time he would give up his job with it, have nothing to do with them. He was sick of it, the sly young men, the officious ones, the deadly pyramid of paper, the ten thousand reins of reason that were crossed and tangled without purpose.

II

The conference had been in progress since eight o'clock in the morning. Now it was nearly two in the afternoon. None of the earnest young men of the Psychosemantics Division appeared at all fatigued, although a few of the medical staffmen were flushed and irritable. The political analyst was a weak-eyed man with thick glasses and a drooping mustache that gave him the appearance of a diffident walrus. He had said practically nothing in the conference that had virtually resolved itself into a quarrel between the two medical members of the conference and the three spirited psychosemanticists. The recording of Burden's words as they were spoken under the influence of the drug had been played eight times and referred to more than twenty times. The arguments had raged back and forth during the morning.

Lark had presided over the conference since its beginning, his chin sunk into a cupped hand, one bony, sharp knee drawn up so his shinbone pressed against the edge of the table, his large, pale eyes watching alertly at times, drooping deceptively with sleep at other times. He had not slept at all during the previous night except for a cat nap in a hard chair while waiting for Burden to be brought down. His clothing was rumpled, his fingernails grimy, and he smelled the stale sweat of his body. By two in the afternoon he had heard enough and dismissed the two medical staff members.

"Thank you, gentlemen, you've been most helpful," Lark said pleasantly as the two doctors rose and looked angrily at the members of the Psychosemantics Division.

"Of course, sir, I trust that you will carefully weigh the opinions of a traditional, tested science against the bastard offspring of two minor systems of inquiry," one of the older doctors said severely.

"I will, Doctor," Lark said without a smile. The doctors nodded formally and respectfully to Lark and left.

After they had gone one of the more disrespectful of the psychosemanticists sniffed and asked calmly, "Did he call us bastards?"

The political analyst stifled a smile under the large, shaggy mustache and watched Lark out of the corners of his weak eyes.

"I think the doctor was most justified," Lark said with a touch of severity in his voice. "Medicine is a respected and established science. You hooted at it, sneered, and deprecated it all morning with as much grace as a gang of hooligans. You fully deserve their contempt."

"The fact of the matter is, sir," the eldest psychosemanticist said carefully, "Burden is not medically insane. I found nothing inconsistent in his statements or in his reactions. Nor do I suggest that the consistency of his thought derives from an obsessive delusion. In the terms of Burden's understanding of the words he uses, he is both consistent and sane. Burden will not be cured by narcotic suggestion or therapy. Essentially Burden is a problem in re-education. He must be retaught the meanings of words like a bright child who has, without instruction or guidance, constructed a world of words that sound the way he likes them to sound, mean what he likes to think they mean, and uses them the way he prefers to use them. After all, a man without words is a blank. We have to erase Burden's understanding and begin again. Change his appreciation, understanding, and use of words and you will change the patterns of his thoughts and the motives that move him. You will only then permanently erase the basic heresies that he maintains." Apparently the other two members of the department agreed, for they both nodded sharply.

"And what shall we do with Burden's nonverbal personality?" Lark asked gently.

"With all respect, sir," the eldest continued firmly, "There is no such thing as a nonverbal personality. Even the most illiterate and brutish of men can find interior verbalizations of his motives. He may not be able to communicate those motives to you, but to himself they can be made quite clear if he is forced to think about them.

He can verbalize far enough to feel that he doesn't like this or does like that. *Like* is a word, sir. If he can express it to himself he is a verbal personality. The only nonverbal personalities are vegetative, which turn toward light or water by instinct that has nothing to do with choice. Where an element of choice is involved and one is selected over another, verbalization is indicated; for the very acceptance of one implies yes and the denial of the other implies no."

"Then all we have to do is to unscramble Professor Burden's vocabulary and he'll cease to be a heretic?" Lark asked gently.

"Basically, that's the problem," the spokesman said, and his associates agreed.

"Thank you, gentlemen," Lark said, bringing his knee down. The psychosemanticists rose, collected their books and papers, and left without speaking again or nodding. After the door had closed Lark surveyed the litter of paper, the cups of water, the ash trays filled with tobacco and bits of scrap. His eye drifted on to the figure of the political analyst. "Well, it seems that we're alone, Doctor Wright."

The older man's head nodded gently, sadly. Lark slumped further in his chair, his eyes turned to the ceiling. "What do you think of our Professor Burden?" Lark asked.

"He is an unhappy man," Doctor Wright said softly.

Lark turned to look at the political analyst. This made more sense than all the gabble of the doctors and psychosemanticists and investigators. "What is he unhappy about?"

"To live one way and to believe another always leads to unhappiness, restlessness, to ultimate failure. It's as true of people as it is of nations."

"Tell me more about that, Doctor Wright."

"There's nothing to tell, really. It is an old dichotomy found again and again in history. Do you know your twentieth-century history well, sir?"

"Fairly well."

"There was a minor dictator of Italy in the early part of the century named B. Mussolinus or Mussolino—I forget the name. But this dictator had romantic dreams of ancient Rome. He sought to restore Italy to its Roman emotional climate. Well, quite brutally and crudely he badgered the poor country into disciplining and organizing itself. And on this industrially primitive and backward nation he forced a helmet, in the fervent belief that the helmet made the warrior. Unfortunately it did not. When he thought he had an Italy that was again Roman he went on his first tiny adventure. It was the subjugation of a barbarian prince—the Negus of Ethiopia.

"He won his little war and was so delighted with himself and his new Roman armies that when the second of the world wars broke out he put his Roman armies in the field—to discover that, after all, they weren't Roman, that the tradition was dead, that Italy did not have the industrial resources, the technical equipment, or the spirit required for modern warfare.

"In the end they succumbed to the only real Romans of the century—the Americans. The Americans were the new Romans of the middle of the twentieth century and they were invincible." Wright paused and shrugged his shoulders. "Well, you know what it led to. You know how much our State owes to that American-Roman tradition. World federation, our own State's almost total Americanization, the bastardization of a thousand social cultures." Doctor Wright stopped and smiled apologetically. "I'm afraid I've wandered from the subject, sir."

117

"No, no," Lark said, entertained and interested. "Go on, please. I'm willing to wait for the point."

"Well, briefly, the analogy of the soft, diffused spirit of a country being artificially heated, hammered, and drawn into a semblance of a war shield to Burden's spirit artificially being drawn into a semblance of conformity to the society in which he lives stands up. Burden may wish to conform. He may see all the reasons in the world for conforming, as the twentieth-century Italians may have wished to be a warrior folk, may have seen all the glittering, ego-warming reasons for being warriors. And yet both failed. They failed because the capacity to become what you *wish* to become is a great deal smaller than the capacity to become anything at all. Burden wishes to conform, the Italians wished to become warriors; but neither could successfully see that wish through. Burden could conform to all outward appearances as the Italians could appear to be warriors, but in great crisis both illusions fail."

"Very interesting," Lark said thoughtfully, "that remark about illusions. Burden can't abide illusion. You notice the stress he placed on the paper flowers?"

"An unsuccessful illusion."

"More than that. It was not the lack of success of the illusion that disturbed him. That I understand. That we all understand. A thing that does not faithfully fulfill its function bothers us. If paper flowers are intended to deceive and they do not, then we have every right to be angry. But Burden objects to the attempt at illusion. And he objects still further when he is partially deceived."

"Deception is something we all undergo, in some form or another, in all our lives. Some men object, some ignore it. Burden is one who despises it," Wright said.

"Then if Burden despises deception, he must equally

despise manipulation, which simply means that he must despise the State."

"Or would, if he understood it completely."

"There you are wrong," Lark said, shooting out a bony forefinger. "He would admire the State and approve of it if he understood it completely. I feel that Burden is a soft humanitarian. Notice in his interview with Richard his concern for Conger. Now, why should he be concerned about Conger if Conger had treated him so badly?"

"I can only suggest that he didn't feel Conger treated him badly."

"Guilty conscience?"

"Perhaps," Doctor Wright plucked at his mustache thoughtfully, "or perhaps deep down he felt that some of Conger's reproaches had some justification—in part, anyway. He saw the justice of his punishment and accepted it."

"And could not bear the thought of Conger's suffering for being correct, and so defended him to Richard?"

"Probably."

"Which suggests that justice is more important to him than pity. An interesting thought. It means that Burden is not a humanitarian at all. I thought we were dealing with one of those soft, fuzzy-headed sentimentalists. But Burden is not a sentimentalist. An interesting and arresting thought, Doctor Wright." Lark paused, placed his long slender fingers together in a churchly figure in front of his long nose. "What if—" Lark began, paused, and began again, "What if Burden were made to see that conformity was no more or less than the inevitable outcome of logic—would he conform then?"

"If he could be made to see that," Wright said.

"Logically it is, you know," Lark said, looking at Wright with innocent eyes.

Doctor Wright shrugged his shoulders.

"Don't you believe that?" Lark asked gently.

"Don't ask me about that. I'm a heretic," Wright said with a smile.

"So am I," Lark replied, smiling back. Doctor Wright looked at Lark sharply. "Yes," Lark went on, "what is happening to Burden happened to me. When I was fourteen years old I was taken out of school and brought here. They worked on me three years, as an experiment. They won, but the expenditure of time and effort were enormous. Haven't you ever read the Larsen-Kohn reports? Incidentally, that's where I got my name—Lark—a simple contraction of the two names of the men who were closer than fathers to me for three years. I was never out of the company of one or the other for all that time. Haven't you ever read the accounts?"

"No," Wright said, looking at Lark with eyes both shocked and curious. The reports were classified and not available to all who were interested. In essence, of course, everyone knew what the reports contained.

"Almost fourteen volumes this thick," Lark gestured with his thumb and forefinger. "I've read them all so many times that if they were destroyed tomorrow I could sit down and write them out, word for word, footnote for footnote—all fourteen volumes. Intensely interesting, one's own soul. Kohn died of a massive cerebral hemorrhage shortly after the conclusion of the experiment and before the last volume was completed. Larsen is an invalid. The doctors say I killed Kohn and crippled Larsen. But, of course, that was nonsense. I didn't harm them at all. They did it to themselves trying to rid me of heresy, to understand the mechanism of heresy. I've tried to visit Larsen—he doesn't live too far from here. But the doctors won't let me. Larsen gets uncontrollable when my intentions are even hinted at. Somewhat like the poor dogs Pavlov worked on. Even the sight of the laboratory building made their salivary glands operate, caused them to howl and twitch and otherwise seem possessed. In my case, the curious thing was that the experimenter and not the experimental animal was affected. Poor Larsen. He and Kohn were the only family I knew. I loved them both. But I proved to be too much for them," Lark concluded with a strange, half-lit smile that was at once turned toward Wright and toward some inner vision.

"Well," Wright licked at his lower lip nervously, "if they were successful with you—I don't see why you can't hope to be successful with Burden."

Lark looked at Doctor Wright for a long moment. He knew that Wright was a heretic. There were a few working for the Department in sections where a conformist would produce false results. While it is pleasant to have everyone believe as he should, it is fatal to depend upon them for all necessary opinions and decisions. A political analyst who was not a heretic was useless. He could produce analyses only to the taste and liking of the State. A government could not afford such flattery in critical matters; political analysis had to be clear, cold, absolute, without any taint of state loyalty or social conformity. There were other heretics in government of great importance and their opinions were highly valued. However, their heresy had been carefully charted. Wherever they worked, whatever they did, their superiors knew the full extent of their hostility. Wright, for instance, could not be relied upon for political analyses concerning the manipulation of intellectual thinking. He was bitterly opposed to it and denied that it could be done successfully. However, no one asked his opinion in this field or, if his opinion were asked, his conclusions were viewed in the light of his emotions. Lark knew Wright well enough to know that the man had a compulsion toward honesty in his work and could no more lie about his conclusions than he could voluntarily cease breathing. The one thing Lark knew about Wright and all other heretics employed in government was that they were required to show superficial social conformity outside of their work. It was required to keep heretics from enlisting others in their ranks, and to keep confusion from the minds of those who did conform and saw no reason for not conforming. It was a wise state that knew when to excuse heresy, and Lark felt that his was a wise one.

"Doctor—we're going to be successful with Burden. But not because Larsen and Kohn were successful with me. You see, they had all the time in the world. What was more, I was young and still impressionable. There was a certain elasticity of thinking involved. Burden will not be available to me for three years and his mind is rather rigid. He is not a child. He is an adult male of fairly good intellectual powers. The problem becomes immensely more difficult with these two added factors."

"Perhaps impossible," Wright said.

"That's a hope, Doctor," Lark smiled, "not an opinion."

"It could be both."

"Yes, except that I am even stronger than Larsen or Kohn. I am, in fact, a synthesis of those two men plus the heretic who was first brought here. Who can tell you more of the horrors of drink than an articulate ex-alcoholic? You see my point? I can succeed with Burden because once we might have been brothers—dearly beloved brothers. I know more of what goes on in the heretic's mind because I, too, was once a heretic."

"That statement reminds me faintly of the Inquisition's

opinion—certainly there were no more zealous inquisitors than the redeemed heretics who had renounced their heresy."

"The difference between those inquisitors and myself is that I want heretics to come out into the light, to cast off the very things that set them apart from their fellow citizens, to live happy, useful lives."

"It may interest you to know that there is still no difference."

"But there is. I am not interested in creating more inquisitors—I am interested in creating happy men and women."

"That is what they thought, too."

"Ah, but they failed, and for a very good reason."

"What reason?"

"They burned their failures at the stake publicly."

"And your failures are buried out of sight?"

"My dear Doctor Wright—you know the ordinance against punishment. It no longer exists as a social concept."

"I've wondered about that, sir. What does the State substitute?"

"Science, patience, benevolence."

"When those fail?"

"They never fail, Doctor. The State is immortal. It never loses its patience or its benevolence."

"Which probably means that you hound the poor devils for life."

"For life? No, not at all. Only until their heresies are truly rooted out of them."

"And those who won't give up their heresies? Can't give them up?"

"But there are no such persons. Burden is an example of

a man hagridden with heresies—some of which he does not even know he holds. And yet, in two weeks or slightly less he will be free of them."

"If heresy is so easily removed—then why wasn't mine?"

"Because to erase your heresy it would be necessary to remove your independence of judgment, my good Doctor. It happens that the State has need of your heretical judgment. You may be unhappy being a heretic. In fact, I know you are. But for the good of the State you are expected to bear up under this unhappiness."

"In other words, I'm a hero?"

"No, you're not quite that," Lark smiled indulgently, "but you are missing your fair portion of happiness. Happiness, my dear Doctor Wright, comes from conformity—comes from being exactly like your fellows. Your joys, your sorrows, your aims, your hopes, your dreams when shared and felt with others make for happiness. Man is a social animal and the State is helping him to the realization of the perfect society—a complete identity of common interest, where all feel a part, take a part, are a part."

"It sounds like a prayer when you say it."

"It is a prayer," Lark said gently, smiling at Wright.

11

Burden slept fitfully until the late afternoon, his bones and muscles aching, a profound sense of exhaustion filling him. The day seemed to pass so quickly. He had slept after eating a lunch of soup and crackers and was awakened by the nurse taking his pulse.

"Please," he said in a voice that felt hoarse, "I'd like to leave here. Couldn't my clothes be brought in? I want to go home."

"Oh, you're too weak to get up right now. You've been sick."

"No, it was just the aftereffects of the sedative the doctor gave me this morning."

"Oh, now you know that isn't true. No sedative could make you sick."

"But it did. It made me weak and flushed. I must have caught a chill."

"Now, now, don't disturb yourself about that. You'll be fine as can be tomorrow or the day after."

"The day after? That's Monday, isn't it? I can't be here

Monday. My wife is expecting me home tomorrow night."

"Well, you may be able to leave by tomorrow night. But that's up to you, you know. If you stay in bed under the covers and behave yourself you might get that fever fully licked and you could be out of here. Now, won't you help us to help you get home by tomorrow night?"

It was useless, Burden decided. They had made up their minds that he was sick and he would have to do as they asked. In God's heaven, how they wore a man down. He rested against his pillows, holding the thermometer in his mouth. The nurse read it. But when he asked her what his temperature was, she smiled and said nothing and then took the temperature chart out of his room. Hopeless. Completely hopeless. To get enmeshed in the official red tape of a large organization was to be frustrated completely. There was no way out but the one they indicated. He would have to do as they asked until they were satisfied. He touched his forehead. It felt cool. But perhaps he was running a slight temperature—he could feel it in his bones. The doctor had probably given him something too drastic. The old fool. Well, it was no more incompetence than he could expect of the Department. Hadn't Conger been an incompetent? And that Richard? Oh, he was learning a bitter lesson about the fallibility of governmental organizations. The benevolent State, unfortunately, was also the bungling State. Burden napped for an hour because it was the easiest thing to do, now that he had determined that he would stay until the following night.

He was awakened by the sound of the door opening and when he opened his eyes he saw the old doctor who had administered the sedative. He awoke so quickly and sharply, so intent on the doctor, that he barely noticed the tall, crane-thin man with curious light eyes and long pale face who came in behind him.

"Would you mind telling these people that I am not sick?" Burden demanded loudly. "They've kept me here in bed, taking my temperature, treating me as if I had undergone some kind of siege. You know as well as I there's nothing wrong with me except that perhaps that sedative you gave me had a bad aftereffect."

"My dear Professor Burden," the doctor said calmly, "you were suffering with the onset of grippe while I was examining you. The sedative had nothing to do with your present condition. It neither brought it on nor aggravated it. As a point of fact, it should have helped to weaken it and that's exactly what it did do. You are sick, although I can see you're much better. Your eyes are clear. Do your bones and muscles ache?"

Burden hesitated. It was quite possible that the doctor was right. Damn it, but why should the grippe have followed so closely on the sedative? Surely he was well before he went to the examination room. Or was he? "Well," Burden reluctantly admitted, "it is possible I had a touch of it. I do get it every winter. Although I don't recall having a chill or anything like that."

"You'll feel better tomorrow. You'll probably be out of bed by Monday."

"Monday? But I want to go home tomorrow night! My wife's expecting me."

"Oh, I don't know about that." The doctor's eyes narrowed dubiously. "Tomorrow night might be a touch too soon for you to get out of bed and do any traveling. These things tend to complicate if they aren't nipped in the bud. Better to stay in bed an extra night than to take a chance."

"If you don't mind, I'll take that chance," Burden said

testily. It was getting out of hand now. Their medical caution could keep him in bed for a week. If he was going to be sick he might as well have Emma to take care of him. At least he'd be comfortable in his own home, away from these official bunglers and their eternal red tape. Burden looked again at the tall, slender young man with the silky black hair who stood slightly behind the doctor. The large, pale eyes seemed abstracted and yet they seemed to be staring directly at him. "Are you a doctor?" Burden asked the young man.

"Oh, no," the slender young man said with a pleasant smile.

"Oh, excuse me, Professor Burden," the doctor said, "you don't know Lark."

"Lark? Don't you have a first name?" Burden asked, conscious of the fact that he was being rude. But then, if he was not a doctor he didn't belong in his room.

"I'm very pleased to meet you, Professor Burden," Lark said, ignoring Burden's question.

"I'm sorry if I snapped at you, Mr. Lark," Burden said, deciding that it was unfair to be rude to someone he didn't know. He might be a friend of the doctor's accompanying him on his rounds. "The fact of the matter is that I've been treated abominably in here." Burden fixed a cold and angry blue eye on the doctor. "Abominably," he repeated.

"I'm sorry if you feel that way, Professor," Lark said with a regretful look.

"You work for the Department, then?" Burden asked, wondering if he was on the staff. He wore a plain sack suit but he might be on the administrative staff.

"Yes, I'm Mr. Richard's superior," Lark said.

"There's another fellow without a first name," Burden

said, his annoyance with Richard and Conger returning.

"Julian is his first name. Julian Richard," Lark said politely "The doctor tells me you're well enough to talk, so may I stay awhile and chat with you?"

"Chat away," Burden said grimly. "It's been so overpoweringly dull in here I'd chat with the devil himself."

"Thank you," Lark said with a fleeting smile. The doctor nodded.

"You won't tire the professor too much, I hope?"

"My word, Doctor," Lark said, faintly suggesting a bow. The doctor nodded and patted Burden on the shoulder, a gesture from which Burden shrank on the grounds that it was an unnecessary condescension. Last night it hadn't bothered him but now it did. It annoyed him far out of proportion to its importance.

"I hate people who pat others like stray dogs or children," Burden said after the door had closed behind the doctor.

"Yes, it smacks a little of superiority, doesn't it?" Lark said, sitting down on the chair beside the bed.

"It smacks of a great deal more than that. It smacks of a damned lot of familiarity," Burden said, slightly surprised at his own swearing and vehemence. This place brought out of him things and expressions of emotion that were almost alien to him. Of course, there had been a great deal of provocation. Had been, and still was. But still, it was odd the way he had changed since coming to the Department—sharper, more irritable, quicker to anger, as though his nerves had been brought closer to the surface.

"I'm sure it has something to do with the sense of power that every doctor must feel," Lark said.

"That's an interesting thought," Burden said, eyeing

129

Lark. "It would suggest that the strong are gentle with the weak only because they know their own strength is so much greater."

"I don't see why the thought should be so startling, Professor."

"Oh, but it is. You see, by extension it means that the powerful owe a great obligation to the weak because of their strength. And if by the powerful you substitute the Department, and if by the weak you substitute myself, then you see the Department owes me some consideration. For instance, it is obliged not to show its strength over me by keeping me here."

"But you are not being kept here," Lark said, faintly disturbed. He didn't want Burden to feel restricted this early in the game. There might come a time when they would have to point out to him that he couldn't leave, but this was far too early for the employment of such a tactic.

"But I am. Perhaps I am sick. But I'm not so sick that I couldn't leave and recover at home. My wife is quite an accomplished nurse and I would feel happier there."

"Oh, I see," Lark felt somewhat relieved. Burden hadn't yet sensed a pattern behind all that had happened to him.

"So, if you have any influence—and I suspect that you do—I wish you would see to it that I'm released tomorrow morning or afternoon so that I could get back to my family."

"I wouldn't like to use my influence and endanger your health, Professor."

"My health is my business, Mr. Lark. I'll risk it as I choose."

"Professor Burden, aside from the fact that that is a foolish thing to say, it is a heretical thing to say."

"What?" Burden's eyes opened wide with surprise.

"Why, yes, of course. I'm surprised you didn't recognize it. The health of every citizen of the country is the concern of the State since the health of the citizens affects the production of the State. We would not think of allowing garbage to accumulate in the streets, nor would we allow people to live under unsafe or unsanitary conditions. Your health is of primary importance to us. In brief, it is our business and quite properly so. When you deny that you're uttering a heretical statement."

"I suppose in the largest sense you're probably right. I didn't think of it just that way."

"Not only in the largest sense but in the particular sense. You're a teacher, whose occupation is important to the welfare of the State. If you should sicken and die, the State would prematurely lose your skills which are so sorely needed. I would be endangering your life if I arranged for you to leave before you were fully recovered."

"I doubt that I am in any condition remotely as dangerous as you suggest, Mr. Lark."

"My dear Professor, I don't presume to be a judge of your condition. I am not a doctor. I have heard the doctor say that it is risky for you to leave before your illness is completely cured. Do you presume to know more than the doctor?"

Burden paused, looking at the thin young man. There was something sharp and yet insinuating in his speech and in his reasoning. He was not crudely baiting him the way Conger had done, nor was he stickily insinuating after the manner of Julian Richard. He was quite a different personality, and Burden decided it would be best to be cautious with him. "Well, we always like to feel that we know more than our own doctors, Mr. Lark, don't we?"

"You know, Professor Burden, it is always a little surprising to me, the way in which you consistently fall back on the vanity principle. One should understand this, that, or the other thing, but one doesn't because one prefers to trust his own vanity. Is vanity a bad thing, Professor?"

"Rampant vanity, of course, is always bad. It brings out the worst in men. It makes them unreasonable, selfish, silly, and quite vulnerable."

"Controlled vanity, then, is the desideratum?"

"Yes," Burden said, watching Lark carefully.

"Of course, my own feeling is that control in everything is desirable. What was the old saying about moderation in everything, denial of nothing—something, something, something. I'm very poor at quotes."

"Mr. Lark, would you mind telling me just why you're here?"

"Why?"

"Does it have something to do with my hearing? I mean, I thought Mr. Richard covered all the routine questions."

"I suppose he did."

"Well, if he did—what do you want?"

"I don't know, Professor. I really don't know what I want from you. Perhaps all I want to do is to see you face to face. I've heard and read so much about you the past twenty-four hours I grew curious to see what you were really like."

"I didn't know people in the Department had the time to satisfy their idle curiosity."

"Oh, but that's exactly how I do occupy my time, Professor," Lark smiled.

"Well, if you've satisfied your curiosity, Mr. Lark," Burden said coldly, settling back against his pillow, "I wish you'd leave. As you pointed out, I'm a sick man."

"Good, I'm glad you recognize that," Lark said, showing no intention of rising from his chair. "However, you're far sicker than you think, Professor."

Burden looked at Lark questioningly, an uneasy sense of danger beginning to crawl across his mind.

"Yes," Lark went on, "you see, Professor, we have every reason to believe that you're a heretic. A very determined heretic, in fact."

"What?" Burden asked softly, half rising from his pillow.

"I know it must disturb you to hear that. But it's the truth. In fact, we have a mimeographed booklet of around a hundred and forty pages listing each of your heresies and the sources from which the heresies were found."

"I don't believe that."

"Oh, but it's true. It took a good deal of reading and research and a lot of listening to recorded conversations, but the list is very complete. And very discouraging—to us, at least."

"They can't be true," Burden said, sitting upright in bed now, his eyes fixed on Lark, his mind a jumble of thoughts that he couldn't arrange.

"Professor Burden, these heresies are taken from your own reports, from recordings of your own voice. They don't derive from hearsay or the reports of others. These are things you yourself have written or said. And to us they represent only the visible fraction of an iceberg. Just from what we can see of your heresy, Professor Burden, we know the rest must be of enormous size and importance."

"I've always been loyal to the State," Burden said faintly, feeling his voice failing him.

"The fact of the matter is that you have not. You are a heretic—a deeply profound heretic whose emotions and thinking and, yes, actions, too, are fundamentally at variance with custom and doctrine of the State and the society in which you live. You're a rare animal, Professor Burden—a strange, exotic, unhappy animal in our midst."

"This is incredible," Burden said, his voice now hollow, his senses numbed. "Of all the errors that have been made this far, this is the most terrible, the most incredible. I can't believe that any organization can be this stupid. I can't believe it of the Department. I simply can't believe it."

"You will be given a copy of the booklet containing a list of your heresies, Professor Burden. You will be allowed to read it, question it, study it, and then decide for yourself. But would you like me to quote some of the heresies we have discovered about you?"

"I defy you to name those heresies," Burden said, waiting, alert now, his heart pounding. Now they would have to be specific. Now he could pound at things that had dimension, limit, surface, and meaning. Before it had been a kind of slippery, elusive intellectual game of hide-and-seek.

"Let us go back to your first interview with Frank Conger," Lark said calmly. "When you first met him you said—and I'll try to remember the exact words—*I had the rather naive idea that I was going to be complimented, officially, for my work.* Do you recall that, Professor Burden?"

"Yes, I do. I said something very much like that."

"It's most important that you remember exactly what you said—particularly the choice of words. I am especially thinking of the word *naive.* Did you use that word?"

"I think I did. Yes, I suppose I did."

"Do you remember using it?"

"Well, get on with it, Mr. Lark. What does one word matter more or less?"

"Well, I'm afraid it matters quite a bit, Professor Burden. You see, the word that first comes to your lips is a revelatory word. I suppose you know the elementary principles of the word-association test in psychology?"

"Yes, I know that," Burden said, pondering the significance of *naive*. It meant innocent, unsophisticated. What sinister meaning did it have in the catalogue of heresy?

"You used the word *naive*. Believe me. I have heard the recorded conversation a dozen times and I know you used the word. However, if you don't believe that you did, I can arrange to have the recording equipment with the recorded electrical tape brought to this room and you may have the entire conversation repeated for you."

"No, no, don't bother with all that, Mr. Lark. Please get on with this."

"Now, don't hurry, Professor. This is not a minor point. I want you to believe me when I tell you that you actually said these things in the way I am repeating them to you. That's important. It's important that you believe me. It's important that you trust me. It's also most important that you have no doubt that I am quoting you correctly and fully."

"I trust your memory, Mr. Lark," Burden said, confused now and watching Lark carefully.

"Professor Burden," Lark said in a softer, more kindly tone, "I'm not here to torment you, or to frighten you, or to accuse you. Heresy is serious but it does not throw us into a panic. It must not do so to you. You are what we call an unconscious heretic. Very simply, that means you want to believe in the State, you want to conform, you want to be a good citizen, but in spite of your intentions you hold certain beliefs, certain prejudices, certain emotions which make you a heretic."

"As if I were possessed of an evil spirit?"

"Yes," Lark said solemnly, "in earlier centuries that's what would have been said of you. We're more enlightened now and we know that a man is the sum of many things over which he has little control. A heretic is a person who has been badly formed, a person who is sick. Heresy and the grippe are the same except that the grippe is simple and heresy is not. In your case, the heresy is most complex and most serious. That means we want your co-operation; we need it if we're going to help you."

"You really mean that, don't you?" Burden said thoughtfully, looking at Lark. Lark nodded silently and waited for a moment. Burden leaned back against his pillow, his brows knit, the tumult in his mind easing somewhat. It was a strange feeling to discover that the Department was not wrong, had, in fact, never been wrong—that he was carrying about in him an illness he never knew possessed him. He had never gone into the subject of heresy very fully. In his own mind heretics had always been cranks, embittered obstructionists, men and women who resented order, peace, the normal routine of life. The idea that a man who was in complete agreement with himself and at peace with the world could be in complete disagreement with the world without knowing it struck him as faintly frightening, vaguely mystifying. He understood now why the Department referred to it as an illness—as if heresy were a strain of virulent bacteria hidden in his bloodstream. "Go on, Mr. Lark," Burden finally said.

"The word *naive* occurred in your statement to Mr. Conger. Now, what does the word *naive* in that context suggest to you, Professor?"

"You mean in the statement I made to Conger about the award? Well, I guess I rather romantically supposed that I had done a splendid job of being a correspondent and that I deserved an award."

"Now, let me tell you what our interpretation of the word *naive* is. When you say *naive* you are referring to yourself as an innocent person, a person without guile. And yet you don't mean that at all. You think of yourself as a person with a great deal of sophistication, a person with a great deal of *savoir-faire*, a cultured and learned man. When you used the word *naive* you were doing two things, you were first of all deprecating yourself, hiding your true opinion of yourself—that you are a man of great talents who should be officially appreciated and deco-rated—and secondly, you were implying that our awards are naive ceremonies which you are quite above being impressed by. However, you are quite willing to let us decorate you with the rather condescending understand-ing of how much importance bureaucrats attach to such things as decoration ceremonies." Lark spoke very sharply and quickly now. "Please don't try to be evasive, Profes-sor Burden. It's vitally important that you be honest. No matter how bad a light it seems to throw either us or you into—admit it if it is true. We have to know the exact na-ture of the illness with which we are dealing. Now, is the analysis substantially correct?"

Burden paused, admiring this thin, intense young man. As he listened he was able to evoke the thoughts and the feelings that had come over him during the interview with Frank Conger. "Yes," Burden said, "it is quite correct. Not very polite of me, but hardly heretical. At least, I see no heresy in it."

"Let me go on with the first interview with Mr. Frank Conger. Mr. Conger, if you remember, seized on the word *naive.* He pursued it because it was a sort of danger signal to him."

"Yes, I remember," Burden said, wondering now if Conger was, after all, as clumsy and stupid as he had thought. Evidently not.

"He tried to make you explain what you had meant by it but you kept retreating, modifying what you had said, deprecating yourself further and further until finally you wound up lying."

"Lying?"

"When Conger finally pressed you to the point of admitting whether your work deserved an award or not and suggested that a realistic appraisal of your work indicated that you didn't feel you deserved an award—what did you say?"

"Well, I think I said something like—I guessed my work didn't deserve an award."

"That was the lie," Lark said, extending a skinny forefinger.

"Yes," Burden admitted honestly, seeing it now. "I guess it was a lie. But you see, Conger kept at me so aggressively—trying to twist my words. Well, not twist, exactly. But to derive meanings from what I said—meanings I had no intention of—" Burden stopped abruptly, oddly blocked.

"Yes, Professor Burden?" Lark asked with a soft smile.

"Well, what I meant to say was that Conger suggested meanings that were false."

"You're evading again. Finish the sentence you started a minute ago. The sentence that began, *"but to derive meanings from what I said—meanings I had no intention of—."* Lark paused, waiting, a slight smile on the heavy, sensual lips.

"Well, false meanings," Burden offered weakly, knowing now how the sentence should have ended.

"No," Lark shook his head, " '—meanings I had no intention of *revealing*,' " Lark ended the sentence. "That was the word. *Revealing*. It was a word you were going to use next but didn't because it implied that Conger was correct in his suspicions. You were concealing something. You are still trying to conceal things from me."

"Yes," Burden said thoughtfully, "that was the word. I realize it only now that you point it out."

"Don't feel badly," Lark said with a smile, "I am not offended by all of this. This concealment of yours is partially involuntary. I expect it. I shall keep on pointing it out to you. Just continue to be as honest with me as you have been and we'll do a lot for you, Professor."

"But the heresy. Where's the heresy?"

"The heresy is implicit, Professor. If you will think about it for a moment you'll find it for yourself. Let me help you. Who is it that you feel is really naive, Professor? Surely it's not yourself. It's the Department—Conger probably, or his superior, or perhaps the person to whom you have been writing your reports. We are the naive ones, the unsophisticated ones. To believe yourself more knowing than an official organ of the government is a heresy, Professor."

"But surely not a serious one, Mr. Lark?"

"Quite serious. Let's examine the nature of its danger to the State. Let's presume that you are a platoon commander in the Army. That would make you a lieutenant. Let us presume that your nation is at war and that in some tiny corner of that war you hold a certain responsibility—a small bridge, the stream that runs under it, the banks on both sides for a few hundred yards, and a small clump of trees across the stream on your right. You know that the enemy has a machine-gun emplacement in the trees, that their line of fire covers the approaches to the bridge and covers the stream as well. Let us also presume that somewhere, outside of your command area, there is a mortar emplacement which has your area taped for fire. You receive an order from the company commander who, of course, has received it from the battalion commander and he, in turn, from the regimental commander. You are ordered to enter the area, attempt to cross the bridge or ford the stream, according to your own appraisal of the likelihood of either—but, in any case, to get across, past the machine-gun emplacement, and destroy the mortar platoon which is hidden somewhere out of sight in the woods. Now, to attempt that without some artillery fire is well-nigh suicidal. So you request fire on the opposite bank of the stream and on the clump of trees that hides the machine-gun nest. But you are refused artillery support. What can you do?"

"Try another way."

"Well, you're not a student of military tactics so I won't go into it further. But briefly, there is no other way. A platoon is too small a force to attempt to overrun a machine-gun position—especially when a bridge must be crossed or a stream forded. In short, the entire attempt is suicidal without artillery support. But you are denied that support. What would you do then, Professor Burden?"

"I would do the best I could. Perhaps wait for night or something."

"But you would obey your orders?"

"If I were a soldier, yes."

"Yes, of course. You would obey those orders even though you knew they were unrealistic. That because you are under the tension of war. Orders given in combat have a certain crucial urgency, the situation is surcharged with compelling drama. You are a soldier, with all that means. You are a commander—your soul, your actions, your judgment, your bravery or cowardice nakedly exposed for your men to see. All these special conditions compel obedience to orders from a higher authority. You cross, and you are killed in the attempt."

"Poor theoretical lieutenant," Burden said with a smile.

"That is war. Those were soldiers. They were battle conditions. Even the dullest of men understands how important orders—even wrong orders—are under such conditions. But let us suppose that it is peacetime. Let us suppose that you are a clerk in a governmental agency, or an inspector in government service. In other words, you occupy a small position of responsibility—roughly comparable to our poor, dead lieutenant who was placed in an untenable position. You receive an order from a superior. Roughly speaking, an order as manifestly foolish as the order our dead soldier received. What do you do?"

"Protest it. Try to reason with my superior."

"Let us suppose you do as much in that direction as our dead soldier did. But to no avail. You must obey."

"I suppose I would obey."

"Yes, you might. In war, your failure to obey would be flagrant. You would probably be shot on the spot. But in peace, in the dull routine of a government department—you would not be shot, you might not even be fired. And you are a person who feels that he is more knowing than the people above him. Perhaps not in everything, but in this small thing, this tiny province of yours, you know more than the others above you. What would you do?"

Burden nodded, understanding now. "I would probably not obey the order—or find some way to get around obeying it."

"Exactly. That lack of obedience, that evasion, that deception arises when someone feels better qualified to judge than the people appointed above him. Multiply such an attitude—on small matters, mind you—by ten thousand government employees and you have anarchy, chaos in the administration of this nation's affairs. Multiply that attitude millions of times by the citizens of this State and you will find lawlessness rampant."

"But surely you're very much exaggerating the importance of one man's feeling. Even if I tried, I couldn't throw the country into a turmoil."

"Professor Burden, heresy is an illness in many ways. We feel heresy is contagious. One man is bound to communicate it to another and that other to two others and so on."

Burden felt uncomfortable. There was some justice in what Lark said and yet it was such an innocent vanity, hardly worth all this effort. "I suppose strictly speaking you're right. But what can I do about it?"

"Cease thinking that the government is less sophisticated than you are. After all, the government is an accumulation of many brains and personalities. Surely among them there are some at least as sophisticated, as well-educated as yourself."

"Yes," Burden said with a smile, looking directly at Lark, "I see that now."

"I am not an exception, if that is what you're thinking, Professor Burden," Lark said solemnly. Burden smiled, almost laughed. "I read your mind then," Lark said seriously. "It wasn't difficult to do. I'm not psychic at all. I merely understand you."

"Well, let's say that's one heresy that's laid to rest, Mr. Lark," Burden said, rather liking this young man, appreciating the keenness of his mind.

Lark regarded the professor for a moment. The heresy had not been laid to rest at all. It was a far more complex process than Burden imagined it would be. It was a far more painful process than Burden dreamed it could be. But it was best to make it seem easy at the start. Lark had very little time in which to accomplish a great deal and it would be best to keep Burden's co-operation as long as possible, to tell him as much of the truth as could be told to him. The painful part of the reclamation would come soon enough, and soon enough Burden's resistance would tighten. Now the honeymoon was still in progress and now was the time to secure Burden's help as far as possible. "Yes," Lark finally said, "we have done some good with you already, Professor. I must warn you, however, that there is still a great deal ahead of us. That's why I want you to stay here in the Department."

"Oh?" Burden lifted his eyebrows, puzzled.

"I know you want to go home to your wife and sons, but this is most important. If you could spare a week?"

"Oh, no, it's out of the question," Burden said, shaking his head.

"We've just barely touched on the heresies, Professor Burden. I'm sure you'd want to co-operate with us."

"Well, of course I'm willing to co-operate—but I have classes to teach, my wife, my home, my work."

"Couldn't you spare a week to rid yourself of heresies?"

"Well, of course, but—"

"Believe me, Professor Burden, it's a profound experience. You'll be a happier, more useful person when we're done. I've spent a great deal of time and effort in preparation for working with you—I'd hardly know how to explain it to my superiors if you proved unwilling to go through with it."

"My purging you mean?" Burden said with a smile.

143

"Yes, Professor—your purging," Lark said solemnly.

"Well—"

"We can arrange for your leave of absence from the college for one full week and you may telephone your wife to explain if you wish. I wouldn't tell her the truth— but make some plausible excuse. I leave that up to you. She might, conceivably, be upset by news that you've been delayed here."

"Yes," Burden said, biting his lower lip, "she might, at that. I think I can satisfy Emma with a story of some sort. But—" Burden looked at Lark, "is this quite necessary? I mean, I am loyal to the State; I approve of our society, its aims, its methods—I have always been a supporter of the benevolent State and all it stood for."

"That is why we are going to this much trouble, Professor Burden—we consider you far too valuable a person to be lost in a confused limbo of heresy. It's my job, Professor Burden. Please let me do it."

"Well," Burden sighed, "all right. But I'm afraid you're wrong. I'm not a heretic."

"You are," Lark said evenly. "We'll prove it to you. But I think you've had enough. Have a good night's rest, Professor."

12

Lark returned on Sunday, the eighteenth of October, while Burden was having his lunch. With the doctor's permission he was out of bed and the tray was set on the low table in front of the couch. He had been brought a faded blue bathrobe to wear over his pajamas. His temperature, according to the nurse, was normal.

"Good day, Professor," Lark said as he entered, picking up the chair from the bedside and bringing it over to the table.

"Oh, hello, Mr. Lark. My lunch," Burden gestured at the small dishes, "I'll never get fat on it but at least it's hot."

Lark smiled a faintly appreciative smile.

"You know," Burden continued as he cut a limp asparagus stalk with his fork, "I did some thinking last night after you left."

"Good, Professor. I'm glad to hear that. Mind telling me what you thought?"

"This whole concept of heresy—isn't it rather exaggerated? I mean, after all, what does it boil down to but some disagreement with the mores of society, with some official concepts, with some popular notions? Is that so terrible? Surely there is some latitude allowed for differences of opinion?"

"There is nothing wrong with differences of opinion provided the differences have to do with alternative courses of action or conduct. But a difference of opinion on—let's use your own words—'mores,' 'official concepts,' 'popular notions' is quite important. A difference of opinion here is heresy, without a doubt. Let me illustrate this with a homely example. While you and your wife might disagree on the placement of furniture in your home and still remain happily and completely married, you could not disagree on the very need for a home and expect to maintain the marriage."

"Oh, I see—principles, fundamentals."

"Precisely. In the same relationship of citizen to state, agreement must be obtained on 'principles,' 'fundamentals,' to use your words again."

"But on principles and fundamentals I do agree with the State, Mr. Lark."

"I'm sorry, but you do not."

"Oh, my black book of heresies. I forgot about them. It seems that we erased at least one heresy yesterday—my feeling that I was more sophisticated than the government. You proved me to be wrong."

"I did no such thing. I merely demonstrated that one public servant could be at least as sophisticated as yourself. I proved myself to be your equal. But I do not constitute the government. You retain the heresy with a modification, a certain weakening. You surely believe that you are far more sophisticated than the vast majority of government workers, perhaps including some of the highest executives and administrators of the government. Don't you?"

"Well, yes, I rather feel that you are an exceptional case."

"I am not," Lark said flatly.

"You're not admitting, are you, that your intellectual equipment is on the same level with say, Mr. Conger's?"

"I am admitting that. For the sort of work Mr. Conger does he is every bit as successful and astute as I for the work I do."

"Well, yes, perhaps that's so. But Conger's intellectual level is much lower, isn't it?"

"No."

"I see you're no heretic, Mr. Lark."

"You think I'm responding like some official automaton, don't you?"

"We-lll—"

"That I say one thing and believe another? That I am not being fully frank with you?"

"Mr. Lark, I can't see into your mind as cleverly as you appear to be able to see into mine. All I can say is that Mr. Frank Conger may be fully able to handle the sort of work he does but that's only because the work is not as demanding as the work you do."

"Suppose I were to tell you that Conger and I regularly exchanged jobs as a matter of administrative routine?"

Burden gave Lark a look of surprise. "Really?"

"To be perfectly honest, we don't. But it is quite possible, and in neither case would our work be impaired in any way. You find this remarkable?"

"I think you're stretching matters a bit to make a point —the absolute standard of equality. I know it exists in theory but I'm afraid it doesn't work out well in practice."

"It exists in theory and is being put into practice by

the State. Notice how many more people who would never normally go to college are attending your classes."

"Unfortunately that's so. Don't raise your eyebrows. I did say unfortunately. The intellectual level of the freshman classes keeps going down semester after semester."

"By your standards."

"By any standards."

"By 'intellectual level' what do you mean?"

"Ability to learn, the capacity for original thinking, the ability to understand abstract relationships, the appreciation of knowledge, the ability to retain, assimilate, and use the knowledge we pass on to our students."

"Curiously enough, those things do not determine what standards the State has created for intellectual levels."

"What?"

"The intellectual level is an arbitrary and rather romantic notion as you have described it. For instance, it could very easily encompass people who are irresponsible, unstable, treacherous, lazy, callous, indifferent, weak."

"Well, yes, I guess so."

"Do you think it is of any value to educate such persons?"

"No, not if the aim of education is to create useful people."

"Precisely. And yet such persons might easily meet all the standards you describe as coming under an optimum intellectual level. The official State definition of intellectual level is quite different. Intellect divorced from character is meaningless. Society has no use for brilliant anarchists, for gifted idlers, for educated cynics, for clever nihilists. The State prefers its educated people to have character, to be honest, to be energetic, to be loyal, to be trustworthy. Such are the people who will take over the government, and eventually all governments."

"Character before ability? It's an odd concept. Why not both?"

"That is our hope, our goal—to combine both standards, yours and ours."

"Well, that's always been the aim and hope of education."

"But, unfortunately, in the choice between the two, ability has always won and character has always lost. That's because teachers have always had a *mystique* about ability. I would rather live in a nation of moral morons than in one of scintillating parasites."

"Well, the choice is never that extreme, you know."

"No, it isn't. There is hope for training the morons. There is never a hope of reclaiming a parasite."

"But the products of the local schools are so bad, Mr. Lark."

"They will improve. Of one thing we are certain—the local schools turn out young men and women who believe in the principles and fundamentals of the State, who are hard-working, serious, anxious to learn, and equally anxious to be of service to their fellows. That is paramount."

"I suppose you could improve the scholastic qualities of such young people in time," Burden said thoughtfully.

"We will. But, as you say, time is needed. First things first. And character comes first. The State demands character above all. Intelligence without character is intolerable. You remember the illustration of the platoon commander? The world could get along very well on a minimum of brains and a maximum of character. I shudder, however, if the situation should be revised."

"But my dear Mr. Lark, the world has done without either of the two for such a long time."

"Yes, and you know what a world it was—selfish, stupid, cruel, callous, allowing some nations to starve while others gorged themselves, living in a constant state of tension, the big nations hysterically jockeying for power and the small nations terrorized at the prospect of being ground between the millstones. You are not a historian, Professor Burden, else you would not so blithely suggest that the world has done without brains or character and could continue to do so. I must introduce you to a real historian one day—a Doctor Wright. I find him most stimulating."

"I would like to meet your Doctor Wright," Burden said, deciding that if Lark truly represented the character of man the State was trying to create it would be a remarkable world in fifty or seventy-five years. Lark was a remarkable man. The only thing Burden vaguely distrusted was Lark's insistence that he was merely a routine product of the benevolent State. Lark might believe that but Burden knew it wasn't true. Lark was head and shoulders above all the men Burden had met in government service. Burden decided that the curious blind spot in Lark's make-up was that although he talked a great deal about reality he was intensely idealistic and romantic. Burden smiled at the thought.

"Are you smiling at me, Professor?" Lark asked.

"No, not really," Burden said, again puzzled and faintly upset by Lark's sure instinct for guessing what he thought. "I was smiling at what I thought was an amusing reversal. You think of me as being a romantic and yourself as a realist—whereas it just occurred to me that you are the romantic and I am the realist."

"I am not much of a philosopher," Lark said patiently,

"but reality is something that undoubtedly changes in time. In the Middle Ages there were pious folk who thought angels could fly, but in reality no one could fly. In modern times even pious folk conceded that angels only flew metaphorically speaking but in reality almost anyone who was so inclined could fly. So what was reality in one age was quite different from the reality of another age. A state ruled by men of character for men and women of character was no reality in past ages. It is becoming a reality now."

"Then you don't believe in the immutable aspects of human nature?"

"Human nature is a myth. The human characteristics are the ability to laugh, the capacity for tears, the erectness of carriage, and opposed digits. Otherwise humans are indistinguishable from apes."

"Reasoning?"

"Many animals can reason, Professor Burden, as many animals learn from experience. No, mankind is not a divine mystery. He is a riddle that demands patience and care and skill, but he is solvable."

"But his creation—that's a divine mystery, isn't it, Mr. Lark?"

"Professor Burden—you're descending to quibbling. The State has no desire to create men. It only desires to shape them. While science cannot create matter, the simplest technicians can shape it to desired ends and characteristics. Only God can make a tree, as the old poem goes, but ordinary workmen can change it into several thousand sheets of ordinary white paper."

Burden smiled. "You know, I enjoy these talks, Mr. Lark. You're a stimulating and sharp-witted young man. But what has all this to do with heresy? Aren't we wasting our time?"

"Not at all," Lark said, easing forward in his chair. "Our conversations actually amount to instruction—one of the therapeutic specifics for heretics."

"Instruction, eh? I'm afraid I've always thought of instruction as something more formal."

"You see now how wrong you are. Instruction can arise from conversation as random as this and be effective. Is it effective, Professor Burden?"

"Oh, I guess so. Except that it seems to be such an enjoyable way of learning that I can hardly believe that it is learning at all. I mean, it sounds to me as if we're both having a splendid time passing the hours, but not actually accomplishing anything."

"We're accomplishing a great deal, Professor. You see, pediatricians and child psychologists tell us that children learn from playing, that what seems to the adult to be random, pointless manipulation and childish handling is actually hard work that involves an enormous amount of instruction to the child on the sort of world he lives in, the things in it, its textures, shapes, colors, weights, and so on. So, like a child, Professor Burden, you are learning about the world in what may seem to you a fairly random and purposeless fashion—but you are learning. May I suggest some of the things you have already learned about yourself?"

"Please do," Burden said, leaning back and watching Lark with interest.

"For one thing, you have learned that you hold some erroneous notions about the State, its functions and your attitudes toward it. You have learned that while you feel superior to the bureaucrats of the government you should not feel so—that there is justice in what they ask of you and all citizens of the State. You may continue to feel superior to these people but only at the expense of a faintly guilty conscience. You will check that feeling of superiority from time to time. You will think of me. You may even wonder how many persons like me are engaged in government. You may wonder if perhaps the government isn't, in some ways, at least as sophisticated as yourself. You will cease thinking of every government functionary as some sort of shortsighted bumpkin with more power than is good for him. You have also learned that there are other valid standards of measuring the worth of college students than the ones you have been applying for years. You may also begin to weigh in your own mind the values you hold against the values the State finds important. You may even decide that perhaps the State's values are more important for the immediate future, and that your own values, while quite worthy, are something to be realized sometime farther off. Think a little of all the things we have discussed, Professor Burden— see how your thinking may have been modified slightly here, sharpened slightly there, changed a little in direction. You have learned quite a lot in a short time, Professor Burden. For my part, I feel you've made good progress."

"Mr. Lark, you should have been a teacher," Burden said with open admiration.

"But I am, Professor Burden. And I am teaching what is probably the most vital subject in the world—the purposes, aims, and methods of the benevolent State. No state can hope to succeed by fiat. Historically such states have failed. A state must persuade its citizens to accept the premises on which it exists and functions. In some cases persuasion is quite simple, in others, difficult. But it must be accomplished with every citizen—particularly the intellectuals. You know, Professor Burden, that in other times and in other cultures you would have been shot out of hand for disagreeing with the state. I am not mentioning this to make you feel any gratitude. We know such methods are false, that they accomplish nothing, that they postpone the inevitable—that, in fact, they strengthen the ultimate rebellion. To display a weapon is to use your final argument—it is the pathetic threat of a threadbare political system. The Department has built its reputation on reason, justice, and benevolence. We have been successful, Professor. In fact, we have never had a failure. And yet, if we had chosen to be an instrument of terror, to insist upon conformity, the grounds surrounding these buildings would be filled with the graves of our failures. The State is immortal, it cannot concern itself with the immediate success—it must think generations ahead and behave in the present so that the following generations will accept it willingly, gratefully, understandingly. That's why I am a teacher. That's why all of us in the Department are teachers, and all of our functions are those of teachers. Even Mr. Conger, whom you tend to despise, is a teacher. He taught you to think about what you were saying, taught you to examine your motives. You learned from Mr. Conger—learned more than you realized. Think on what Mr. Conger's instruction was and you'll see that I was right. Think on it and you may even come to amend your opinion of Mr. Conger."

"I think you may be right at that," Burden said, puzzled now, wondering if he hadn't, after all, made a complete fool of himself, acted arrogantly when he had no right or reason to act that way. Lark had a curiously sure instinct for awakening thoughts, for instilling doubts, for provoking self-questioning. Burden looked at him more closely, wondering exactly how important Lark was in the hierarchy of government. A man with such talents ought to hold an immensely important position and yet Burden wondered if he did. Could his own case of heresy be so minor that Lark was nothing more than one of a battery of investigators? He had said once he was Richard's superior and Richard had spoken as if he were Conger's superior. Then Lark was at least two cuts above Conger. But now high was that?

"Well," Lark said, rising, "the doctor tells me that you ought to be out of bed and on your feet by tomorrow afternoon. I'm glad, Professor. It will make things more convenient for both of us."

"It certainly will," Burden said with a smile, "and what's more, I'll be able to get out of these pajamas. You don't know how immoral it makes me feel to spend whole days dressed this way. Oh, by the way, you said you would send down that booklet listing my heresies. Remember?"

"I'll see that you get it, Professor. But not right now. I think perhaps we ought to hold it until the end of the week. Then at the end of the week I think you can read it and understand the extent of your heresy and the progress you've made."

"Ummm," Burden said, thoughtfully, "er, would you mind telling me what I can expect during the coming week?"

"Oh, a rather intensified number of conversations of the sort we've been having, various tests, questions. You see, the problem is a double one—to acquaint you with your own heresies, and to disabuse you of them."

"You mean, I have heresies of which I'm not even aware?"

Lark nodded.

"But if I'm not aware of them—how can you know?"

"Partially because some things are evident to us as heresies which are not evident to you, and partially by extension. We've made educated guesses at the extent of your heresies and if our guesses are correct—and by the way, we're rarely very far wrong in our estimates—then your patterns of thinking, your system of values, your entire conceptual processes are heretical and must be changed."

"That's a tall order," Burden said. "Do you really think it can be done in a week?"

"You're a reasonable, logical, educated man, Professor Burden. I think that we can demonstrate the validity of our thinking to you so conclusively that you will give up your heresies."

"Let's hope so, Mr. Lark," Burden said with a smile.

"I hope you're not going to be hostile, Professor," Lark said coldly.

"No, of course not," Burden replied, suddenly unsettled by the tone of Lark's voice, "I want to help."

"Good," Lark said, turning to open the door, "I'll see you in the morning, then. Good day, Professor."

"Fine, Mr. Lark. In the morning," Burden said, as the door closed behind the inquisitor. Burden sat back against the couch, vaguely troubled. The cold tone of Lark's voice was quite out of keeping with the young man's manner. It disturbed him somewhat, impressed him with the fact that Mr. Lark did have a temper after all. He shouldn't have been quite so flippant. It wasn't fair to Lark. He *did* want to be rid of these heresies if they were as important as Lark felt they were. He did want to justify Lark's faith in him, see some good come from all the work the young man was putting into his case. After all, he respected Lark and could even come to like him if Lark would unbend. You had to respect a man with so much basic integrity. No, he thought, he would co-operate actively, he wouldn't make the job any more difficult for Lark than it was already. Perhaps he was wrong—perhaps subconsciously he was a danger to the State. After all, he was a teacher, he had a duty both to the State and to his students. Had he ever flavored his teachings with heresy? Was he breeding heresy in the work he did? The State deserved loyalty. Especially such a state as the one that presided over their society. It was a small nation, but it had grown from the enormous cultural heritage of the English-speaking world.

He knew something of early history. He knew about the psychotic tensions of the twentieth-century world, the terrors, the brutalities, the incredible bestiality recorded in the history books. It had been a sick, tortured, frenetic world in which life became nearly intolerable. It had to be made over in a new image. The benevolent State was the new way.

Lark was right. Terror had failed and reason was being tried, reason and science. People, the eternal problem, were also the answer. Hence the State that concerned itself totally and exclusively with its citizens, their thoughts, their attitudes, their habits, the conscious remolding of their characters to more social, more humane, more peaceful patterns. He had agreed with those principles long ago. His father, too, had agreed. All thinking men had decided that man must be master of his fate, captain of his soul. The mercantile philosophy, the concept of their cultural progenitors, had failed; the myth of self-gratification had failed; the great religions had failed; terror had failed; war had failed; technology had failed. Character was the only thing left—the deliberate, systematic, tortuous method of breeding humans of character, believing in one another and in their systems of government. It had been under way just thirty years. Its first generation of seedlings were now coming into maturity and the country was showing its effects. For one thing, crime had fallen away to virtually zero figures. The only criminals actively operating were adults in their forties and fifties. Juvenile delinquency was nonexistent. Burden knew that insane asylums were dwindling in number, that alcoholic wards handled no adults under thirty.

There was a great deal more family participation in self-entertainment. Reading of books and magazines had zoomed. Automobile registration had fallen enormously. Restlessness and wanderlust had decreased. People preferred to stay near home. The various churches had been delighted at the renewal of family life, the decrease in crime, the easing of emotional tensions, but they were disturbed by the empty places in the houses of worship. The Church of State was taking stronger and stronger hold. It was a strange religion. It could not be called wicked or immoral. It contained so many of the precepts of the Judaeo-Christian ethic that religious leaders were at a loss to criticize it and yet they wondered and puzzled and sought to understand why they were losing their worshipers. They lost them by the hundreds, by the thousands, by the tens of thousands. The Church of State was a church without ritual, without ceremony, without a *mystique*. It was moral, upright, simple, and stressed the fellowship of mankind. It had no ordained members. Any member of the congregation might get up and lead the others. Members lost their identity once they joined. Their contributions to the church were made directly from a small, uniform deduction from their salary. No one could give more even if he so desired and the application for the deduction was voluntary. It could be withdrawn at any time without comment or censure. The church had no synod, no over-all ecclesiastical direction. A State Church could be built by the government upon application of fifty adult citizens partially from funds contributed by the fifty and from the general fund of the church which was administered by two paid church employees, an accountant and his secretary. A government employee supervised the keeping of records and regularly examined the books but he was the sole official connection with the church. There was no other.

Burden had never thought deeply about the society in which he lived. It seemed to work well, but he didn't have the basis of comparison that older people seemed to have. Most of the older people, when you spoke to them privately, agreed that this society was better, but that it was puzzling, one they did not fully understand, and so did not quite trust. There were so many good things in it that one couldn't complain, and yet the vague feeling persisted that the society had a catch in it, a joker that had not yet been shown. Burden had pursued this point a few times in the hopes of describing it in his reports. But the older people seemed unwilling or incapable of pinning down their thoughts. One professor had complained that the society had "no zest, no verve, no drive, no sense of excitement." Burden thought it a rather childish comment of an old man. Only one colleague, a professor in the Physics Department, had ever made a valid point about the old days. "Nowadays," he had said, "you get the feeling that no one really gives a damn about physical sciences. Nuclear physics used to be the most important thing in the world. But now, what if I do come up with a process for extracting maximum energy from a lump of coal? All you can use it for is to drive a ship to the stars. But who the hell wants to go? People don't even want to stir out of their houses at night—how in God's name can you expect them to want to reach the stars?"

At least that much was true. There seemed to be a lack

of interest in things that had once absorbed mankind. The preoccupation with the outer world had fallen off. There was more looking inward. Psychologists, social scientists, and others who studied man were delighted. Their work was considered important and was subsidized by an interested government.

The integrity that the government sought to instill in its citizens was seeping into business. A buyer's market—a very moral, very sober buyer's market—existed, in which appeals to vanity or to hedonism were considered immoral, wicked, and heretical. But there appeared no undue amount of unemployment. Food consumption was high, home construction booming. The population growth, surprising in its steadily rising curve, provided a half dozen industries with continuous work. Labor-saving devices for the home were always in demand and there was a steady pressure for the development of automatic machinery to cut down the length of the working day. People wanted to be home more often for longer periods of time and marriage figures topped their previous highs with every counting. Divorce, on the other hand, steadily decreased.

Burden had heard all of these things. They constituted, he knew, a picture of the society in which he lived. But he had grown up in that society, and he was not old enough to make comparisons, to know whether it was a good society or not. Strange, he thought, how we need rulers by which to measure our own happiness. Stranger yet not to know whether a society was good or not unless one had lived in an earlier, different society, The young people, of course, completely accepted their society. To them it was approaching the state of perfection. That much he got from talking with all of them. They were quite free in their ideas; free and identical. Differences of opinion did not seem to exist for them, except at home. Burden recollected that quite a few had trouble at home —particularly where there was a disproportionate difference in age between themselves and their parents—late parenthood or cases of children born of second marriages. The beginning of the new society had caught Burden in midstride, he decided. He was just twelve years old, not a child, not an adult. His father had been in favor of the new society—his brother Ralph dubious. To Burden it had always seemed a good society, a vital one. Then where had his heresies come from? Not from his parents, not from his observations. From his colleagues? From Emma? From Emma's parents? Burden rested against the couch pondering the question that he knew Lark would ask him. Lark would want to know. Lark, in fact, was entitled to know. He himself did not know the answer. It would require thought—as much as he could do on his own without Lark's astute guesses, although he knew that Lark would help him. The discovery of one's own soul was a fascinating experience, Burden decided. He found himself looking forward to the week ahead with something that resembled excitement.

13

Because he was in need of fresh air, Lark left the building for the walk to the conference room. The air was cold and the brilliant sparkle of the Sunday afternoon was disappearing very quickly. It gave him an unhappy sense of confinement to walk between the buildings, their sheer walls rising on all sides of him, broken only by the cross bridges of the intrabuilding shuttles. He wished that the designers had not chosen such a pattern but something a little more open, perhaps a group of low buildings scattered over all the acreage available to the Department. The construction of the buildings suggested that they existed for the mechanical efficiency of the Department and not for the personal efficiency of the staff. Perhaps he ought to do an investigative monograph on the implicit heresy of the architects who designed the buildings. The question, of course, was whether the buildings existed for the sake of the workers who were to occupy them or for the convenience of the functions they were to perform.

Lark smiled and stowed the thoughts away in his mind for later inspection. Now his chief problem was Burden.

It was moving along well. Burden had effected a transference. The psychiatric division had predicted the transference, had suggested means by which it could be established quickly. They had been right. Burden liked him, respected him, perhaps even needed him. Lark thought that perhaps they might go into Burden's sexual fantasies at the next session in which Burden would be drugged.

When Lark arrived at the conference room he found Conger sitting at the long table, fussing, as usual, with his short-stemmed pipe; Julian Richard was drawing pointless doodles on a pad of paper; Doctor Emmerich was chatting with his assistant, a youngish man with a sturdy, earnest face whom Lark did not know. Doctor Wright, plucking absent-mindedly at his mustache, was seated in a discreet, distant corner of the table apart from the others. He had been called to the conference because Lark felt the political analyst was a stimulant to the discussion.

The psychiatric division had hinted broadly that it would like to place a representative on the conference board but Lark had avoided decision by suggesting a separate psychiatric consultation. There was no point in overloading the conference board on Burden. Lark preferred small groups. They worked better. He had witnessed the painful effects of mass conferences in earlier years. Where departmental and divisional convictions ran high, a synthesis in open conference often exhausted more time than it was worth. Perhaps one day he would be reproached or perhaps even examined for the arrogation of authority. For the moment, he was careful to acknowledge the assistance of each of the divisions of the Department and to take no steps without consulting the necessary divisions. But the over-all plan was still in his own hands, where he intended it should remain.

"Well, gentlemen, I think we can begin," Lark said, taking his seat at the head of the table.

"Sir," Doctor Emmerich, the elderly doctor who had first examined Burden, spoke up, "do you contemplate questioning under narcotics again?"

"Yes, Doctor," Lark said, pulling Burden's folder toward him, "every night for the next two weeks or until I'm satisfied there is no point in it."

"I should like to point out that the drug is rather dangerous, in that continuous administration over a period of two weeks may permanently damage the heart and other organs," Doctor Emmerich said.

"I'm not interested in Professor Burden's health, Doctor," Lark said crisply. "If I fail, he's lost. If I succeed I don't imagine he would reproach us for a weakened heart. I think the psychiatric division's recommendation that this method is the quickest is a sound one. I intend to continue with it. Yes, Frank?"

"I was thinking," Conger said mildly, "couldn't we possibly have these injections made at some other time than three or four o'clock in the morning?"

Lark smiled mechanically. "Sorry to break up your sleep, Frank, but it's part of the pattern. Burden's going to catch on to those injections. Perhaps this morning, perhaps the next morning. That's what we want. I don't have three years in which to amiably coax Professor Burden out of his heresies. I have exactly twelve days left now, and every one of them has to count."

"But aren't you afraid that if Burden understands that he's being systematically drugged and questioned he will freeze up?" Richard asked, leaning forward on the table.

"What is needed here is a thread of terror—a bright, red thread of terror. Just enough to let Professor Burden know that we are not merely holding conversational hands with him."

"Then you want to frighten him?" Conger asked, sucking at a flame held over his pipe bowl.

"Fear is necessary, I'm afraid. We want to speed up Professor Burden's reclamation. We can conceal the reason for the injection. Make up anything that seems plausible to you, Doctor." Emmerich nodded. "But he is bound to wonder about the injection," Lark went on smoothly, "and we'll hold off telling him."

"That's the shocker," Conger said, finally satisfied with the light in his pipe.

"Yes, that's the shocker. It might drive Professor Burden forward. It might retard him. If it deeply frightens him I'll discontinue for a night and see if we can't persuade him it's for his own good—which, of course, it is," Lark said blandly. "The emotional pattern is fear, recovery from fear, increased faith in me, suspicion, doubt, confusion, and fear again."

"And once he's terrified?" Conger asked, puffing placidly.

"He turns to me. Then we begin to break down his inner resistance. He wants to believe because intellectually we've shown him how wrong he's been."

"But what if he reacts to fear with courage?" Doctor Wright asked. The others turned to look at him.

"I always trust you to come up with the difficult question," Lark said, favoring Wright with a smile. "Well, let's presume he becomes brave and resists. Whom will he resist? Me? Certainly not. I'm the one who is working so hard for his own good. I am his friend. I am the one person whom he knows well. I am a quantity he understands. The Department, on the other hand, is a vague, threatening entity which he does not understand. He has had some painful, minor experiences with it. If he resists he must have some basis on which to rest his resistance. What is it he objects to? To being held? But he is being held for heresy. He has admitted heresy—or will, when we have come up to that point. We are effecting a cure. He wants it now—the cure, I mean. He wants it in a slightly intellectual, vaguely social way. It is not imperative to him that he conform. He'd like to, if only to please me, but if it becomes inconvenient for him to conform he won't. Not at this stage. The strength of terror is that it is implied, never stated. A man can face anything if he knows how terrible it will be, or imagines that he does. You can threaten him with beatings, with torture, with death. Well, he says, they can beat me senseless, they can torture me until I faint, and I can die only once. I'll trust the thresholds of pain and death to save me from things I can't bear. But what if he has no knowledge of what terror we are saving for him? What if the terror is never named? What if the terror is never limited? He has so many things to be frightened of—all the things that are buried deep within him. He supplies himself with his own whips, racks, chains, acids, fires, and hells. He'll do a more awful job on himself than we could ever hope to do. And too, of course, you know the ordinances against physical punishment."

"You don't call this punishment," Doctor Wright said dryly, watching Lark through the thick lenses of his glasses.

"Punishment as a social concept no longer exists," Lark said patiently. "I would not dream of harming Professor Burden. I seek only to rid him of his heresies. If I enlist his help in doing so, am I punishing him? You see what I mean, don't you, Doctor?"

"Yes," Doctor Wright said calmly, retreating behind the thick glasses, the heavy mustache.

"You don't seem convinced, Doctor," Lark said, conscious of the fact that the others at the table resented Wright's presence and his remarks. "I may not punish a man but I cannot help it if he punishes himself. He would not be punishing himself if he had no sense of guilt. The sense of guilt derives from his heresy. Deep down he suspects the Department of cruelty. That's an error. That's a heresy. If he were not a heretic, the concept of official cruelty would never suggest itself to him and he would be anesthetized to all suggestions of terror. In short, he would not believe that we would harm a hair of his head. Which we would not."

The others waited a moment to see if Wright would answer, but the political analyst nodded his head vaguely and retreated still further.

"Now," Lark said, addressing the others at the table again, "I have a question to ask of you. I want your opinions—but briefly, if you please. Would there be any value in evoking Burden's sexual fantasies in a drugged session? Doctor Emmerich?"

"Yes, I believe there would be," Emmerich said. "We know how much motivation of human behavior is based on sexual desire and, after all, we are primarily devoted to the investigation of Burden's motives. It would be useful."

Lark nodded and turned toward the fat investigator with his pipe. "Conger?"

"I see no value in it. It appears to me to be a waste of time. Burden is an intellectual, and while all human motivation is somehow enmeshed with sexual drives of one sort or another, Burden's problem seems to me to stem from ego, from a strong sense of individualism—from intellectual processes rather than from any other process. I know that there's a sexual link somewhere in there, but I don't think it's worth exploring."

"Richard?" Lark snapped.

"I agree with Frank Conger basically. Burden is a conventionally sensual man. He's happily married, has two sons, has no record of adultery, and as far as we know had had no intercourse with anyone before marriage. We went further back in the records and have failed to find any indication that adolescent sexuality was overly important. At least, no record of any family concern on the matter."

"Doctor Wright?" Lark asked, deliberately seeking to draw the political analyst back into the discussion.

"I'm not a psychoanalyst," Wright said calmly, "but it might be pertinent to discover which of his two parents was more important to him. You know the theory of the strong state as representing the father, as dictators representing father-images and so on. If he was in rebellion against his father he might be in rebellion against a strong state—rebellious, in general, against supervision. That's only a guess, of course."

"And a very shrewd one, as usual," Lark said admiringly. Lark felt the tiny stir of annoyance from the others at the table. It pleased him, in a mysterious way, to annoy his subordinates with his attention to Wright. Someday he would have to go into an analysis of their hostility and his desire to provoke it. "Well, then, gentlemen, I think we've concluded our conference. I have an idea for the story we're going to give Professor Burden, Doctor Emmerich—

concerning the injection. I want to go over it in my mind for a short while."

"All right, sir," Emmerich said, his assistant following his lead and rising with him. Conger and Richard followed suit. But Wright remained seated, a fact that made Lark smile inwardly. Wright knew that he was not being dismissed.

The others left, with only Conger casting a backward glance at the political analyst. The fat man's face had no expression as his eyes traveled between Lark and Wright but Lark had the feeling that a mental note was made that Wright lingered, apparently with Lark's approval.

Lark said nothing for some time after the door had closed and Doctor Wright waited patiently. The inquisitor slumped in his chair, drew up a knee, rested it against the table, and stared at the cover of the folder that contained reports and analyses of Professor Burden's heresies.

"Do you approve of my methods, Doctor Wright?" Lark finally asked, not looking at the political analyst.

"I think you may succeed," Wright said. "I approve of the choice of methods as leading to a probably successful conclusion—yes."

"But morally you disapprove of my methods?"

"There is no morality in your method. You are a peculiarly amoral man. You lie when it pleases you, cheat when it suits you, terrorize when it is convenient. You manipulate this man as if he were a cardboard figure. You are not interested in this man's heresy—you're involved in a game of slowly driving the poor devil out of his mind."

"It's no game, Doctor," Lark said grimly, "it's quite serious. Tell me this—what is your analysis of the probable course of our State during the next seventy-five years?"

"You don't want my opinion on that subject, sir. Don't you know that I am never consulted on that subject? Haven't you heard of the bias index? Didn't you know I rate at the top of the index on such questions?"

"I'll discount your bias, Doctor. Give me your opinion."

"There is no such thing as a benevolent state without tolerance. Yet this State purports to be exactly that—a state which knows all, tolerates no deviation from established doctrine, and operates for the good of all. That's nonsense. A state which tolerates no deviation from established doctrine is a state which suppresses deviants. The longer the State continues in power the greater the area of its control. You know historically that there is no such thing as a state which stays in power without increasing its power to rule bit by bit. This encroaching blanket of power continues until crises arise—war, famine, religious dissension, technological improvement, scandal in government. And then the rebellion sets in. An inflexible government very often falls—as many of the monarchies of Europe and Asia fell. Only a government which is willing to yield, to relinquish portions of its power manages to survive—most notably, the royal house of England, which underwent a progressive deterioration in power and so remained, while its sister houses of royalty met challenge and crisis inflexibly and fell. This State is broadening and deepening its control every hour, every day, every year that it continues. And it is an inflexible state which yields nothing."

"But such a state is only in danger when a crisis occurs," Lark said, knowing full well what Wright would reply. "I think you said war, famine, religious dissension, technological improvement, and scandal in government. The State has rather neatly undercut these crises, has it not? After all, the age of the military adventuring state is over and our State would be the last to resume it even if the World Federation tolerated such a state—which it would not. As for famine—modern agriculture makes famine a ghost out of the past, scary, but not effective. And as for religious dissension—the Church of State is growing at an enormous rate. In twenty years it will have swallowed up the major religious groups. And technological improvement—well, we don't encourage that, do we? And as for scandal in the government and in the conduct of state affairs—like Caeser's wife, we are all above reproach. We see to that ourselves."

"Yes, I'll admit that the State's plan has been very shrewd. Yet there's been a new factor of crisis—a rather modern factor. It was growing rapidly until it was struck down by this State—our benevolent State. I'm speaking of the intellectual—the person you call a heretic—the individual. The concept of individualism has been growing for a long time, sir—it now has earned the right to be called a crisis matter. I think in seventy-five years you'll find that it's grown enormously. And the harder the State squeezes its citizens into the mold, the more heretics will appear. They'll grow rapidly and they will include the thoughtful, the gifted, the honest, the brave, the moral. In short, the best elements of the society will be arrayed against the State. That's what's going to happen in seventy-five years, sir, and this State, inflexible as it is, will break."

"Yes, Doctor Wright," Lark said, pleased with Wright almost as if Wright were his protégé, a protégé who had performed brilliantly, "that's exactly what I told the Commissioner. That's why he's allowed me two weeks in which to rid Burden of heresy. You see, if we can take the intellectuals, the people you so poetically call the thoughtful, the gifted, the honest, the moral, the brave,"—he paused, smiled, "did I get the sequence right?—and enchant them into conforming, we'll have whipped the last crisis. That's why Burden must be reclaimed. If Burden can be purged of his heresies, then we can purge anyone of his heresies." Lark paused, not quite certain that Wright's face hadn't paled slightly, trying to find out what emotions coursed behind those weak eyes, trying to see whether or not the lip under the heavy mustache didn't tremble faintly. "There aren't many in the government who see these things so clearly. To Conger, to Richard, to Doctor Emmerich and the others Burden represents a puzzle, a test of our resources. If we fail, then it only means to them that we must improve our methods, re-evaluate our techniques, and perhaps add to our equipment. None of them realizes how deadly failure with Burden can be to all of us—to the State, to everything. You realize it, and I do, and perhaps, vaguely, so do a few others in the Department including the Commissioner. But no government ever wants to believe that its existence depends upon some minor point, some insignificant citizen. It rather offends official vanity, which is every bit as real as personal vanity. A state is immortal— a concept that is very necessary to its proper functioning. If a stooped, balding professor of English at a small college can topple it by remaining obstinately individual— well, that's unthinkable, isn't it? Unthinkable and untenable. But it's true. This State's destiny is locked up inside a man named Professor Burden who likes to think that he is an individual."

Lark's eyes glittered, his lips parted more than usual. He brought his knee down from the table. "The key to this man has always been his pride, his vanity, his unwarranted belief that he is a creature apart, that he possesses some single, indefinable identity that is his and his alone. And it is the retention of this one idea that stands between the State and a thousand years of rule—a thousand years which will mean a golden age for man. To me such a thing is monstrous!" Lark's hand, slender, hard, pale struck the table like the slash of a whip.

Wright remained motionless, his weak eyes hypnotically fastened on Lark's face.

"Do you know what I'm going to do, Doctor Wright?" Lark asked, his chest heaving slightly, his eyes large and pale in their concentration. "I'm going to pulverize this man's identity. I'm going to reduce him to a cipher, from one—" Lark shot up a bony forefinger, "to nothing." Lark's finger curled back on itself to make a bony, angular symbol of zero. "That's the whole problem. Break that outer shell of individuality and you can rake up the heresies with a common gardening tool. Would you be interested in watching the process, Doctor Wright?"

"You can't do it," Doctor Wright said and Lark, with keen satisfaction, noted the huskiness of the doctor's voice, the overstressed negative suggesting Wright's deepest fears.

"You're invited to watch us, Doctor," Lark said.

14

For Burden it seemed to be the repetition of a bad dream. The dark room, himself asleep, the chill air, and the hand—bony, sharp, insistent—calling him.

"What?" Burden said, sitting up in the darkness, the faint reflection of light from a starched white blouse.

"The doctor wants to see you, Professor Burden," the attendant said.

"In God's name—at this hour?"

"Yes," the attendant said and reached over and picked up his robe which was resting across the foot of the bed. Burden slipped out from the warm covers and felt the chill on his feet. What did they want now? Was there some sort of madness loose in the medical department that they awoke him at such an hour?

"Do you have to go to the bathroom?" the attendant asked as Burden put his slippers on and got into the bathrobe.

"No."

"Good," the attendant said, and Burden felt the strong

fingers at his elbow guiding him. The door opened on the same corridor, endless, looking even longer than the first time he had stepped into it. And yes, he saw the small, distant figure, working silently, patiently on the floor. Burden knew, before he looked, that it would be the same attendant—the one with the broken, fighter's face. It was.

"It seems to me that we've done this before," Burden said. The attendant said nothing. Burden seethed with annoyance. Surely they did not have to wake him at this hour. He decided he would tell Lark—would, in fact, insist that his sleep not be broken up by such nonsense. After all, he would need a clear mind if he was going to help Lark.

Again the same large room with its screened cubicles, leather-topped examining tables, the gleaming copper and porcelain tubs. This time the doctor was waiting for him at the examination table. It was the same gentle, elderly doctor who had come in with Lark, the same one he had seen that first morning.

"Doctor—what is this?"

"Get up on here, Professor Burden," the doctor said kindly, but not smiling.

"Would you mind telling me what this is all about?"

"Do you recall yesterday that you were asked for specimens of your urine and blood?"

"Yes."

"Unfortunately, the lab has just informed us that your blood shows that you are suffering from syphilis."

"What?" Burden was stunned, incredulous, uncertain whether he had heard correctly or the doctor was completely insane.

"Would you mind taking off your bathrobe and rolling up your pajama sleeve? Right arm, please."

"Now, wait a minute. This is impossible. Y-you can't be right." Burden found himself stammering slightly.

"Professor Burden, there's no mistake. The test is quite simple and quite conclusive. Your blood shows the presence of *spirochaeta pallida.*"

"It's impossible." Burden's voice was hoarse now, his eyes large with shock.

"Professor Burden, I'm not going to argue the morals of the matter. The disease exists and is very probably beyond the secondary stage. At least your skin seems clear. Have you had any rashes or lesions on your body the past few years?"

"No." Burden thought quickly, frantically, before realizing that he was accepting the doctor's verdict. "And I have no such disease. I've been married for sixteen years to the same woman."

"Then it's possible you've contracted it from your wife," Doctor Emmerich said calmly. "Your sleeve, please."

Burden's hand shot out and caught the doctor's coat in rage. "You're lying," he said, feeling himself trembling, his muscles growing weak, his head bursting.

"Professor Burden, I know it's a shock to learn that you're suffering from a venereal disease. But please have the courtesy to respect my professional status and my judgment. I wouldn't lie to you, nor would I seek to embarrass you. Syphilis is acquired in just two ways—by heredity and by direct physical or, more particularly, sexual contact. Now, we know yours is not a case of hereditary syphilis and so it must have been acquired by sexual contact. You assure me that you have not had adulterous sexual relations and I believe you. Hence the only other conclusion is that your wife must have had adulterous relations."

"In God's name," Burden said softly, feeling sick as he let go of the doctor's coat, "it can't be true."

"The important thing at the moment is cure, Professor Burden. Fortunately we have specifics to deal with all stages of syphilis. They're very successful and very quick. But the sooner we start the treatment the sooner we'll arrest internal damage. Now, if you'll take off your bathrobe and roll up your sleeve, please—"

Burden obeyed the doctor's orders numbly, staring sightlessly into the darkness of the room. He hardly felt the needle, his mind a chaos of images and thoughts, of the sounds of Emma's words, the voices of his sons, the particular shape of furniture in the house, the light soap scent of Emma's hands, the faint delicate animal smell of her mouth, the melting look of pleasure in her eyes when they were in bed together. Ten thousand things that he had forgotten sprang into his mind—the surprising sensuality in Emma that he had discovered on their honeymoon, his delight and pleasure in it, the sharp, rising fierceness of her desires. He had been a withdrawn young man and had supposed Emma as innocent as himself, and on their honeymoon he didn't equate the eagerness of her body with anything but love for him. He knew Emma had been popular and it had both surprised and pleased him to know that she preferred him to other young men. Emma had seemed so completely out of the world in which he lived. College, for her, had been a social engagement filled with the attentions of young men, the giggling mysteries of sorority sisterhood, the games, the rallies, the dances, the holidays. Why had she chosen him? He was cynical enough to know that it is always the woman who chooses the man for a love object, so he knew that she had chosen him. But why? Was it because he was steady, prosaic, and showed promise? Had she chosen him for the gratitude he would show her? He had been grateful for many years. But more recently—he didn't know just when—he had ceased being grateful, had perhaps taken Emma for granted. Was that when she had looked for a lover? In God's name—his Emma? The two boys, the house, the routine of their life . . . oh, no. And yet, there was the remark she had made. What was it? About his going out every night—what did she say? That she used to pretend that he met some woman? Was it, then, a guarded, guilt-struck admission that she met someone else? That she had lain naked in someone else's arms and had accepted the taint of his blood?

"Yes, she did."

What? Who spoke? Again, someone speaks and—who is it?

"She was naked in his arms and she squirmed and cried out and bit him."

No, please don't say things like that.

"But of course it happened just that way. His apartment—or perhaps even in your own house."

No, no, Emma wouldn't.

"But she did. There's the proof—signed in your own blood."

Oh, my God.

"She's a passionate woman—she couldn't wait for desires to mount in a placid, pale grub like you. She tore her clothes off to be naked for her lover."

No, no.

"She was eager for it. Don't be a fool. You never satisfied her. Perhaps there was more than one lover. A woman as lusty as Emma Burden could use more lovers."

I trust her. It's not true.

"Think back, Burden. Weren't there times when she

wanted more of you, more than you could give? Didn't she retreat into the darkness, still hungry, her body straining, a deep sense of being cheated filling her?"

I don't know. I don't know.

"After all, Burden, you're not a passionate man. You couldn't hope to satisfy her. Be realistic."

It was my fault, not hers.

"She's probably with her lover now. Emma has smooth, warm thighs, doesn't she, Burden? Her lover probably knows more about them than you. He probably knows her body as intimately as a—"

Stop! Stop! In the name of God, *stop!*

"Man is an instrument of woman's will, Burden. Emma married you for comfort, for security, for prestige. She probably never expected you to excite her, to fulfill her. She found that elsewhere. Face up to it, Burden—you're only half a man as far as Emma Burden is concerned."

No, no, she's happy, she's content.

"Happy with your position, with the home you've provided for her, with the attention you've given her, with the security you've furnished. But when her body demands a man she seeks him out, hungry for him, aching for him—not caring whether he's diseased or brutal or stupid. Do you think he respects her? Cares about her? Do you think she wants any of those pointless, weak little things from him? She can have that pap from her husband. From her lover she wants the darkness, the flesh, the pain, the excruciating light of completion. He may spit on her, beat her, humiliate her, but she will twitch with desire, hunger for the final depravity, the deepest instincts of her womanhood reaching, clinging, desiring—"

Won't you please stop? Please, please, please?

"You're not quite the hero you imagine yourself,

Burden, are you? Not quite the complete man, the perfect man, after all. You can't arouse a woman, satisfy a woman. Your wife pities you when she thinks of you at all."

What do you want of me?

"Stop lying to yourself, stop taking on airs. A man who can't fulfill the primary functions of manhood has no right to assume he has any importance. Your sons—are they really your sons? Do they look like you? Perhaps they are another man's sons. You can never be sure. She's found joy in other men's arms, a joy you could never give her. Perhaps your sons are born of that joy—that pure white-hot joy you could never give her."

I don't know any more. I don't know.

"You know nothing, Burden. That's the secret of your life. You have always been uncertain—of yourself, of your skills, of your manhood. How can you pretend to be something when you know that you are nothing? You're less of a man than the brute who enjoys your wife. You're less of a man than Doctor Middleton who speaks his mind—who voices his heresy. You conceal yourself, you're afraid of it—you are sly and slippery and nauseating. You're a spy—a State spy. Do you really think no one at the college knows it?"

But surely they don't.

"They do. They all know and they have contempt for you as Emma has contempt for you. What's happening now in your own home? This minute? Is Emma with her lover? Is—"

The voice went on, vicious and insinuating, detailing the scene in the bedroom, in the darkness. It was Lark's voice. At the far end of the room Doctor Wright drew back into the darkness, his face pale, his hands shaking. Doctor Emmerich crossed over to the political analyst, who watched Lark leaning over Burden's supine form, talking, talking.

"What's the matter, Doctor?" Emmerich asked softly.

"When is he going to stop?" Wright said, feeling cold sweat on his face.

"It's part of the personality readjustment," Emmerich said blandly, glancing over his shoulder. Doctor Wright unexpectedly put his hands to his ears, his small, weak eyes seeming to bulge into the thick lenses of his glasses.

"It makes me sick," Wright gagged, "they'll drive him out of his mind."

"Nonsense," Emmerich replied, turning around to watch the group clustered about the examining table and Burden's drugged body.

II

It was early in the afternoon of Monday, the nineteenth of October, when Burden awoke. It was an awakening with a shudder since it instantly recalled the words of the doctor who had administered the specific.

Burden shrank back against the bed, his head throbbing, his bones aching, his mind endlessly running a circular track, exhausted, feeble, tortured, but forced to keep to the track. It wasn't true, it couldn't be true. It was merely an obscene error—the worst they had committed thus far. He had had dreams—he knew what the dreams were—tangled, shadowy pale figures quivering under the awful tensions of desire, mindless, seeking only the touch, the kiss, the bite, the pain, and the completion of pain. One of the figures had been Emma. Or had it?

Burden passed his hand over his mouth in shame and shock and felt the dry heat of his lips and the stubble on his chin and over his upper lip. No, he shook his head weakly, he would never believe it. Dreams were not things to be trusted. The doctor was wrong, the examination of his blood was an error, names had been mixed, slides mislabeled. In God's name, how could such errors continue? Or had it been an error? Burden's pale blue eyes searched the room vacantly. Had they lied to him? Deliberately? But why? What reason could they have for such a lie? What purpose did it serve? He shook his head exhaustedly and forced himself upright. He could not think in bed. The aching of his bones and muscles dragged at him as though he were wading through water waist-deep. It sapped his strength, sucked at his resistance. It was the whole business of being in bed, in a hospital, that kept him from thinking clearly. First it was the sedative, and then the grippe, and now this—if it really existed.

Burden forced himself out of bed. He was no invalid, they would not make him an invalid. What were they trying to do to him? Lark had told him it was to disabuse him of his heresies. Burden shook his head at the confusion in his mind. He could not pick up the string that held the beads. First things first, he told himself firmly. If he tried to consider all of it at once it would merely compound the confusion, paralyze him with its contradictions.

He huddled on the couch although the room was not cold, and wondered where they had put his bathrobe. The slight rattle of the window made him turn his head. All he could see was hard, flat light. It might be any sort of day outside—cold, sharp, raw, mild, bright, dull. He had no way of telling. The wall opposite his window began to depress him. He longed for a view of open spaces. It was impossible to think inside this room. If only for an hour he could get outside. He had to speak to Lark about it.

To begin with, he thought grimly, Emma was not un-faithful. That was false. He knew it as certainly as he could watch the level of water rise in a glass under an opened tap. Whatever his dreams, whatever the diagnosis suggested, Emma was not the disordered, pale, frantic figure in his dreams. And he could answer as certainly that he had never been false to Emma. That meant the diagnosis was wrong. But how wrong? An administrative error? A clerical mistake? Or a deliberate error? But if it was a deliberate error, what was its purpose? To confuse him? Would that help them rid him of his heresies? How? What purpose did it serve to make him think that his wife had been unfaithful? Was it intended to shake his beliefs in things he held sacred? Was this the begin-ning of a succession of such attempts to shake his faith in everything he believed? If that was the reason behind the deliberate lie, did it follow that if he lost his beliefs he would lose his heresies? Or was it something even more basic? Did they have to sweep his mind clean before they could attempt to rid him of his heresies?

Burden's jaw tightened; his hands opened and closed just once, and then remained closed. Lark would arrive shortly, Burden knew, and this time he would find out the truth. Perhaps Lark had nothing to do with this part of the treatment. It was quite possible that his purging was a matter of concern for several departments and that each would be trying its own methods. If that were the case then it suggested an over-all direction. But who was responsible for such direction? Lark? Burden could not believe that. And yet Lark had a formidable mind. It was possible he made all the decisions. But if he did, would he be on such intimate terms with his subject? Burden rather felt that the head of such a project would stay aloof from any particular phase of it, watching all the activities, weighing all the results. Lark would not fit as the head under such circumstances. It would be someone higher, someone more important—Lark's superior, or perhaps someone even several stations above that. Burden wondered how important he really was to the Department. Lark had taken a very serious view of heresy. He remembered the illustrations Lark had given him—the platoon lieutenant, the clerk in government service. But how serious was it, after all? The fact of the matter was, it was a fiction. A platoon commander did not alter the course of a war, a clerk in government service did not alter the affairs of a nation. War and politics were too huge to turn on such minor pivots. Perhaps a thousand platoon commanders, a thousand clerks made a difference—but not one. Curious, Burden's eyes narrowed at the thought, how much stress Lark placed on the dangers of an individual. He did not say the individual was important—he said the individual's disobedience or attitude was important only in so far as it differed from the attitudes of all. It seemed a remarkable twist of reasoning to ignore the importance of an individual except when he deviated. It was as though Lark had no concept of the individual unless he did wrong—held heresies.

Burden halted that line of thought and forced himself back to the consideration of the first question. Had the doctor committed a deliberate error? Had they lied to him? That question had to be answered before he could reason any further.

Lark arrived at four in the afternoon, looking pale, rumpled, his pale eyes tinged with red fatigue, a smile on his face. As usual, he brought his chair over to the couch where Burden sat.

"I'm glad to see you looking so well-prepared for our chat," Lark said.

"Did you know that last night I was taken to the clinic and told that I was suffering from syphilis?"

Lark hesitated for a moment. "Yes," he answered softly.

"Do you know what that news has suggested to me?" Burden asked calmly, his eyes fixed on Lark.

"I wouldn't go into the morality of it," Lark said, "if you were thinking of that. After all, the flesh is a mysterious envelope. I don't think it's worth-while to explore what a man will do, or what a woman will do under certain circumstances. Don't let it disturb you too much, Professor. It's a disease like any other, and it can be cured."

"It's more than a disease, Mr. Lark," Burden said carefully. "Some people consider it a moral judgment. Almost any married man would consider it a revelation of a secret. Since I have been faithful to my wife it can mean only one thing."

"Professor Burden, I don't want you to be upset about this. I'm sorry the doctor informed you of the condition. Actually, there was no need to. You could have been treated and left here at the end of the week completely cured. Of course, as a matter of public health, your wife will be contacted by public health authorities and given the same examination and treatment. She will, of course, have to be told. And whatever other sexual contacts she's made will also have to be found." Lark paused. "I'm sorry if this is painful for you. You may believe me when I tell you that I have formed no derogatory opinion of your wife because of this."

"Neither have I," Burden said slowly.

"Good," Lark said, nodding agreeably but soberly, "I'm glad to hear that. When I first discovered what had happened last night I was disturbed to think that it would upset you—prevent us from going on with our most important work."

"Mr. Lark," Burden said, bracing himself, "I believe my wife has been faithful to me. I know I have been faithful to her. That means the diagnosis of syphilis was in error. The question I want to ask you is this: Why did they lie to me?"

15

Lark hardly paused before answering. "That's a surprising conclusion, Professor Burden. Why should anyone lie to you about anything? Especially about something that carries such grave moral implications?"

"I don't know, Mr. Lark. That is what I am asking you. I know they lied. But why?"

"Well," Lark shrugged his shoulders, "perhaps they didn't. Perhaps there was some error in the labs."

Burden shook his head. "No, Mr. Lark, I don't think there was. I think we once discussed my feeling more sophisticated than people who ran the government. And I think you showed me the fallacy of such thinking. Well, I've rid myself of that heresy, Mr. Lark. I think the doctors, the laboratory assistants, and the administrative workers of this Department are capable enough to avoid such errors. So I will not accept error as an answer. The only other answer is deliberate falsehood. Why was it necessary?"

"Professor Burden, you manage to be flattering and insulting at the same time." Lark smiled wryly. "On the one hand you credit us with infallibility, only to prove that we are damned as liars. Couldn't the truth be simpler and less flattering to ourselves—that a mistake was made somewhere?"

"Let me ask you another question—"

Lark nodded soberly, waiting.

"Evidently purging me of heresy is a matter of some importance with the Department. And since it is, I suppose quite a few branches of the Department are in on this project. And if that is the case there must be some over-all direction, some person in charge of all phases of the operation. Is there such a person?"

"No," Lark said softly.

"You mean to tell me that there is no one person in charge of this project? That you allow everyone and anyone to do with me what he will?"

"Professor Burden—what is it you really want to know?"

"Was I lied to deliberately?"

"But you say it was a lie. Would you believe me if I said it was not a lie?"

"I know it was a lie," Burden said softly, determinedly.

"Let's set the matter aside for a moment," Lark said quietly, "and pick up the question of the over-all authority. You are quite right. I am not the only person involved in this matter of purging you of your heresies. It is a co-operative enterprise. Why should you assume there is some one in charge of the entire enterprise?"

"It seems to me that an elementary sense of organization would suggest that when a number of people or agencies are engaged in working on some one thing there be a supervisor over all the workers."

"And your elementary sense of organization tells you that there's someone sitting in an office somewhere reading reports on you, criticizing techniques, making value judgments, issuing orders on your treatment?" Lark noted Burden's grave, steady look. He smiled. "Well, you're wrong. Actually there is no such person. What you call the over-all authority is a book—a manual. You see, the Department is the society in microcosm. We deal with you—each division—in accordance with certain regulations and rules printed in black and white in a manual. Each division has a specific function to perform according to the manual and only that part of the manual which concerns the work of that particular division is in the possession of that division. I don't know how I can best explain it, but it is as if a man were performing some tiny function in the manufacture of a very delicate and complex apparatus. Of course he knows what the finished product should look like, and he probably knows, generally speaking, its function. But he does not know the interrelation of all the parts or the particular relationship his own small contribution has to the other parts or they to his."

"That's monstrous," Burden said, genuinely shocked and amazed. "You mean I'm dealt with as if I were a machine—like any other?"

"It shouldn't shock you," Lark said, pleased at his own improvisation and its success in touching Burden so deeply. Burden's sense of individualism had sprung up like a tongue of fire, naked, glowing, gorgeous in its anarchy. "The manual is extremely complex and the product of many years of experience and the efforts of many sophisticated and intuitive minds. I've never seen a complete copy of the manual myself, but I should imagine it would be huge—laid on its side it might be three or four feet thick. Our own section is three hundred pages long of fine type and it isn't a bit discursive. It's all quite to the point."

"There are others like me?"

"Of course," Lark said blandly. "You didn't think you were unique, did you?"

"Does the manual call for lying about a woman's fidelity?" Burden asked, angry now and bitter that he should be treated in accordance with the instructions in a manual.

"I have no idea what the medical division's section of the manual calls for. It's quite possible all this is misleading you and you actually do have a social disease. Or else we have made an error."

"I don't believe it is an error. I believe it was a deliberate lie. And if that's what your damned omniscient handbook calls for—it isn't worth the paper it's printed on!" Burden was aware that the final epithet was weak, and was angry with himself for not finding words strong enough to match his indignation. He watched Lark, still feeling the shock at the thought that Lark's intimacy and friendship were probably nothing more than the treatment advised in the manual for heretics. For all he knew, Lark's arguments were taken bodily from the manual, carefully worded arguments designed to meet any situation. Burden looked at Lark with new eyes. This was the man who had once said that he and Conger were of the same intellectual level. Perhaps it was true. Perhaps this was a dull-witted man, as literal, as fanatic, as thick-skinned as Conger or Julian Richard. Burden looked at Lark more carefully. He had accepted this man as a friend, as an equal. Was he either?

"If it was a lie," Lark said, sensing now a new avenue of exploration based on the nonexistent manual, "then it was told to you to help you rid yourself of heresy."

"Then it is a lie. You've admitted it," Burden said.

"I've told you, Professor Burden," Lark continued calmly, "I don't know whether it was a lie or not. If it was a lie and it has upset you, I'm sorry. I have no control over these things. I can only follow the procedures outlined by the manual. In fact, I should not be suggesting to you the possibility of the existence of a lie."

"Violating an ordinance in the manual?" Burden asked with a faint sneer.

"In a sense, yes," Lark said gravely.

"I'm afraid this time that tactic won't work, Mr. Lark," Burden said, hearing his own voice more loudly and clearly than he had expected. "Mr. Richard tried the same stunt. I'm afraid you two gentlemen have got your tactics mixed. He tried to lure me into the trap you've just presented to me."

"What trap is that?"

"Pretending that you're willing to violate an ordinance or a rule or a regulation on my behalf. Mr. Richard tried to get on my better side by pretending disgust with Mr. Conger. It was a disgust he did not feel. There's something chameleon about you and the other people in this Department, Mr. Lark. You're too quick to be obliging, you're too ready with glib explanations. I've trapped you in a lie before and it seems that I've trapped you again." Burden rose from the couch, feeling fine now, feeling his blood tingling through his body, giving him a sense of alertness he hadn't felt since he first entered the buildings of the Department. "For instance, I'm beginning to feel that there's been a calculated succession of lies from the very first. Conger had no reason to suspect me of heresy. I doubt whether Conger ever read my reports. The hearing I also suspect was a farce. I don't know. There's a great deal I don't know. But I'm beginning to feel that your explanations aren't explanations at all. You say I'm a heretic. Perhaps I am. But I cannot see that I am dangerous to the State, I cannot credit my heresy as being very important. I cannot believe that I am the center of an enormous investigation. Toward what end? What have I said or done to harm the State? You *tell* me I have heresies, you *tell* me they're serious, you *tell* me I will find out about them, you *tell* me you will purge me of them. But I don't believe that. I don't believe any of it. I'm sick and tired of being held here as if I were an invalid. I'm not an invalid. I want to leave. I want to leave now. I am willing to sign any statement of loyalty or conformity or what-have-you, but I want to leave. Just as soon as possible. I don't care whether I'm happy or not with my heresies. I don't care about any greater or more perfect happiness I can reach by being completely in tune with my fellows. I have enough. I'm not an ambitious man; I have gone far enough in my career. If you don't feel I deserve further advancement, or am competent enough for a higher post at the college, I'm satisfied with your judgment. I'll go on precisely as I have before any of this happened. Just have them send me my clothes and the necessary papers and I'll leave before dinnertime." Burden was breathing a little heavily now, his eyes bright with excitement and decision, his stubbled face flushed pink with determination.

Lark listened calmly. Then he decided to use his bright, red thread of terror. "I'm sorry, Professor Burden. Evidently all this talk of a disease has upset you greatly. I'll be perfectly frank with you. The medical division has lied to you. You have no syphilis. What you were given early this morning was a drug calculated to reduce your inhibitions. In order for us to determine the extent and nature of your heresies it was necessary to have your complete co-operation. We sought that co-operation, we still seek it. Nothing can be done against your will."

Burden stiffened. "Then the sedative I got the first evening here was also a drug?" Lark nodded. "Why?"

"Because, Professor, only under narcosis can we ask you certain questions with the assurance that they will be answered truthfully."

"If I told you I was willing to co-operate, why were drugs necessary at all?"

"They were merely used as a supplement. We don't have an unlimited amount of time and it is a complex task. As for your leaving here—I'm sorry. You can't. Not until you rid yourself of your heresies."

"But you said you can't do anything against my will?"

"Quite right. That's why you will have to remain here until you are willing to rid yourself of your heresies. They are major heresies. You cannot pick up the life you once led without having those heresies purged. That's mandatory. I can do nothing about that. As for our lying to you—well, lies are sometimes necessary. They are not intended to injure you in any way. They are used to help us help you. It's unfortunate that you discovered them; it's more unfortunate that you misinterpreted them."

"What page of the manual does this small speech come from, Mr. Lark?"

"I won't say that this is an unprecedented situation—heretics have been known to glimpse part of our techniques, to grasp some of the methods being used. This speech, however, is in no way routine. Let me tell you something that is not in the manual, something you should not know, something, however, which you may find out after a long, long time." Lark paused. Then, deliberately, he stitched in the thread of terror. "You can never leave here until you have satisfied us that you no longer hold any heresies. It may be a week, a month, a year, or the rest of your natural life. It is a curious sentence to be under. You are your own judge; the length of your term is entirely up to you."

Burden grew pale but it was the pallor of shock rather than of fear. "You're not serious."

"I am. Completely serious. The drugs, the questions, our conversations are all designed to help you reduce that period of time. We can proceed no faster than you will permit us to proceed. Your co-operation is vital. If we must wait for you, then we shall. The State is immortal and the State can wait for a man."

"I thought that punishment had been abolished as a social concept," Burden said, feeling hollow and weak.

"It has. Please do not regard this as punishment. You are sick. Within the terms of modern psychiatry, you are a sick man, at odds with yourself, with the world about you. We do not punish you by treating you. We have no intention of punishing you when we keep you here. You would not consider doctors very ethical if they allowed their patients release merely because the treatment of a disease would take too much time or effort. It isn't fair to the patient. It isn't fair to you to abandon you because the task would be difficult."

"Benevolence—your damned, awful benevolence," Burden said softly as he sat down.

"Think of it as a disease," Lark said gently, "which it is, of course. There are diseases in which the sufferer feels no pain. But he is diseased nevertheless. And the disease works its deadly way in his body whether he is discomforted or not. You are suffering from a disease. You say that you have no cause for complaint. That, to us, is a bad sign. It means that you are not aware of your illness. We must make you aware of your illness. We must impress upon you the gravity of it, the absolute need for treatment."

"It may take me the rest of my life just to believe that," Burden turned his eyes toward Lark.

"It won't. I promise you that it won't. Help us, co-operate with us, desire to be cured, and we will cure you."

"In God's name!" Burden said suddenly, desperately, putting his head in his hands, "How can I feel there's anything wrong with me when I know there isn't?"

"Yes, that's the first truly difficult hurdle. But you must clear it. You absolutely must," Lark said flatly. "You need to examine yourself, study yourself, ask yourself questions. I warn you—there's no way for you to fool us. We *know* when a heretic has purged himself."

"I'll die here," Burden said, turning his face up to Lark, "I'll die or go insane. I can't even begin to do what you want me to do."

"You don't want to live here the rest of your life," Lark said quietly, "and you don't want to go insane, do you? You want to go home to your wife, your sons, to your work. Well, look into yourself. Ask yourself: where am I different from my fellows? Why have I felt this way? Have I reason to feel this way? Have I a right to feel this way?" Burden shook his head helplessly. Lark went on, softly but relentlessly, "You will continue to ask these questions of yourself until they are answered. And then you will ask yourself: how can I rid myself of these poisons? How can I find the road that leads me back to my fellows, to humanity, to the State? You will keep asking these questions until you feel lost and frightened, your hand out for guidance, for comfort, for friendship. Then perhaps your heresies will die. Then you will leave here, Professor Burden. But not before."

Lark rose, replaced the chair, and left, closing the door gently behind him. Only the soft click of the lock penetrated Burden's consciousness. He raised his eyes and looked at the closed door and felt his throat drying. They didn't realize what they were asking. They were all out of their minds. They were madmen. How could he possibly begin? What did they want of him? In God's name, how could he ever satisfy them? What had he done wrong? Did they want him to lie? But they said he could not lie. But how would he ever be able to satisfy them? By lying to himself? Could he lie to himself successfully? Men did it all the time. But perhaps, underneath, they knew the truth. The drugs would push aside the lies and find the truth. Burden trembled. They were insane. It was impossible. They did not want him to do anything but lose his mind. They could not expect him to rid himself of everything he had ever thought, or heard, or read, or felt.

Burden rose and moved to the bed, his legs stiff, his hands groping, as a man moves who is desperately ill and must, at all costs, lie down before he dies.

16

Night came and Burden did not sleep. He rested on the bed staring at the ceiling, his mind a blank. The air grew cold and he heard the ward attendant outside the door but he did not rise until he felt the hand on his shoulder, bony, calling.

"Yes, yes," he said and got out of bed, finding his slippers, putting on the bathrobe the attendant gave him. Again the long, circular hall, gleaming, cold, deserted except for the sweeper. Perhaps it was not a human thing at all under the distant yellow light. Perhaps it was some sort of gray, formless machine. Burden closed his eyes and walked, listening to the whisper and slap of his slippers, aware of the hard presence of the attendant.

The clinic was the same, as in a recurrent nightmare, and Doctor Emmerich advanced toward him. The doctor did not speak. He slapped the top of the leather table and again it sounded like a hand striking bare flesh. Burden stretched out full-length, chilled, frightened, his stomach churning. He waited gratefully. Perhaps they would discover while he was under the influence of the narcotic how hopeless it would be for them to succeed. Perhaps they would let him go then as a bad case. He said a prayer to God as he felt his sleeve being rolled up by the doctor.

"Please, please, dear God, let them know that it is impossible. Let them know that a man can't do what they ask him to do. Let them know. Let them, please, please."

The drug seized him as ice in his blood, bleeding away the heat in his body. He felt his heart slowing, the gorge rising, and then he felt what might have been a block of wood being pressed against his windpipe, but it was only Doctor Emmerich's forefinger pushing against his throat. The nausea began to subside and the blood to flow more evenly, heating his body.

"Do you know how long you must stay here now?"

Yes, yes, forever, forever.

"Only until you rid yourself of your heresies."

Never. Never. I can never do it.

"It can be done. You must do it."

Never, never.

"You will do it."

I cannot.

"You will or you will die here."

Then let me die soon.

"You will die when you must. But not for a long time."

I will die sooner.

"You will not. You will live out your life."

I will beat my head against the wall until I die.

"You will not die. You will become unconscious and go on living."

I'll hang myself if you keep it up too long.

"You will have nothing with which to hang yourself."

I will find a way to die if I must.

"You will not. Take our word for it. You will not."

I can't do what you ask.

"You must. Who told you you were brighter than your friends?"

My father, my mother, my brother, my teachers, everyone.

"They were wrong."

No, they were right. I could see that.

"They used the wrong measure of intelligence."

They didn't. They used the correct measure.

"An intelligent man is a happy man, is he not?"

No, he is not. My father was intelligent but he was not happy.

"Your father was not intelligent. The aim of life is happiness. Without happiness a life is without meaning."

The aim of life is reason. Without reason life is without meaning.

"Would you rather be happy than rational?"

A lunatic can be happy without being rational. You are all lunatics. The moon will change its phase and your madness will pass as your happiness will pass. The dark side of the moon is coming and with it your unhappiness.

"We want you to be happy. Is that so awful?"

You want me to go insane.

"You would not be happy if you were insane."

Of course not.

"Then why should we want you to go insane? We desire your happiness."

Leave me alone. I'll be happy if I'm left alone.

"No man can live alone."

I can. Leave me alone. I'll be happy.

"Suppose we do leave you alone and you discover that you are unhappy. What then?"

Please, please, leave me alone.

"*Alone* means without company of anyone."

Yes, yes, I understand the word properly.

"Then we will do that. We will leave you alone. But you must remember that you were the one who decided the basis of your happiness."

Yes, yes, I'll remember.

"Do you believe that we think only of your happiness?"

No.

"What is it we want?"

To drive me insane.

"Toward what purpose?"

Because I will not conform.

"*Will* not or *can* not conform?"

Will not.

"Then you could conform if you so desired?"

I don't know.

"Can't you decide?"

I could not conform.

"You will conform."

I can't. Stop telling me that I will.

"You will."

I can't. I can't.

"Wait and see."

II

Burden's first awareness was that he was naked and the room was cold. He opened his eyes and saw only the gray light. He thought for an instant that he was lying naked on the floor of the corridor. It was not the corridor, nor his room in the hospital section. It was a bare, enormous room, perhaps two stories tall, and it was so huge that it curved almost out of sight. There were no windows in it, not a stick of furniture, nothing but the soaring monotony of rough concrete. The floor was smooth and cold to his bare feet. Burden rose and walked slowly. There was enough light for him to see the room in its entirety. It was perhaps twenty feet in width and fifty feet in height and it curved with the building. Cautiously Burden followed the wall, looking for a door, a window, a break in the concrete. But there was none. He followed the curving wall for what seemed two hundred feet and came up against another wall, twenty feet wide and stretching fifty feet toward the ceiling. The light appeared to come from the ceiling. Burden's first thought was that the room was once an immense storage place. High up along the curving walls there seemed to be ventilators but they were far too high for Burden to reach or to see clearly. The light of the room was unvarying and strange. It didn't seem like daylight and yet it did not resemble artificial light. It was a uniform, flat gray. Burden crossed to the opposing wall and, brushing his hand lightly against it, walked back the curving length of the room. It brought him back to the opposite wall. The room was so long and so curved that he could not see from one end to the other. How had he been put in the room? Lowered perhaps from somewhere on the ceiling? There seemed to be no breaks in the ceiling and yet he felt that his eyes probably deceived him.

Burden sat down on the floor, his back against the wall. The room was cold, so cold that goose flesh began to rise along his arms and legs, prickling his buttocks. The cold was not intense, but it would not be easy to bear. What sort of room was it? Why had he been put in it? He began to long for his pajamas, thin and dirty as they were, for the slippers, cold and sleazy as they were. Nakedness was an awful feeling. A terrible sense of vulnerability began to seep into him. He drew his knees up and clasped his hands across his shins, looking up at the ceiling. They would not leave him there to starve. They had to give him food. He would see then where the food came from, perhaps find out from the person who brought it how long he would have to stay in the room. Or would it be lowered from the ceiling? If it came down on a rope he could seize hold of it and refuse to let go. They would either have to haul him up or cut the rope. In any case he would have something in the room with him— even if it was only a rope. Burden shuddered at the thought of being left so utterly alone. He had read of dungeons, of prisoners left in the darkness without the sound of a human voice, without the sight of a human face. But this was not a dungeon. It was a large room, it was not at all dark, and its shape was more interesting than a box. It suddenly occurred to Burden that someone could enter the other end of the room that curved out of his sight and he would not see him. He rose and walked to a spot he judged to be the exact center of the arc and sat down again on the floor, able now to see both opposing walls. But he discovered that in that position there were at least two corners of the room he could not see. A sobering though struck him then. No matter where he sat in the room there would always be some part of it he could not see. Was that how they intended to get his food to him? To watch him from the ceiling, determine his position, and then allow someone to slip in, leave the food in the blind spot, and then slip out again? Burden rose to his feet. It was a devilishly planned room if that was the plan. It meant that he had to keep walking to be certain he missed no one who entered. But how could entry be made? He saw no signs of doors. Perhaps there were ordinary doors behind the concrete, with knobs and locks and wood paneling. Perhaps the walls were not so thick as they seemed. Burden struck the wall with his fist hard enough to hurt himself. The wall seemed solid, at least several inches thick. The question, he realized suddenly, was whether the inner curved wall faced a corridor or the other wall. Burden looked at the two walls and felt foolish. One was inner and the other outer, but he did not know which. The walls were of equal length and it was the trick of perspective that made one seem longer than the other. The question was, did the room follow the inside curve of the building or the outside curve? If he knew that he would know which curved wall opened on a corridor and which formed part of the building's limit.

Burden sighed at his own foolishness and sat down. It was a pointless question. Why did it matter at all? Except, he thought, rising again, the wall which faced the corridor would be the wall in which he would find the door—if there were such a door. Burden crossed to the opposing wall and struck it with his fist. It felt as solid as the first. He leaned his face against the rough concrete to see if he could hear through the wall. There was no sound but the steady throbbing of his own blood, the hollow roaring one could hear when cupping a hand over an ear. Burden sighed again—a sick, small, helpless sigh. He sank down to the floor and crossed his legs. It was then that he noticed what seemed to be a stain on the sole of his foot. He took hold of his ankle and turned the sole of his foot toward him. The hair on the nape of his neck rose with terror. Someone had carefully, with ink or with iodine, printed in small but clear letters across the sole of his foot:

"You will be alone until you can no longer bear it."

Burden uttered a small cry that echoed in the huge

room and began to rub at the words with his fingers. Dirt peeled away from the skin as he rubbed, but the words remained. He rubbed until the skin grew pink and then angry red. He spat on his fingers and his foot became streaked with dirt and spittle. But the printing remained. Suddenly he gave up and sank back against the wall, his eyes traveling over the floor and the walls and across the ceiling. He felt as if his head were bursting. They were treating him like an animal, caging him. They would not win, Burden swore. His eyes stung. He shook his head; he did not want to cry. If they were watching him they would want him to cry. But he would not. Instead, he scraped at the concrete with his fingernails freeing a few flakes. Carefully he pushed them together into a tiny heap on the floor. The heap was too small for his fingers to pick up so he bent over and with his tongue licked them up, brutally squeezing the bridge of his nose to fight off the impulse to gag. Carefully he licked the flakes into the palm of his hand and then rested, fighting the nausea that rose inside him from the pain he had inflicted on himself. A few tears came down his face as he carefully collected spittle in his mouth and let it drop into the palm of his hand with the flakes of concrete. He stirred them with his finger for a moment and then crossed his legs, brought up the sole which had been written upon, and pressed his palm against the sole, grinding the spittle and the concrete flakes against the offended flesh. He felt the grit biting into his skin and he winced, but he kept it up until finally the grit disappeared. When he could look he saw that he had succeeded in drawing fine scratches across his skin, some of which were bleeding. But, what was most important, the lettering had become indistinct. He rested then against the wall, keeping the sole of his foot off the floor, resting on his heel, feeling the sting of warm blood seeping from the scratches.

He knew that they were in dead earnest and he would soon have to find a way to kill himself, or go insane. He could not do what they asked. He could never do it. They had no right to ask it of him. They had no right to ask it of anyone.

17

While Burden slept in nude exhaustion, his arm thrown across his eyes to shut out the flat light, a six-foot square section of the floor dropped out of sight. The hole remained dark and gaping in the floor and after a brief while light shone through it and there were the soft hum of voices and machinery. The floor rose back into place and on it were two ward attendants with a gleaming white porcelain cart on rubber wheels. They wore soft, canvas-like shoes and worked quickly and silently. The tray was rolled over noiselessly beside Burden and one of the attendants took a hypodermic syringe, filled the hollow needle, and stooped beside Burden and waited for his companion to kneel on Burden's other side. His companion held a small gauze mask and a can of ether. At a nod, the attendant holding the needle gently lifted Burden's arm away. Burden stirred and the attendant with the ether mask quickly placed it over Burden's nose and mouth. Burden started to move but the attendant with the needle leaned his weight heavily on Burden, pinning him down, one hard hand pressing on his forehead and covering his eyes. In a short while Burden's body relaxed and while the ether was being administered the injection was made in Burden's arm. When the two attendants were satisfied that the injection was working the ether mask was removed. One of the attendants went to the table and picked up a collapsible metal stand while the other went to the elevator section of the floor and gently rapped on it. The floor section dropped out of sight. Within a few moments the attendants had set into place the metal stand with its curved arm, suspended the heavy bottle upside down in its wire holder, and had begun feeding Burden intravenously. The floor lift rose, bearing Lark and a man dressed like a mechanic. The mechanic briskly lifted a heavy black suitcase and stepped off the lift before it had come quite level with the floor. He hurried to Burden's side and gently placed the suitcase down on the floor.

"One hour, sir," one of the ward attendants said softly as Lark came over to Burden's body. Lark nodded and watched Burden while one of the ward attendants precisely adjusted the drip valve of the feeder and the mechanic busily and professionally opened the suitcase and began to adjust dials and switches from the mass of electrical equipment that the suitcase enclosed. Once satisfied with that, the mechanic opened another compartment of the suitcase and produced two reels of thin electrical paper tape. Quickly, with practiced fingers, he stripped the protective wrapping from the reels and ran out a few feet of the sensitized paper, turning it first one way and then the other to check it. Lark leaned against the wall, looking down at Burden's face, gray, drawn, and yet relaxed under the dirt and the stubble. He noted from the streaks on Burden's face that he had been crying. It was a good sign, Lark thought. Lark's eyes coldly drifted over Burden's nakedness, the blond-haired slender flabbiness of his thighs, the thin, darker hair of his pubis, the shadowy scar of his appendectomy, the collapsed softness of the belly moving gently with his breathing, and the pale skin stretched over the rib cage with its thin line of long, fine blond body hair. Burden's shoulders, narrow, cramped, were covered with faded freckles and on one shoulder was a puckered old scar of the sort that came from an early childhood accident.

After tapping his reels with a final gesture the mechanic looked expectantly at Lark. Lark nodded slightly and kneeled beside Burden.

"You're alone now. Does it make you happy?"

No.

"You see how wrong it is to think that being alone will make you happy?"

Yes.

"You need the company of others. Man is a social animal, isn't he?"

Yes.

"If it really makes you happy to be left alone you can spend the rest of your life in this room."

No, God, please.

"It isn't what you want, is it?"

No, no, please, please.

"Good. Now, listen. You will be instructed on the aims and purposes of the State."

No, I don't want to be instructed.

"You want to rid yourself of heresy, don't you?"

No. I don't.

"But you must. Otherwise you will never leave here."

Please!

"You will never leave here. Don't you want to help yourself?"

What do you want of me?

"Listen. That's all that's required of you. Listen."

All right, I will listen.

"Good." Lark glanced at the mechanic who nodded and brought out a small earpiece from which a long, rubber-covered wire ran into a plug. The mechanic slipped the plug into a gleaming jack on the face of the machine and then leaned over and fixed the plastic earpiece in Burden's left ear. Lark nodded and the mechanic snapped a switch on the machine. It began with a soft mechanical hum and the reels began to turn slowly.

"You are a citizen of the State," the far-off mechanical voice of the tape said flatly. "As a citizen of the State there are certain obligations you assume. All citizens of the State assume the same obligations. If they did not, there could be no State. If there were no State, there would be chaos. The strong would rob the weak, murder the helpless, rape the women, degrade the children. Man is an animal and like an animal he has no morals, no character. Without the State he reverts to the nature of the animal. The State is the only check man knows. The tiny strength of one man is multiplied a million times in the form of the State. The State, then, is stronger than any man. It protects each man from his own animal nature. This is the function of a state. This is the reason men have states and governments. For the safety of every citizen the State is necessary. In order that you or any citizen may live in safety, in happiness, free from attack, from plunder, from outrage, you must uphold the State. You are a teacher. In order to teach, to do the work you love, to have the home you have, to raise your sons, to protect your wife, you must have the protection of the State—the combined strength of all your fellow citizens. You cannot exist alone on the earth. There must be fellow citizens to protect you, to build your home, to feed you, to clothe you, to send their children for you to teach, to print the books you use, to keep you safe from disease, disaster, fire. You are helpless without the State. The State is your protector, your father, your mother, your family. You are helpless without the State." The voice went on and on but Lark had long since ceased to listen to it. He tapped the mechanic on the shoulder and the man rose respectfully, waiting.

"You'll repeat the reels twice." The mechanic nodded. Lark turned to one of the ward attendants. "If necessary, he'll have another injection this morning so that he can hear both reels through twice completely."

"Yes, sir," the ward attendant said.

"How long will the feeding take?" Lark nodded at the stand with the inverted bottle.

"The drip is set for an hour, sir," the attendant said.

"Tell me, do they feel hungry after getting that?"

"Well, it's funny. If he doesn't know that he has had it, he will feel hungry. If he knows he has, he won't. I've seen people claim they were dying of hunger when they weren't at all. Hunger is sometimes all mental, sir."

"It's curious how many things are mental," Lark said with a faint smile and glanced again at Burden. He realized suddenly that he had no time to spend with Burden at the moment and hurried to the floor lift. He hit the floor with his heel a few times and then felt the floor lowering. The drop was very short and quick and the floor bobbed against hydraulic pistons before it leveled and a door opened with a quick hiss of compressed air. Lark stepped out into a long, cold, waxed corridor. His footsteps made a hurried pattern as he went down the corridor. It was the morning of Wednesday, the twenty-first of October, and the target date was just ten days off.

In his office Lark pulled the dictation machine over, flipped the switch, and spoke evenly into the mouthpiece.

"From Lark to Operations Division: We will need the body of a man in his early forties as close an approximation to Professor Burden as you can find. Please check the identification section on Burden's vital characteristics and photographs. I suggest an auto-smash victim or an industrial accident case. This will have to be done quickly, since Mrs. Burden is expecting her husband home at the end of the week. Please contact Boyd University correspondent, Doctor Ellis Wilson. Inform him that he will accompany the body to Templar College. You will supply him with the fact sheet accompanying this order. See that he fully understands it. Please also prepare a new identity for Burden. I suggest the name should be something commonplace—perhaps Hughes. I suggest a minor clerical background. You might make him a widower with no children or close relatives. Please send me your thoughts on this matter as soon as possible." Lark snapped the switch on the machine and pushed it away. He stifled an enormous yawn and then shuddered slightly from the cold. His letter to the Operations Division had started the wheels of Burden's official destruction.

Lark depressed a button on his phone and called through to the lift operator. "Will you please have the audio engineer come to my office when he's done? Thank you." Lark put down the phone, cocked his long legs up on his desk, and slumped in his chair. Another enormous yawn escaped him, one he did not try to stifle, and he fell asleep.

The mechanic awoke Lark.

"What time is it?" Lark asked.

"Seven o'clock, sir," the mechanic said. "It took almost three hours."

"Did he need another injection?"

"Yes, sir. It had something to do with subconscious attention, I didn't understand."

"But you went through the reels twice."

"Yes, sir."

"Any reaction? Did he speak out? Did he stir?"

"A few times he said something under his breath. I couldn't catch the words, sir."

"Did he groan or make any other sounds?"

"No, sir. Once or twice he drew up his hands."

"How?"

"Something like this." The mechanic cupped his hands and brought them up in front of his face in the manner reminiscent of a small, shy child.

"Did he keep his hands there long, like that?"

"No, not long. Perhaps for a moment or so."

"When did it happen? On the first reel or the second?"

"The second, sir."

"The first time he heard it or the second time?"

"I think it was both times. That is, both times he heard the second reel."

"In approximately the same spot on the reel?"

The mechanic puzzled for a moment. It was obvious he hadn't thought it was a significant fact to remember.

"Never mind," Lark finally said, "it isn't important. Did you ever do that when you were a child?"

"Do what, sir?"

"Put your hands up in front of your face like that?"

"No, sir, not that I can remember."

"I did," Lark said. "I was being scolded at the time by my father."

"Yes, sir," the mechanic said, and Lark realized that it meant nothing to the man.

"Thank you very much. We'll go on with this series tomorrow morning at the same time. If he does it again, please mark the spot on your tape."

"Yes, sir, I will," the mechanic said. Lark knew he wouldn't fail.

"All right, thank you again. You did a fine job."

The mechanic bobbed his head in acknowledgment and left. Lark picked up his phone, depressed a button, and got through to the Medical Division. He asked for the supervising nurse and got the night supervisor.

"This is Lark. What are the names of the two ward attendants who were on special detail this morning?"

"Just a moment, sir," the supervisor said. Lark heard the crisp sound of stiff sheets being handled. "Mr. DeGrey and Mr. Lehman."

"Thank you. Will you please tell Mr. DeGrey and Mr. Lehman that I deeply appreciated their work this morning and would like them to be assigned to the same detail tomorrow morning?"

"Yes, sir, I'll make a note of that."

"Will you please make a note of the fact that I personally thought they handled their jobs very well and see that they hear of it either from yourself or from the day supervisor before they go off duty this morning?"

"Yes, sir. I'll see to that."

"Thank you," Lark said and hung up. He yawned again and decided he had better get his hair cut and his face shaved before he took a nap. It would be a busy day. He rose and yawned again; his bones and muscles felt stiff. He thought again of the gesture Burden had made and smiled bitterly. A man was borne back, against his will, to the dark currents of his childhood. He became small, frightened, lost, and dependent under the narcotic. Anything could be done to him then. Unfortunately it was a temporary state and Burden came back against the current into adulthood, into heresy, into resistance. Well, Lark thought, perhaps enough trips backward might soften him. The room was working beautifully on Burden and Lark was pleased that they had been able to prompt him into a desire for solitary. Perhaps they would not need it much longer. But Burden would have to go deeper into despair before Lark could hold out a hand. Much deeper.

II

The black and blue bruise on his arm told the story, Burden decided. They had somehow come during the night and fed him intravenously. He remembered dimly a moment of wakefulness and the cruel weight of a man's body, a strong hand against his forehead, and then the sickeningly sweet smell of ether. His mouth had been swabbed out with something sharp and medicinal. He did not have the strength to get up and so he rested on his side on the cold floor, feeling his body aching and heavy. He had a memory of someone talking to him for what must have been hours and yet he remembered nothing. Nothing at all. He was in the hands of the State. And the State must be obeyed. He rolled his head slightly against the floor and closed his eyes. Who had told him that? Had it been his father? But his father had never said "the State." Never said it in just that way. He referred to it as "them," or "they," but not "the State." "They" wanted things "their" way and you had to watch "them." You could not fight "them." That's the way his father had spoken.

Burden sighed a long, shaky sigh and turned over on his back to stare at the ceiling. His arm ached from the needle. He would not starve to death. They would not let him starve to death. They would not let him die. The State wanted all to live. He was a citizen of the State and he had a right to live. Burden still stared up at the ceiling. Where was the light coming from? It was gray and yet it was not daylight. What sort of day was it outdoors? Burden groaned. No, he couldn't lie there naked like an animal. He had to get up.

Painfully he used his arms to raise himself to a sitting position but he immediately felt lightheaded and would have fallen backward had he not put out an arm stiffly against the floor. He let his head droop forward, waiting for blood to fill it, to clear the pale fog that began to close in front of his eyes. He tried to move his legs but they felt inert. Burden rubbed his hand along the shinbones. They felt cold and sharp, as if they did not belong to his body at all. Burden sighed helplessly and was grateful for the concrete walls and the concrete floor. Behind them was intelligence. Behind the walls was reasoning. He was not alone in the world—not if he never saw another face or heard another voice. They came into the room and they had fed him while he was unconscious. He was not left alone in the world. He existed in their minds, in their talk. There were places warm and cheerful and well-lit where his name was spoken, where he was remembered, where he existed. No, it was not the same feeling as being abandoned on a glacier, naked, forgotten, facing the horrors of a hellish night of indifference. They knew he was there and from this Burden drew a thin stream of warmth. No matter how cruel, how brainless, how sterile the room was, it still breathed human life. Human hands had built it and human minds remembered it existed and that he was in it. As long as he could cling to that they could not make him suffer the worst. But it was not they who wanted him to suffer, was it? The State desired only the happiness of its citizens. It was its reason for being. What of this citizen? What of this chilled, aching, bearded, naked citizen? Did they want his happiness, too? Burden shook his head. Merely to sit upright was too exhausting. He despised himself for it, but he lowered himself to the floor, to stare up again at the ceiling, his body throbbing its deep thankfulness.

His father had been a small, precise man with cultivated speech and perfect manners. He had never heard his father shout but he had seen rage in his father's face and he had heard it, under control, in his voice. Burden, as a child, could not face the rage. He felt that something awful, something terrifying would happen if his father looked that way, spoke that way with the fury rushing like a swift, angry, cold-white mountain stream under the clear glass of his controlled temper. As a child Burden had thought that no one could look at his father's rage and not turn to stone, like the men in the fairy tale of the Medusa. When his father was very angry and his face grew pale, Burden had clapped his hands to his face so that he would not turn to stone, so that his voice would not be locked within the stone, unable to get out, to be heard.

Burden put his hand to his throat and caressed the skin, feeling the scratch of his beard. To turn to stone and to keep one's soul inside, unable to close the stone lids over the stone eyes, unable to open the stone lips, to move the stone tongue, to utter a sound. It had been the nightmare of his childhood that one day his father had pulled away his hands and he had had to stare into the face and see that overwhelming fury and then had turned to stone. As a child he had wondered what they would do with him. Would they keep him in the house, out of sight of visitors? Or would they set him up in the garden with a ring of bleached pebbles around his feet and never pretend that he was anything but a piece of sculpture? And if they turned his back to the house he would never be able to see into the windows, never be able to move his stone feet and his stone limbs, never be able to hold out his stone arms to his mother, to put his stone hand against her warm, soft, living hand of flesh and bone. He would stand until his soul broke with weariness, with the desire just to sit, to lie down, to rest. He would stand while the house aged and dried and rotted and his mother and father died and Ralph died and all of his friends and neighbors died and people would come into the neighborhood who did not know him and no one would ever know that there was a real boy inside the statue that stood in the garden with its back to the house.

Burden smiled gently. He had not thought of that fantasy in many, many years. Except that now the nightmare had come true. He was imprisoned in stone and it was not as horrible as he had thought it would be. And yet, Burden frowned, the fantasy had come true in just the terms he feared it might. He had looked upon the face of the State and it had turned him into stone. But the State was not his father. Or was it? Burden turned his cheek toward the cold floor and looked along its length, feeling the chill seeping into his cheek. Could he give to the State what he could not give to his father? He respected his father, he feared him, but he never loved him. He could respect the State, he had learned fear for it, but love? Yet it held him in its arms and offered its gross lips and waited. He knew that if he loved it he would no longer be a heretic.

Burden rolled his head so that he stared directly at the light that came so mysteriously from the ceiling. Why did they not vary it? Just the least bit. Darker or brighter. Its constancy sickened him as a moon might that remained forever fixed in the sky. Could he ever get out of this room? How would they ever know how he felt unless they asked him? Or had they asked him in the dead hours of the morning? Did they ask him under the influence of the drug? And what did he answer? Did he say to them that he wanted no more of the room? That he wanted no more of the loneliness, no more of the nakedness and the cold, and of the light that never changed? Did they hear that from him under the drug? Or was he even more stubborn than he knew? Burden exhaled desperately and felt his head throb. He must want to get out of the room. He must want to get out so desperately that he would tell them so under the drug.

He rested on the floor, his brain aching, his will sharply urging his mind. Tell them, tell them to let me out—in God's name, tell them I want to get out.

18

At four o'clock on the morning of Thursday, twenty-second of October, the ward attendants DeGrey and Lehman listened to Lark speak to Burden, dirty, chilled, supine on the floor, his arm receiving the drip from the dextrose and glucose bottle.

"What is the State?"

The State wishes me to live.

"Yes, the State wishes you to live and to be happy."

I am not happy.

"That is because you are alone."

It is awful to be alone.

"Yes, it is. Would you like to be with others?"

Yes, yes, yes, yes.

"You will be with others soon."

Please, please, soon, very soon.

"Yes, very soon. Do you know the State wishes you to be happy?"

Why does it treat me this way?

"Because you wanted to be left alone."

I don't want it any more.

"Then you'll be kept with others. Will that make you happy?"

Yes, it will.

"And if it doesn't?"

It will. I promise. I know it will.

"The State will help you to be happy in any way you think you will be happy."

I'm glad.

"The State knows the true path to happiness."

Please don't leave me here any longer.

"Would you follow the true path to happiness?"

Yes, I would.

"If the State shows you the true path will you believe it is the true path?"

Does the State know?

"Yes, it does. Don't you believe that?"

I don't know any longer.

"The State does know. Believe that."

Yes, I'll try.

"You must trust the State."

I'll try.

"You have been very sick."

Yes, I know.

"You're getting better. But you must help yourself."

I'll try.

"Good." Lark then rose from his kneeling position beside Burden and nodded to the mechanic who leaned over and fixed the earpiece securely on Burden. He then reached over and flipped the switch.

"The true path of happiness lies in loving one's fellow citizens," the recorded voice said evenly, calmly. "To understand what this means think of a family. Not your own, perhaps. Think of a family you might have chosen for yourself as a child, if you had had the power. The father loved the mother and the mother loved the father. The parents loved all the children and cared for them. And the children, in turn, loved their parents and obeyed them. It was a home without fear, without pain, without unhappiness. It was perfect and complete in every way. You belonged there and you were welcomed there. You could always return no matter where you had been or what you had done and be loved and understood and accepted. The State is like that. The State is your family and your fellow citizens are your brothers and your sisters. You need not do anything to earn your place in the family. You must only believe in it. You must only trust it. You must only love it. The State does not care if you are wise or stupid, handsome or ugly, brave or cowardly. The State wishes you to belong, to be happy, to be at peace with yourself. The State will always care about you no matter what you have done. If you are sick it will nurse you to health. If you are tired it will provide you with rest. If you are frightened it will protect you. Your brother and sister citizens are ready to embrace you, to call you their own. Come and join them. Don't remain frightened and unhappy and bitter outside of the family. Come and be one of us." The recording droned on as Lark walked up to Lehman.

"He will be taken to the Psychiatric Division after you're done in here," Lark said softly. "They'll be expecting him in the locked ward."

"Yes, sir," Lehman said respectfully, watching Lark.

"Nothing else except that I want to tell you and Mr. DeGrey again how much I appreciate this work. You're helping this man enormously."

"Lehman can see how miserable he is," the attendant said softly, looking at Burden with pitying eyes.

"Are you Church of State?"

"Yes, sir."

"Do you think he would be happy in the Church of State?"

"It would mean a new life for him, sir."

"Yes, I think you're right. But we'll have to cure him first, won't we?"

Lehman nodded grimly, looking at Burden with determined eyes. "The people are one. He will come to us and join with us and he'll never have to lie naked and groaning on a floor like this. It is an awful thing to have a troubled spirit."

"Awful," Lark agreed.

II

It was a room and he was still naked in it but there was a difference. The light. It was no longer gray. It was brighter and clearer, almost like daylight. Burden stirred and knew now that he was no longer on a floor. He was on a bed. His heart bounded inside him. He looked up at the ceiling. It was low, no more than eight feet above him, and it was simple, blessed white plaster, glowing with daylight, with ordinary fluorescent fixtures set into it. An involuntary small cry of joy came from Burden as he ran his shaking fingers over the bed sheets. They were warm and clean and the walls were not rough concrete but a smoothly painted white surface that gave back the glow of daylight. Burden rose on an elbow and saw that his bed was one of a row of beds. Bedclothes were rumpled, speaking volumes to him of people who had been in them just a few moments before. Burden's sense of lightheadedness overcame him and he had to fall back, but an enormous wave of gratitude swept over him. He had told them and they had believed him. He was not alone. Others used the beds, they would be back, wherever they were now. Burden stretched out, his stomach churning with excitement. He had been taken out of the room with its awful gray light, its curving walls, its idiot emptiness. He was no longer an abandoned animal left to madness.

There was no need now for him to get up, to walk. He could wait and rest. Someone would come and speak to him in a while, surely. It was that certain knowledge that made it possible for him to lie in bed, his eyes closed, softly thanking God.

Burden heard the soft slap of a slipper and turned his eyes. A tall man wearing loose pajamas and backless slippers came down the aisle. He walked carefully, with a great air of self-possession. Burden watched his progress with almost hungry eyes. He did not seem to be a sick man. In fact, he managed to give the shapeless hospital costume a certain air of dash, of sartorial elegance. He had plain, straight black hair that was freshly cut and carefully combed. He was closely shaven and his skin had been dusted with an aftershave powder so that his severely classic face seemed to be chiseled out of marble. His eyes were an electric black and looked like the eyes of some proud, wild bird. He paused when he was just a bed away from Burden and he leaned slightly. It was only then that Burden realized that he was leaning on a cane. But it was not the sort of cane an invalid used. It was altogether different. Burden had only seen one other like it in his life and that was in a photograph taken of his grandparents' wedding. It was what used to be called a "dress" cane. It was polished black wood with an old ivory top. Burden suppressed the smile. It was appropriate to the man, incongruous to the place.

Burden waited for the man to speak but he did not. He

merely leaned on his cane, regarding Burden with those sentinel eyes. For a reason he could not fathom, Burden began to feel that the man's eyes were unfriendly, that the look on his face was harsh and disapproving. Burden was about to speak when he heard footsteps at the far end of the room. As he turned his head to look, the man spoke sharply.

"You're filthy! Filthy!"

Burden turned his eyes bewilderedly back to the man with the cane. Before he could reply, the man straightened up sharply and smacked the point of the cane loudly on the floor. "Don't you understand the common decency of remaining clean? Your body stinks! I can smell it from here!"

"I'm sorry," Burden murmured, but his words only seemed to infuriate the man with the cane.

"Hideous! Absolutely hideous! I won't be able to stay in the same room with you! You ought to be placed under scalding water and scrubbed with a common brush!"

The nurse whose footsteps had distracted Burden came into sight. She was a motherly woman. She came up behind the infuriated man with the cane, passed him, and stopped at Burden's bed, placing her plump, capable hands on the footboard of the bed.

"Well, you're awake. That's nice," she said in a voice so devoid of any malice that Burden immediately warmed to her. "Are you hungry?"

"I don't know," Burden said, keeping an eye on the man with the cane who continued to glare at him. "I think maybe I could eat some soup or something light."

"He's filthy!" the man with the cane virtually shrieked.

Burden started at the sound but the nurse behaved as if she had not heard at all.

"Well," she said, patting the bed, "I think we can manage some soup for you."

"Clean him, clean him!" the man with the cane shouted at the nurse, but she behaved exactly as if he did not exist.

"I think perhaps I would like a bath," Burden said softly.

"If you wish," the nurse said with a smile, "after you eat."

"I'll return after that's been washed," the man with the cane said indignantly, and marched down the aisle out of the room.

"I'm afraid I've offended him," Burden said softly after the man with the cane left.

"Oh, don't mind him," the nurse said with a short laugh, "he's a fanatic on cleanliness. If we spent all our days and nights scrubbing we wouldn't be half clean enough for him. It's very odd, too, because he has some disgusting personal habits."

"Such people generally have," Burden said quietly.

"I'll bring you some soup and a bathrobe. After you wash and have your shave and haircut I'll see that you get fresh pajamas."

"Thank you," Burden said gratefully.

"That's all right," the motherly nurse smiled, "you'll feel better with a bath and fresh clothes and some food." She started to go and then stopped and turned back, "Oh, there's just one thing," she said. "My name is Miss Funston. I'm on duty for eight hours and then the night nurse comes on. You probably won't see him if you're a good sleeper. Most of the boys in here are good sleepers. They hardly ever get up in bed." She smiled again and started to turn but remembered and checked herself. "Oh, there's one more thing—that man with the cane. His name is Victor. I wouldn't talk back to him or get involved in any discussion with him. All the other boys know him and leave him alone. If he thinks you've insulted him he's liable to use the cane on you."

"Oh," Burden said, making a small sound, "but why don't you take it away from him, then?"

"He'd be completely miserable without it. And since everyone knows him they stay well clear of him and so there's really no danger. Just pretend he isn't around. After a while he stops roaring and goes off." She smiled warmly. "That's what all the other boys do and they're quite right. It works perfectly."

"I see. How many—" Burden hesitated and then with a self-conscious smile used her term, "boys are there here?"

"Twelve now. Including yourself."

"Where are they all?"

"Oh, various places," she said with a vague smile. "getting their hair cut, or reading, or in some class lecture, or talking. They'll drift back in time for dinner, though."

"I see," Burden smiled and nodded. Miss Funston smiled back at him and then walked down the aisle, one plump hand in her dress pocket so that she looked like a fat soldier marching in an outlandish salute position.

There was one thing Miss Funston had omitted to tell Burden. He discovered that for himself when the "boys" came back from the barber's, the reading rooms, the classroom lectures, and what other places they had been in. The eleven men who shared the room with Burden were insane. Completely, hopelessly, incurably insane.

19

The room creaked with their silent agonies and it was most awful when it was most quiet. Everywhere Burden looked he caught the glint of madness in the eye. Victor took off his shoes when he rested in bed but the cane remained by his side and he stared at the wall with those piercing bird eyes as if he could see through it to the horizon. They did not speak to one another and Burden was as alone in the ward as he had been in the curved room. They remained wrapped in their inner terrors, private, separated from one another as if each were alone on an island, helplessly marooned, incapable of seeing any but distant, visionary ships, deaf to all but private inner voices. The evening meal was served in the ward and Burden noticed that some were given no silverware but had to pick up their food with their hands. Victor was one of these, and Burden began to understand that Victor was not nearly as harmless as Miss Funston said he was. The silence of the room was shattered by an occasional frightful clatter as one of the men, done with his meal, casually threw his metal tray on the polished floor. As soon as that happened one of the small, gray-faced men who had his bed near the door put down his own tray and patiently padded across the floor to pick up the discarded tray. He carried it then to a small wagon and carefully placed it on the wagon as if the tray were made of fragile china. Once done with that he returned to his own bed, picked up his own tray, and resumed eating. The crash of a tray caused Burden to start, but the others seemed insensitive to the sound no matter how sudden or how loud.

Victor fastidiously finished his meal, dabbed at his lips and carefully scoured his fingers with the napkin, and then casually tossed the tray over the foot of the bed. It struck the floor with a sound that made Burden rise from his bed. Particles of food still left on Victor's tray spattered the wall. One tiny wet bit struck Burden's cheek and he put up his hand and wiped it away. Burden's chin sank to his chest in misery. He could not remain in the ward long. He knew it as certainly as if he had spent a year there.

Miss Funston had said that the "boys" were "good sleepers" but Burden felt now it was a lie. Perhaps a good sleeper was someone who didn't rise at night and try to murder the supervising nurse. But Burden dreaded the night.

The small, gray-faced man came up to Burden's bed with the tray and Burden looked at him. Probably he was the most harmless of the lot. Burden looked into the vacant face, drained even of the alertness of madness, the mindless eyes, the weak jaw, the mouse-brown hair, and the stunted, thick body that suggested the man might once have been a circus dwarf who had suddenly grown a few more inches. Burden wanted to speak to the small man but could not. The heavy, dwarfed figure turned and waddled back to the wagon with Victor's tray.

Miss Funston eventually returned to collect all of the trays that had not been thrown on the floor. Burden heard her cheerful voice address each man in turn as she collected his tray and counted his pieces of silverware. But Burden did not hear anyone answer Miss Funston but himself.

"The meal was delicious," Burden said, anxious for her to stay a while.

"And that was only the regular weekday meal," Miss Funston said with a trace of pride in her voice.

"I wonder if I can have something to read," Burden asked quietly.

"Oh, I'm afraid not. The reading room was closed before dinner. You can go there tomorrow if you like," she said, and started to go.

"But tonight," Burden said quickly, trying to check her, trying to keep her with him for a moment more, "I would like very much to have something to read tonight."

"Oh, you don't want to do that," she said with a smile, "it'll just strain your eyes. Why don't you get acquainted with the boys this evening?"

"They don't seem very friendly."

"Oh, but they are. They are ever so friendly. It just takes a little patience. They're mostly shy, you know. That's all—just shy. If you're patient with them you'll see they'll come around your bed to talk to you like a flock of birds." She laughed at that and brushed back a wisp of her hair. "Oh, my, once they're started they can hardly stop—like a lot of twittering and chirping birds."

"No one's said a word since I've been here," Burden said, "except—" Burden nodded his head discreetly in Victor's direction.

"They're shy. You're a newcomer and they won't say a word for awhile until they get over your being here. Then they'll be themselves, all right. And they're very nice boys. One of them dances. Very well, too. I've never seen him dance. He's very shy about it. But I've heard he dances." Miss Funston patted his hand affectionately. "You'll make friends in no time. They'll like you. I can tell generally how they'll act toward someone. They'll like you. I've no doubt about that." Miss Funston smiled again and walked down the aisle with the trays she had collected and Burden watched her go with a slight shudder of fear. He leaned back on his pillow and tried to envision the madmen about his bed, talking and talking *like a flock of birds*. Burden closed his eyes in horror at the image.

The sound of the table rolling out with its load of trays and the faint, distant click of the door behind Miss Funston was like a signal in the room. Burden sensed rather than saw someone leap from his bed. He turned and watched a young man standing in the middle of the aisle, his hands lifted in a theatrical gesture, his body frozen and tense as he half turned on his hips to display a clean, classic profile, a strong, long neck, and a well-shaped head disfigured by hair that was cut without shaping. He stood in that attitude for a long moment as if waiting for his cue. It came, and he did a swift series of strong, soaring turns, rising on the balls of his feet and whipping his arms around. It was done silently except for the faint sound of his bare feet on the polished floor. He came to a halt in the attitude of one who has heard something and stands frozen, afraid of detection, listening. Then he began a series of small, intricate steps, crossing his feet, advancing, retreating, his hands shyly together behind his back, his eyes downcast.

Burden sat up in bed watching him, marveling at the

grace, the control, and the complexity of the man's memory—if it was memory that directed his feet and not some spirit of improvisation. Burden scarcely noticed that the others ignored the man who danced. Victor remained in bed, his fingers lightly caressing his cane, staring through the wall opposite him.

The dancer worked his way down the aisle to Burden's bed and Burden saw that the man was not as young as he first appeared. He might have been anywhere from forty to sixty years of age but his body had been kept marvelously young by dancing so that he had all the whipcord strength of a young athlete. The mincing counterpoint became stronger and the movements more pronounced. The hands came out from behind the dancer's back and he began to move them back and forth, palm down and then palm up, and then he tossed his head up and down to match the movements of his hands and feet. He seemed to be working himself into a frenzy of plunging and retreating. Burden began to marvel at his skill, at the illusion of plunging and springing back that became more and more difficult to sustain. Suddenly the dancer sprang backward in an enormous, horrified leap, his shoulders drawn up, his hands stretched open against his body in withdrawal, his eyes opened large in loathing. He landed with his back heel within a fraction of an inch from the wall. The slightest miscalculation and he would have struck the wall and seriously hurt himself, so enormous and strong had the backward leap been. The dancer remained on the spot in which he had so accurately landed, his body locked in a horror that seemed so real that Burden unconsciously looked about him. The others still ignored the dance.

Softly, slowly, his eyes glittering, the dancer began to advance, turning his body on his hips as he put first one foot forward and then the other. His body became supple and yielding and Burden was shocked to discover how fully the character of the dance and the dancer had changed. The look in the dancer's eyes, the movements of his body, the gestures of his hands all seemed to suggest that the dance was now all feminine, all desiring, flirting, yielding, begging, entreating. The dancer's face had undergone a distinct change. The lips actually seemed fuller, the lids of the eyes heavier, the strength of the man's body changed to the slenderness of a girl's. The illusion was awful in its directness, in its nakedness. The dancer advanced close enough so that Burden could hear him hissing. Burden drew back in his bed slightly. But the dancer was obliquely approaching Victor, who paid no notice, who still stared ahead, soundless.

The dancer had come almost to the foot of Victor's bed. The dance now became more insistent, more urging, the movements fuller, the dancer's sibilant hissing stronger. The deep, voluptuous rubbing motions of the dancer's hands had disarrayed his clothes so that his chest was bared, lean, strong, waxenly white with dark, circular nipples. With a swift turning motion the dancer dropped his pajama top and then, drawing up his shoulders, crossed his hands and delicately caressed his own arms. Burden wanted to look away but found he could not. He watched the half-naked figure turn and dip, touching its own body with hands that kissed and then called and retreated only to advance. When the dancer made a swift turn into the place between Victor's bed and the adjoining bed, Burden had an awful presentiment that something cruel would happen. The dancer leaned closer, his hissing stronger, his face passing within inches of Victor, who stared ahead, oblivious.

The motion was so swift that Burden only caught a

fragment of it. The dancer had turned his back on Victor and was facing across the adjoining bed toward Burden. His face was hungry with a look of desire, his eyes half lidded, his mouth half opened, his hands touching his breasts, his long, thin torso bared and pale. The sound and the movement seemed to come at the same split instant and Burden heard the sound and saw the movement incompletely. It came like a pistol shot and the dancer fell full length across the bed with a shuddering scream. Victor had turned in the bed and Burden saw the cane rise. Before Burden could stir the cane lashed down again on the dancer's back. The dancer leaped under its impact and screamed again. His naked body started to turn as Victor got out of bed and raised the cane once more. Burden lunged across to intercept the blow and caught it half on his forearm but the pain was so intense that Burden winced and screamed involuntarily. His arm grew instantly heavy and dead and fell to his side. Burden rolled and fell off the bed, striking the floor, the pain tearing at his shoulder, making him want to vomit. The blood began to drain from his head and he felt cold sweat break out on his legs, his back, and the seat of his pants. He rested on his back, knowing that he would be unconscious if he did not rise and force the blood back into his head. As if in a nightmare he saw the dancer's face peering over the edge of the bed down at him on the floor and the eyes were fixed and wild, the face contorted in an awful mask of pain and delight. Burden turned away so that he would not see the face. The screams came down at him between the beds like pistol shots and he kept hearing the unbelievably cruel sound of the cane cutting through the air and the explosion of it against flesh. He was aware of feet hurrying across the floor in many directions and disconnected voices and screams and, very clearly, someone giggling with a frenzy that seemed indecent and insane. Then he remembered no more.

Burden came to in his own bed, sweating under heavy covers, feeling his arm throbbing and aching distantly as if he had been given some pain deadener. He tried to move his arm and found that he couldn't. He groped with his fingers to see if his arm had been splintered but it had not. It was not broken. Or was it? Burden found he didn't care. The ward was dark except for the faint luminescence of moonlight, cold and revealing. Victor was in his bed, sleeping quietly, evenly, the classic, severe profile outlined in moonlight, completely at peace with the world. Burden hated him but then, with a tired small sigh, retreated further under the covers. Victor was mad, as mad as the dancer whose hungers were so awful, so twisted, so strange. He could not be alone and he could not be with others. They were strange, sick, tortured animals whose inner realities were far more awful than the outer realities. Burden rested, feeling the sweat crawling down his back, absorbing the lesson. The State's moral was implicit: as long as he held the heresies he was a sick, strange animal like Victor, the dancer, the small gray-faced man with the compulsion toward order and neatness. Who was he to say that his heresies were less dangerous to him and to society than the perverted sexual fantasies of the dancer? How could he be right and all the others wrong? The State was far different from the individual. It had no private advantage to seek. It would roll on as magnificently without him as it could with him. He did not mean that much to the course of the society. Then they were right and he was wrong. It was their concern for him that was innocent and not his concern for himself. That was wrong. It was filled with the evil of vanity and vanity had been the curse of the world since the dawn of man. Were his misconceptions so important to him that he could offend his mind, his soul, his body with them? Would he not be happier if he believed as they did? If he did as they did? Were they so wrong? The ward contained men who had gone their own mysterious, imagined ways to happiness, and what were they but sick, miserable wretches? They did not recognize one another's desperate unhappiness but it existed. It was real. To the State he was as desperately unhappy as any of the others. And he was no longer sure that he wasn't like them. To all insane men there appears a path of happiness, of correctness, and the path is always the chart of their insanity, he thought. Was his path of happiness equally crazed?

These were not profound thoughts on reality, Burden thought critically, but they had more than profundity: they had pertinence, a terrible, sharp pertinence. He could persist in his heresies and if he did he might eventually become like the others in the ward—locked in the chamber of his own making, walls composed of rationalization, doors belted with reason and barred with vanity, and what would he live on within the room he had made for himself? Then thin gruel of being right? Victor was right. He lived on some imperial fantasy in which he waited for armies to return. And the dancer was right. He lived on the sure, feminine knowledge that he was a slender, desirable woman whom all men wanted. And in the small, gray-faced part-dwarf body the world was neatly and correctly aligned without broken walls or irregular shapes, where each thing had and occupied its place.

When the ward attendant with the broken face came for Burden at four o'clock on the morning of Friday, the twenty-third of October, Burden was almost grateful to see him.

"Is my arm broken?" Burden asked softly.

"No. But it will be stiff. I'll help you out of bed," the attendant said. He had brought a heavy bathrobe for Burden and Burden, chilled by the cold air striking his wet body, was grateful for the blanketlike robe. He found it difficult to stand on his feet and leaned heavily against the attendant as they walked slowly down the moonlit aisle. He passed the bed where the dancer lay and the face was serenely turned against the pillow, the fingers limp and faintly curved like a child's. Burden wondered what release pain could bring, what pleasure it aroused, and thought with a sinking heart what a childhood the dancer must have had.

The halls were poorly lit and cold and more than once Burden had to stop, almost too exhausted to walk. The attendant was patient. He waited for Burden to resume without saying a word. When they came up to the door of the examination room Burden was almost pleased to see it again. It was so familiar, so much a part of what he had known. Any sense of pain or anger was gone. It was with gratitude that he saw the room had not changed, that Doctor Emmerich still waited for him at the leather-topped examination table, that the lamp still burned at the far end of the room.

"Good morning, Doctor," Burden said softly.

"Good morning," Doctor Emmerich said.

"Will you tell Lark that I am ready to purge myself of my heresies?"

"I certainly shall," the doctor said with a smile and with the attendant helped Burden up on the examination table. "How does your arm feel?"

"It throbs. I can't move it at all," Burden said.

"Never mind. We'll help you." They did, very gently.

"You won't need the drug any more," Burden said, knowing that it was hopeless to say that.

"Well, you let us decide that."

"Yes, of course, I know. I was just telling you in advance. I've changed."

"Well, I'm glad to hear that," Doctor Emmerich said as he pushed up the heavy blanket stuff of the bathrobe, baring Burden's arm.

"You'll see that I'm telling you the truth," Burden said softly. He felt the needle and closed his eyes, grateful now that they would believe him, that they could see into his mind and find that he was telling the truth. All he wanted now was to be rid of the sickness that infested him. It would bring peace. It would bring quiet. It would bring love and the life he wanted to lead.

"You did not enjoy being with others, did you?"

No. Not those others. They are sick.

"Yes, sick the way you are. Do you believe that?"

Yes, I do believe that.

"They may never recover. But you could."

I want to. I want to very much.

"Will you help?"

Yes, in any way I can.

"Do you believe now that the State seeks only your happiness?"

Yes, I believe that.

"Do you acknowledge that you hold heresies?"

Yes, I do.

"Do you know what these heresies are?"

Yes, I do.

"Do you know how they arose?"

Some of them, yes.

"But not all?"

Some I don't know. They came from—I don't know.

"Do you care where they came from?"

No.

"Would you like to know where they came from?"

No. I don't. I want to be rid of them. Please, please, help me get rid of them. I want to live a happy life. I don't want to live like those other men in rooms they've made for themselves. It is awful to be mad.

"It is awful to be outside of the world. That is what you mean."

Outside of the world?

"Yes, to be alone as those men were alone. Not to be with others in common hopes, common dreams, common feelings."

Oh, yes, I see what you mean. They were all together in the same room but they were all alone by themselves. Yes, yes, you're right. Madness is like heresy—it sets you apart from others. It can destroy you.

"Exactly. Heresy is madness—the most subtle sort. When you do not believe as all others do, then you are mad. You invent your own reality but that does not make it reality, does it?"

But what if all the others have invented a reality? What if there is a collective madness of a state?

"You are beginning to talk philosophically and to talk philosophically is to talk idly. This is not a world of idlers. This is a world of doers. Who is to decide what is real and what is not? The State, as directed by its citizens, determines reality. What everyone believes to be reality *is* reality. That is simple enough, isn't it?"

Yes, but *is* it reality?

"It is reality for all the citizens of the State and that means everyone. To suppose any other reality is to be a heretic. To be a heretic is to be insane and you do not want to be insane, do you?"

No, no, of course not. Then something is real because everyone says it is real? Is that it?

"Of course. Do you remember the story of the man who said the moon had fallen into the well? He saw it in the bottom of the well and showed it to everyone in the village. But when it was pointed out to him that the moon was also in the sky and that what he saw in the well was only the reflection of the moon in the water he gave up his belief. The reality that everyone could see and believe was that the moon was still in the sky. For one man to say that the moon is in the well does not mean it is so. The moon may appear in the well and you may believe with all your heart that the moon is there and not in the sky, but it is madness to persist in the face of what everyone else believes."

And if everyone believed that the moon was in the well —would the moon then be in the well?

"For the people of that village, yes. It would be in the well and any traveler who came through and thought differently would be mad."

But the moon actually was in the sky. It had not fallen into the wall. Physics, science, astronomy would prove it to be impossible.

"Nothing is impossible if people will believe it. That is the strength of common thinking. It eventually makes all the things it thinks come true."

But how?

"By explaining away the apparent differences with discernible fact. If enough people believed the moon to be in the well, a bright person might suggest that the moon in the sky was merely a reflection of the moon in the well, and that would satisfy the appearance of the moon in the sky."

But if the moon moved—I mean, if it was no longer seen in the well but still seen in the sky?

"There would, in time, be an explanation for that."

And it would be true?

"It would be made the truth. What man wills reality to be he can make it become. Will you accept the reality of your fellow citizens?"

Yes, yes, I will. I see now what reality means.

"Then listen and be instructed."

"The State exists for the good of all. Because of this, all must subordinate their desires to the desires of the State. In time the desires of any citizen will be identical with the desires of the State. No conflict can arise for no one man can wish more than happiness for himself and the State wishes happiness for all. You have no quarrel with your neighbor nor he with you. No city has a quarrel with another, no province with another. All are part of the State and all exist for the mutual good. Your life is good only in so far as it is part of other lives. Good citizens marry, have children, love their families, worship God, conduct themselves honestly. You cannot cheat anyone without cheating yourself. There is nothing in the State which is not yours for demonstrable need. But no man may expect the fruits of the State without labor." The recorded voice went on and on, now rising, now falling as Burden listened under the heavy bathrobe, his face pale and covered with sweat.

Lark drew Doctor Emmerich aside as he read Burden's medical report.

"That was a nasty crack on the arm," Lark said.

"I was surprised it didn't break the forearm," Doctor Emmerich said.

"But the locked ward served its purpose admirably. He

will get over the injury. There is one thing now, and that is speed. He will have to be under drugs three times a day for the next week. His resistance is down and the instruction must be continuous. There is also a matter of a new identity. Continue as you have been without mentioning his name or his old identity. We'll begin the shaping of the new identity tomorrow or Sunday. It will all be done under narcotic suggestion. I don't want any overt reference to his new identity before Monday, at the earliest."

Emmerich nodded. "By the way, did you see the corpse the division finally selected?"

"No, I didn't."

"Beautiful job. Right coloring, height, weight, most of the other dimensions. When's the funeral?"

"Probably tomorrow. I know the body is on its way to Templar."

"I suppose the wife will take it hard."

"A man cut down in the prime of his life? Yes, I imagine she will. But accidents do happen. She has the house, her two sons, and she won't lack money under the widows' pension plans and the various monies due her from the college and from Burden's professional funds. She'll be all right."

Emmerich nodded thoughtfully and turned back to look at Burden, stretched out on the examination table, the recording machine beside him softly humming its instruction. "There's something very wonderful about creating a new human personality," the doctor said softly.

"Yes," Lark agreed quietly, and wondered whether Doctor Wright would concede that he had succeeded, after all.

20

Burden's funeral at Templar was fully attended even though it fell on Saturday, October 24. Emma Burden stood at the graveside, pale and frozen, hardly crying, watching the ceremony with dull eyes. Mark and Paul stood sturdily by her side, both boys crying but holding their mother's arms as if she were the one who needed comfort the most.

The leaden-colored skies darkened and an unseasonable fall of light snow began, coating the broken yellow earth, falling into the open grave and onto the coat collars and hats of the funeral party. The snow was light and cold and stirred by a strong northerly wind so that people began to turn away from the grave and the wind in order to catch their breaths. As soon as the gravediggers began their job the funeral party, as if of one mind, began to disperse. The dean of the College of Liberal Arts and Sciences accompanied Mrs. Burden, along with the two boys and Doctor Middleton.

In the Burden home the dean waited a few moments to speak to Emma Burden and then left, but not before drawing the two weeping boys aside in the foyer near the staircase.

"Now, boys, you've got to take care of your mother. This is an awful thing for her and for you, too. But you're old enough now to wipe away your tears and comfort your mother. This is something that could have happened to anyone. You have a very brave and very fine father. I think as you grow older you'll come to appreciate him more and more. He's not dead, you know. He's very much alive—in the books he wrote, in the students he taught, in you and in the love your mother has for him. He's all around you. He isn't gone. You have to understand that." The dean stopped, as if uncertain what to say next, and then clapped both boys firmly on the shoulder and left the house.

In the living room Emma Burden sat on the couch and listened to Doctor Middleton. He was saying much the same thing to her that the dean had said to the boys but it carried more conviction from Doctor Middleton.

"We had our differences, but underneath I always thought of us as friends—good, dear friends. And that's what I want you to feel about me, Emma. You're not moving away. You're staying here, keeping the house. You'll see me and all of his friends. The boys are going to grow up and go to school and they'll go to Templar and nowhere else. So try to remember that life has a way of continuing no matter how impossible the idea seems to you at the moment. And try to remember that there are friends —good friends who care about you."

"Thank you," Emma Burden finally managed softly, and Doctor Middleton squeezed her hand comfortingly and rose.

"If you like I can ask Paula to come over and stay with you for awhile," Middleton said.

"No, no," Emma shook her head, "the boys are with me and they'll be enough."

As if they had been waiting for those words, Mark and Paul entered, their eyes swollen and red. Middleton nodded, squeezed Emma's hand again as if he could think of nothing else to do, and then walked out of the room, patting Mark's shoulder as he passed.

The boys came over to their mother and sat down and snuggled against her. She put her arms around them. All three leaned their heads together and stared at the windows where the snow came in flurries, brightening the window for long moments and then fully dying away as if the storm were over.

"Where are we going to find someone like your father, boys?" Emma Burden said in soft despair and pulled the boys closer to her.

II

"Well, Mr. Hughes, awake, I see?" The nurse was young and would have been pretty if she had not worked so hard to color her face.

"Yes," he answered and wondered why he hesitated over his name. Hughes was his name. Why did he keep forgetting it?

"Are you ready for your bath?"

"Yes, I'm ready," he said, and waited for her to help him but she only smiled and started to walk off. "Aren't you going to help me?" he asked her. The nurse stopped and turned around.

"Help you do what?"

"Help me out of bed?"

"Why, Mr. Hughes," she giggled unaccountably, "you're a flirt."

He looked at her as if the suggestion was astonishing. Her smile disappeared and she moved a step nearer. "You don't need any help," she said gently, "you can get out of bed by yourself."

"I've been very sick," he said, as if he were still not certain that this was the case.

"Ye-ss," she admitted, "but you're fine now. You can get out of bed any time."

He paused for such a long time that she finally pursed her lips with mock annoyance. "Well, if you're going to be a great big baby about it—I'll help you. Now, come on, Mr. Hughes." She held out a strong, rounded young arm. Slowly, not quite trusting himself, he eased part way off the bed, testing his leg. It felt wobbly and he held on to her more tightly.

"Don't be afraid," she said firmly, "you've got to walk by yourself." He could smell the cheap perfume of her cosmetics and her vigorous, rounded young body seemed enormously strong, as if the vitality of her youth were too much for the starched white uniform.

When he was finally on his feet he was glad that she was there and he gratefully held on to her, certain that he would not be able to walk without her help. "I'd better lie down," he finally admitted, knowing that he would fall without her.

"Nonsense. You won't do any such thing. Lying down is bad for people. You're not an invalid. I know what we'll do—we'll go over to that couch by the window and you can sit there. All right?"

He measured the distance to the couch and it seemed miles away. He smiled weakly but he could feel her young body forcing him forward. "Come on," she chivied him playfully, "lift the other foot. That's a good boy. Move it forward and now lift the other. Come on, you can do it."

He clung to her, no longer holding on to her arm but clutching her by the shoulders, negotiating a perilous passage to the couch. She finally released him at the couch and he sank down on it, completely losing control of his legs. For a long moment he listened to his own labored breathing and felt his arms and legs twitch and tremble uncontrollably. She stood over him, beaming and pleased.

"Now, was it as hard as you thought it would be?" she asked, and he noticed that she too was breathing deeply from the effort of helping him. He smiled back with the implicit information that it was not at all difficult. But in his heart he felt that it had been impossible and that both had been lucky he had not died on the way. "Well, now that you know you can do it you can get back into bed whenever you like."

"No," he said with alarm as she started to go.

"Don't be a big baby," she said, wagging her finger, "you have to try for yourself. Stay there, because I understand you have some visitors. I'll bring you a clean robe first." With that she was gone and he could not move or say anything to stop her.

He rested against the couch, grateful at least to be out of bed. She was probably right. He shouldn't pamper himself. He was weak, true, but that was to be expected after an illness. His mouth puckered. That was strange, he thought. He was going to say after a "long" illness. But he wasn't sure how long he had been ill. Had it been a long illness? He looked about the room. It was both familiar and strange at the same time. Certainly he knew it from the many times he had been awake and looked at it. But he could not remember those times except vaguely, as intervals between fevers, headaches, and moments of faintness.

Visitors. She had said that word, hadn't she? Who would come to see him here in the hospital? He had no family, no close relatives. He knew that much. Friends? He didn't recall any.

"How do you know I'll have visitors?" he asked her when she returned to help him into a faded blue bathrobe.

"The supervising nurse told me for one thing, and for another—I saw the appointments chart." She started to change the bed linen and as he watched her he wanted to speak, to ask questions, but her briskness, her concentration precluded any questions and he didn't feel strong enough to insist.

"Now, that's nice and fresh," she said, the old bed linen balled up under her arm. "Don't you go and spoil it before your visitors come."

He nodded to her as she left.

His first visitor arrived within a few moments after the nurse left. There was a timid, uncertain knock at the door and before he could say anything the door opened slightly and then a bit wider, as if the person knocking had to be certain that someone occupied the room. He caught a glimpse of his visitor and the name Cumbers came to his mind. The man was short, middle-aged, with graying hair and faded blue eyes with an uncertain, timid look that suggested a lifetime of routine, minor pleasures and disappointments.

"Hughes, I'm so pleased," the man said, advancing with his hand out.

"Cumbers?" he asked, and the man nodded as they shook hands.

"I'm pleased you recognized me at once," Cumbers said, looking about for a place to sit.

"Take the chair," he said. Cumbers nodded genially and crossed the room, picked up the chair, and brought it up to the table.

"I've been trying to see you for some time. But my appointments were always being disallowed. They said you were far too sick to see anyone."

"Then you know how long I've been here?" he asked.

"Why, yes, of course," Cumbers said with some surprise, "I helped you home from the office. Don't you remember?"

He shook his head. "I'm sorry. But I don't."

"Well, you were in a bad state. I can't blame you for not remembering."

"When was it I took ill?"

Cumbers hesitated and his fingers moved slightly as if he were counting on them. "Oh, at least a month now."

"A month?" It had been a long illness then. "You didn't happen to know what was wrong with me, did you?"

Cumbers turned unmistakably dark with embarrassment. "My dear fellow, if you're worried that I told anyone—believe me, I haven't said a word."

He looked at Cumbers, puzzled and uncertain. Whatever he had been ill from was apparently something shameful, for Cumbers looked genuinely upset. "Please don't misunderstand me," he said to his visitor, "I'm not worried about your telling anyone. In fact, it may seem rather foolish to you—but I still don't know what brought me here. I mean—what was my illness?"

"Haven't they told you?" Cumbers asked with surprise.

He shook his head and waited. Cumbers looked at him narrowly and then began to fidget with the hat in his lap. "I don't know what to say. If they haven't told you perhaps there is some good and sufficient reason for it. I certainly wouldn't want to upset things by telling you something that rightfully they should tell you."

A suspicion arose in his mind at the manner in which Cumbers phrased his sentences. "Tell me," he asked slowly, "was it a mental thing?"

Cumbers looked at him without answering and he knew what Cumbers' tacit silence implied.

"Oh," he said softly, "I understand now."

"But you're much, much better now," Cumbers hastily reassured him. "I mean, there would have been no chance for me to see you if they did not feel your condition was much improved. Now, that makes sense, doesn't it?"

"Yes, I suppose it does," he said carefully, "at least the nurse acts as if I'm on my way to recovery."

"Well, there you are," Cumbers said, leaning forward with intimate enthusiasm, "you're on your way back now."

"I suppose so," he said. "You know, it may seem silly to you—but I don't remember you."

"But you mentioned my name right off. The moment I stuck my head in the door."

"Yes, I did," he said, passing his hand over his forehead. The name had sprung into his mind instantly.

"Don't worry about it," Cumbers said reassuringly, "it's a good sign. After all, in a nervous breakdown a man's memory is apt to slip quite a little. If he forgets things that isn't too serious. It'll all come back to you in time. Why, the moment you mentioned my name like that it was your own, old voice speaking right up. I was more than surprised—I was deeply pleased." He looked at Cumbers' face and there was no mistaking the real warmth and affection that shone in the faded eyes, that lit up the gentle features. He smiled at Cumbers, happy at least that he had one good friend in the world.

"Well, I'm glad you could come around, Cumbers," he said, suddenly at a loss for anything to continue the conversation.

"I have some slightly bad news for you," Cumbers said, but added reassuringly, "however, perhaps it isn't bad news at all. Your room has been let. You don't have to worry about your things. They're all either at my place or in storage. I saw to that. I guess your landlady thought you wouldn't be back for a long time and she needed the rent, so she called me and told me she'd have to let the room to someone else. I'm sure she would have kept it for you had she known how sick you were but I didn't think she ought to know. I decided the fewer people who knew what had happened to you, the better. Of course, I understand that a mental breakdown has nothing to do with a person's sanity." Mr. Cumbers looked at him so anxiously that he smiled and nodded agreeably, showing that he, too, knew that this was the case. "Well," Mr. Cumbers went on in a more relieved voice, "just the same, some people don't understand and it's just as well they don't know. That's why I felt a complete change of environment would be best—room, friends, even a job."

"A job?"

"Yes. I explained the matter to Mr. Hampshire . . ."

"Hampshire," he repeated, vaguely aware that the name meant something to him.

"Yes—our unit officer?" Cumbers added helpfully.

"Of course," he said, knowing now that he did know the name. Hampshire had been his superior in the office. Which office?

"Well, he was very understanding about it and said he would see that when you returned from your sick leave you would be put in another department—away from all the people who knew you and whom you knew. You'll be starting with a fresh slate. Same salary and same rating, of course. But I thought it would be helpful. I hope you agree?"

"Yes, of course I agree," he said, seeing Cumbers' uncertainty. It had been a kind and thoughtful act. He would be happier working with others. "Thank you very much, Cumbers. It was thoughtful of you."

"The only bad part of it is that we won't be working side by side as we have the past eight years. But you'll be seeing a lot of me from now on, don't worry about that. I don't expect to let you stay in your room and brood any more." Cumbers' brows knit. "I guess that was the trouble before. It was stupid of me not to see it. I blame myself for leaving you alone so often."

"No, no," he said, "don't blame yourself. That isn't fair. If I wanted to be alone I don't think you would intrude yourself."

"No, I'm not the sort, you're right," Cumbers said shyly, "but I did owe you a certain duty to keep you company in spite of yourself."

"Good old Cumbers," he said gently, "still the good Samaritan. Well, it looks as if I have a lot ahead of me when I get out of here—a new place to live, a new job, new work, new faces . . ."

"But I'll be there," Cumbers reminded him.

"Yes, yes, of course," he said, smiling again. It was good to know there was such a friend as Cumbers to stand by him.

"Well, I'll be going now," Cumbers said, rising. "I don't want to wear you out on my first visit."

"You'll be back?"

"Oh, yes, of course," Cumbers said, nodding vigorously. "Promptly on time. That is, unless I have some urgent errand to do on my lunch hour."

"Oh, is this your lunch hour?" he asked, concerned.

"Please, don't upset yourself. You know I was always one to gobble my lunch. You remember how you used to scold me for not taking more time over lunch?"

"You must, you know," he said gravely. "It upsets the digestion to eat too quickly."

"The amount I eat for lunch can be taken down in one swallow, my dear friend," Cumbers said as he replaced the chair and came back toward him.

"I'm sorry I can't get up," he said.

"Nonsense," Cumbers said briskly and shook his hand with more strength than he thought the slight man possessed. "Get on your feet and take your time about it. Good-by," Cumbers said and walked backward to the door. He opened it and backed out, waving as one waves to a departing ship.

Cumbers closed the door gently behind him, shook his head and sighed, and then started briskly down the hall. When he came to the supervising nurse's office he knocked the same timid, uncertain knock and entered.

Lark was sitting on the desk with his long legs dangling.

"Close the door," Lark said, and Cumbers securely and precisely closed the door behind him. "Well?" Lark asked.

"He responded quite well. A very nice man, sir," Cumbers said.

"Yes, he is," Lark said. "Did you mention all the points?"

"The room, the job, his change of position, the nature of his illness," Cumbers ticked off each point with a finger, "everything."

"Good. You'll be back tomorrow. You don't have to

stick to the schedule rigidly. If he seems in a more receptive mood any particular day you may cover more of the points. You may use your discretion in the matter. Above all, don't ignore any direct question. It's most important that you answer those questions."

"I fully understand, sir," Cumbers replied gravely.

"Do you think you're going to get along with Mr. Hughes?" Lark asked.

"Yes, I rather think I will. I think we may come to be real friends in the future. Real, good friends."

"Good. I'm glad for his sake. He's a good person, Mr. Hughes. I'm glad we were able to save him from his own anti-social personality."

"It'll be good to have a friend like him," Cumbers said, almost wistfully, losing his briskness for a moment. Lark looked at him closely.

"I'm glad you feel that way, Cumbers," Lark said.

"Is there anything else?" Cumbers asked, once again brisk.

"No."

"Then, if you'll excuse me. I don't have very much of my lunch hour left." Mr. Cumbers tipped his hat respectfully to Lark, opened the door, and left. Lark stared at the closed door for a moment, swinging his long legs slightly, and then hopped off the desk, opened the door, and left the supervising nurse's office. He had an appointment with the Commissioner to discuss Burden's case.

In the Commissioner's office Lark noted the salmon-pink binder that contained the summary of the Department's reports on Burden. He had helped prepare them and knew the positive statements of success at the conclusion of every phase.

"Well, Lark, you've had your way with Burden."

"I'm afraid not. I think I will have to ask you for an extension of time, sir," Lark said calmly.

"That's out of the question. I warned you about that when you began," the Commissioner said.

"Then I'm afraid you'll have to determine for yourself whether I've succeeded or not," Lark said blandly.

"It appears that you have." The Commissioner stirred the pages of the report with his finger. "I'm satisfied."

"I'm afraid, sir, that I'm not. That I can't be."

"What's bothering you, Lark?"

"Burden's personality change may not hold up."

"Well, just how much time do you think you'd need to determine whether or not the change will hold?"

"The rest of Hughes' natural life," Lark said.

The Commissioner smiled. "I see that you're not a man who is easily satisfied."

"I'm afraid there's no other way of testing our procedures, sir. You see, Burden is no longer Burden. For all practical purposes the integrated heretic we knew as Burden no longer exists. What we have now is a new entity—a man named Hughes. A widower, without children, without family or close relatives, with just one close friend, a minor clerk named Cumbers. I think Hughes will live out his life as Hughes, happy and useful in the society about him. However, Cumbers and others will continue to report on Hughes. This experiment is unique. We've been entirely successful as far as we've gone in the past —modifying certain personality traits and, if you recall the Fenton case three years ago, substituting sections of biography. But a complete substitution, a completely new personality, a completely new biography, has been attempted just once—this time, the Burden-Hughes case. If the new personality slips, spontaneously or gradually, then we'll know we've failed with Burden. If he lives and dies believing he's Hughes, a clerk, a widower, then and only then we'll know we've succeeded."

"Charming," the Commissioner said softly with a wry smile. "You really expect us to wait thirty, forty, or fifty years to find out."

"If Hughes lives that long I'm afraid that's what we'll have to do, sir."

"Well, I'm not nearly as timid or uncertain about this as you seem to be, Lark. I'm willing to admit that you've succeeded, and I shall officially record that result."

Lark shook his head. "I don't know. I've wondered about it. The technique may not be completely infallible. This is the first time all the theories have been put into practice. If the personality change breaks down—"

"Well," said the Commissioner, pulling over the salmon-pink colored report, "let's see what prognosis the psych people give us on the personality change."

"You don't have to look, sir. They're quite confident that the personality change will hold up."

"Well, then," the Commissioner smiled as he crossed his hands over the report, "what more can you ask?"

Lark chewed his lower lip gently. "I'm afraid I skirted the actual problem. After all, we were originally planning to peel the heresy from an existing personality without destroying it."

"Any attempt to strip a man of his beliefs, his shibboleths is bound to change his personality."

"But we destroyed his whole personality."

"Then that's what had to be done. If Burden was so heavily riddled with heresy that ridding him of his heresies demanded ridding him of his personality—well —" the Commissioner held out his hand in a gesture of helpless resignation. "Remember your purpose: Cleanse the heretic, make him a useful citizen of the State. No

Burden will ever be hopeless and dangerous, for he can be remade into a Hughes—a psychologically correct, a socially moral personality."

"Yes, sir. I agree with that. But we still do not understand the mechanism of heresy fully. What makes one man believe as his fellows and the other not? There are literally thousands of men like Burden and they are all good citizens. Why is it that Burden is not a good citizen?"

"*Was* not," the Commissioner said. "You forget he no longer exists."

"He does in my mind, sir. I keep searching for the reason, the core of his heresy. Had I found it I would not have had to destroy the man. With every secret corner of his mind willingly laid bare, why couldn't I find it—unless it is something not learned, something not acquired but something instinctive, something so deeply a part of a human creature that it cannot be removed?"

"If it is so basic to mankind then all of us contain the seeds of heresy. Is that what you mean?"

Lark paused and thought for a long moment. It was a dangerous, leading question of the sort he would never have allowed himself to face with any other man. Lark looked at the Commissioner. He had taken chances with this man in the past and he had half decided not to stretch his luck any further when, quite suddenly, he heard himself saying in a small voice, "Yes, I think the seeds of heresy lie in all of us and only require a certain care, a certain set of circumstances to burst, take root, and flower."

The Commissioner's voice was equally soft. "I trust you recognize that answer as being indiscreet, Lark. I shouldn't like to hear you repeat that elsewhere."

"I'm trying to be honest, sir," Lark said, wondering if he had, perhaps, overstepped himself.

"The answer to the question I asked you—the *proper*

answer, is this: Under abnormal circumstances citizens might revolt against the State. But only when the State does not fulfill its primary functions. Our State does and is constantly improving upon its efficiency and achievement. The special circumstances under which seeds of heresy would flower will never exist in this State, so the question becomes both academic and frivolous." The Commissioner paused and then went on, "You will remember that answer, Lark, won't you? It is the accepted and correct answer. If you ever again face that question you'll find my answer is the best to give back to your questioner."

"Yes, sir," Lark replied, vowing never to make such a blunder again, especially not before the Commissioner.

"Well, then," the Commissioner's voice became more brisk, less portentous, "we've settled Professor Burden's case. I understand you, Lark, and your wish for complete, timeless confirmation of success. But you respect the technological integrity of this Department. Well, you must also respect its conclusions. The reports are all favorable, the prognoses cheerful, the conclusions uniformly and distinctly mark this a success."

"If Hughes doesn't slip," Lark maintained stubbornly.

"You act almost as though you wish he would," the Commissioner smiled.

"Of course I don't," Lark flushed, conscious that he had again erred.

"I know you don't," the Commissioner said warmly, reassuringly. "I was just poking a bit of fun at that long face of yours. I think our Department needs a bit more optimism. We snoop and pry and inquire so much that we're apt to fall into a collective crankiness and bad disposition. No," the Commissioner shook his head, "this time there are no knit brows, no worried eyes, no uncertain lip chewings in any of the Divisions. I don't want to see those things in your face, Lark."

"Yes, sir, I'll try," Lark said gravely. "I think, however, it might help if we continue with the present checking arrangements on Hughes indefinitely, sir."

"For thirty, forty, fifty years if necessary," the Commissioner said expansively, tilting his chair back as he put his hands behind his neck. The Commissioner paused for a long moment and his voice dropped a bit, became more intimate. "I'll tell you a secret, Lark—I would never have allowed you to undertake this project if I had any reason to believe that you might fail."

"Your faith in me is flattering, sir."

"Well, I'm something more than just a damned flatterer, Lark," the Commissioner laughed, and Lark smiled politely. "No, I genuinely feel that you're going to go a very, very long way in this State, and I didn't want you to become involved in a Departmental fiasco at this stage of your career. I repeat, I would never have allowed the experiment at all if I didn't think it would be successful. *Now* will you stop your damned unhealthy brooding and expand a bit?"

"Yes, sir, I will," Lark said and wondered why the Commissioner's compliments and reassurances evoked no flicker of interest or warmth within him. He felt lonely. The loneliness and listlessness had been with him since the moment Burden really broke.

21

The second visitor Hughes had in his room was a crisp young woman with heavy glasses from the social welfare office of the hospital. She saw to it that Hughes had books and magazines to read, a toothbrush, a deck of cards, some pencils and paper, and all the other small comforts missing from his room. Hughes was most grateful but, having no letters to write, found little use for the paper and pencils and barely scanned the magazines, reading only those that contained photographs. The books, two light love novels and a true-life adventure of one man's attempt to cross the English Channel underwater with the aid of a mechanical lung, were left unread. The playing cards, however, were a real comfort for Hughes, who played a game of patience that the nurse had taught him.

He could always be found with his cards except when Cumbers came to visit. Then all thoughts of cards were put away and Hughes spent a warm, engrossed half hour with his friend listening to Cumbers' plans and reports of activities. Cumbers told him he had found a room for him in his rooming house.

"It isn't the best room in the house, by any means. As far as that goes, mine isn't, either. The best room goes to the landlady's nephew and God knows there's a waste. I don't think that young tramp has spent a night in his own bed alone. He's always out skylarking, chasing women."

"Not like us, Cumbers, eh?" Hughes asked wistfully.

"Well, he's much younger," Cumbers said.

"No," Hughes said with a slight smile, "I don't imagine you were ever like that—even when you were his age. And I don't remember if I was ever like that. I rather think that I wasn't. But I don't remember."

Cumbers' face clouded with sympathy. "Don't fret yourself. You'll remember everything in due time. And I'm not so sure that you weren't like him when you were younger. Of course, you never told me a great deal about your past. You always insisted that there wasn't anything to tell. But from what pictures you've shown me of your wife—well, Edna was a beauty. Really a beauty, and you must have shown some spirit to get her. It always takes something out of the ordinary to catch the eye of the pretty ones."

"I wish I had her picture here," Hughes said, trying achingly to remember his wife.

"I have it at my place. I'll bring it the next time. It was stupid of me to forget it. Of course you'd want it."

The photograph Cumbers brought on his very next visit (he was a man of his word who never forgot what he promised) was of an alert-looking, pretty woman with heavy, black hair, gracefully combed and pinned at the back. There was a sweetness and delicacy of brow and a gentleness of mouth and chin that Hughes found greatly appealing. When he was alone with the photograph he studied it carefully. It was an old picture and although it was only a head and shoulders likeness Hughes could see by the jewelry and the style of dress that it was nearly thirty years old. It caused Hughes to stop and consider. He did not know how old he was. It had never occurred to him to think of it, but now that it had, he realized that he did not know. He studied his face in the mirror and puzzled. He was not in his thirties. He appeared to be in his middle or late forties. But perhaps he was older. Or younger? The photograph was probably between twenty and thirty years old, and here was a woman in her early or middle twenties. Which meant he was past forty-five or even fifty. It seemed incredible to him that he should remember so little of all those years except as shadows. It was true that Cumbers was always bringing up things that struck responsive chords in his mind. There were names, dates, places, events which, once Cumbers referred to them, he seemed to be able to grasp in rough outline. And Cumbers was always eager to help him to remember. Hughes shook his head. He had never been given an official explanation for his breakdown or any sort of analysis of its debilitating aftereffects. Well, he thought, if they felt it was necessary for him to know such things they would probably tell him. He waited patiently to hear from the doctors.

Meanwhile his physical strength returned and now he was fully dressed most of the day and free of the room. He wandered the corridors and sat in the sunlit reading room. Not for the books or for the magazines, but for the feeling of peace and companionship. Patience was a good card game when one was alone but Hughes did not want to be alone any longer. He looked forward eagerly to Cumbers' visits. Not so much for the pleasure of seeing his friend but to hear about the world in which Cumbers moved. There was excitement about the work Cumbers did at the office. Things people said and did, problems he faced, decisions he made. And from Cumbers' stories of the boardinghouse Hughes began to know all of the people, the landlady who suffered from bad headaches, her nephew who was forever "skylarking and chasing after women," the couple on the first floor who were waiting for an aged uncle to die so that they might claim their inheritance and build a home in the country, the woman who was married to a sea captain who was forever sending her exotic treasures from all his ports of call, the family who had pinned their great hopes on a son who was a gifted flute player. To Hughes they all came alive when Cumbers spoke of the house, of what was said at the meals and during the evenings.

"They must be extraordinary people," Hughes had said once.

"I hope you won't be disappointed when you meet them," Cumbers said guardedly.

"No, no, not at all," Hughes replied, patting his friend's hand reassuringly. "I look forward to meeting them. It will be such an enormous change from this place."

"Yes," Cumbers looked about him. "There's something unhappy about a room where a person's been sick. I mean, they fix it up neatly enough and it's clean and bright and it has all you might want. But it's a sickroom and you can't be yourself in a room like that."

"Yes, yes," Hughes agreed, "that's it exactly."

"I've told them at the house about you," Cumbers said, "and they're all anxious to meet you."

"Ah, that's wonderful. But wait a minute. Haven't I met them before?"

"Why, no," Cumbers said, "don't you remember?"

"No," Hughes said in a small voice. It ached inside of him. He would get excited and caught up in something and then the darkened past would swirl up and chill him to the bone.

"You always insisted that I go to your place. You never came to mine. You've never seen my room. I'll confess that lots of times I felt it was inconvenient and selfish of you but—well, that's the way you were and I had to put up with it."

"Poor Cumbers," Hughes said feelingly, "I've treated you so badly."

"It's forgotten," Cumbers said sturdily, "believe me. I see now that all this illness was responsible for the way you've acted. The illness must have begun long, long ago —long before either of us suspected it."

"Yes," Hughes said thoughtfully, "that must be the answer to all I have forgotten. There is one thing, though, I've got to know. How old am I?"

Cumbers' face grew very small and unhappy. "Forty-three," he said softly, "it's in some of the papers I have for you."

"Then the picture of Edna was taken—when?"

"Oh, twenty years ago, I imagine."

"Then Edna must have been just twenty herself."

Cumbers nodded as one nods when reminiscing of the dead. Hughes sighed. "It's an awful thing to forget, Cumbers," he said quietly. Cumbers watched him with distressed eyes until it was time for him to leave. When he was at the door he took Hughes' elbow and said gently, "Listen to me. Don't brood. I could see you brooding this afternoon and it makes me unhappy. God knows all of us have had our share of misery in our life. Yours came before your breakdown. Perhaps it had all accumulated during those days and nights when you were alone and pushed you into it. Well, Nature has been kind and helped you to forget it. Don't disturb her plan, Hughes."

"Yes, maybe you're right, Cumbers," he said, "maybe if I didn't remember I'd be better off."

"I know a great deal about your life. I'll tell you anything you want to know. But there's a lot you've never mentioned and perhaps that's the dark part and you ought to forget the dark part of it. That makes sense now, doesn't it?"

"The best sort of sense," Hughes smiled, agreeing. Then Cumbers smiled, the two friends shook hands, and Cumbers hurried off.

Cumbers was right. It was best to forget the dark part of his life and not try to revive it. He had a new life ahead of him and as the days went on he grew more and more eager to enter it.

One frosty, clear December morning the doctor made his first appearance in Hughes' room and subjected him to a thorough physical examination. At its conclusion, Hughes waited with a thrumming sense of excitement. The examination could only mean that now he would be free of the hospital.

"Well, it looks as though you're ready to leave us, Mr. Hughes," the doctor said with a smile.

"That's wonderful," Hughes said, barely able to conceal his delight.

"In fact, I don't see why you couldn't leave any time you wished tomorrow morning. I'll speak to the supervising nurse about it."

"Thank you very much, Doctor," Hughes said, and hesitated for a moment before he spoke again. "I wanted to ask you about my illness. My memory isn't all it should be. Will it come back to normal in time?"

"Oh, yes," the doctor nodded his head. "You shouldn't have any trouble with that after awhile. I don't really know how to explain to you simply, nonmedically, about your failure of memory. Let's put it this way. There are things in your past which weighed so heavily upon your mind that a time came when you could no longer cope with them. What happened then is somewhat the same sort of thing that happens when a machine has been overloaded. It breaks down. In the same way, your mind broke down. You lost all consciousness of the present as well as the past. So, during the period of your breakdown a wall was built up between your conscious self and your unconscious, or memory, self. The wall will move back now, allowing more innocent memories through and that process will continue—the wall steadily retreating—until it comes to those memories or memory factors which caused the breakdown in the first place. Then the wall will stop and your memory will stop at that point. Do you understand?"

"Yes, I do," Hughes said. "It means that I won't ever remember the unhappy things in my past."

"I won't say never. You may remember them. The only real cure is to remove the wall, to bring those memories, those thoughts, those fears into the open and discuss them, to understand them for what they are and in understanding them, reduce their power to harm you."

"I see. Then must I stay here until the wall has been removed?"

"That's up to you," the doctor said thoughtfully. "Sometimes an adjustment can be made without a thorough analysis. If the wall operates, then I would not advise disturbing it. However, the wall is not nearly as secure as its name implies. Those things behind the wall do sometimes leak out and you'll find yourself suffering for inexplicable reasons, perhaps moods of depression, or feelings of guilt, or moments of terrible inadequacy. When those things happen you can be sure that you're being affected by something behind the wall which has been exerting an effect on your behavior. Something like a magnetic field."

Hughes nodded solemnly. "How long would it take for me to be fully cured?"

"Months, years, perhaps. Depending upon your resistance, your willingness, many factors."

"Can I live happily without knowing about them?"

"You may live a completely happy life from this moment on. Or you may be happy for a year or so. Or there may be alternate periods of happiness and misery. If you don't wish to undergo analysis which, as I said, may take a long time—then live a full and complete life. Have friends, be interested in things outside of yourself, join a church if you are not already a member, make a conscious effort to be interested in others—in what they do, what they say. All that helps."

"Yes," Hughes nodded soberly, seeing the good sense of what the doctor said.

"Above all, don't worry too much about your memory. Things that are better forgotten are forgotten. You can only make yourself unhappy by trying to recall them without the aid of medical guidance."

"I have a friend who said virtually the same thing," Hughes said.

"Your friend sounds as if he has a good head on his shoulders. I'd listen to him."

"Yes, I will, Doctor. Thank you."

Hughes stayed in his room the rest of the morning pondering what the doctor had said. He felt that he would make the adjustment with Cumbers' help and the thought so increased his warmth and affection for Cumbers that he even surprised himself with the cheerfulness and excitement he displayed when Cumbers arrived.

"They're letting me leave tomorrow," Hughes said.

"Wonderful!" Cumbers exclaimed. "And you're getting out just in time for the holidays, too."

"Why? What's the date?"

"The seventeenth of December. Tomorrow's Friday and a week from tomorrow the holidays begin."

"It's almost as though it were a Christmas present," Hughes said, glowing at the prospect of being away from the hospital for Christmas and New Year's.

"Well, I'll call my landlady from work and tell her to get your room ready, and I'll bring all your stuff from my place to yours. The landlady says we might even have a special dinner for you when you have your first evening home. That is, if you don't feel the excitement would be too much for you?"

"Of course not. I'm fine, Cumbers. Absolutely fine. I've been fit for weeks now. And I've been most anxious to meet everyone at the house. I think the dinner's an inspired idea. Thank her for me, Cumbers, will you? And tell her I'm looking forward to it?"

Cumbers nodded, smiling. He confessed to Hughes that he had been contemplating his usual lonely Christmas and New Year's holidays without much relish. It always struck him most sharply at that time of the year —the fact of his true loneliness. While the people at the boardinghouse were friendly enough, and Mrs. Doughton, the landlady, brightened the halls and dining and sitting rooms with decorations, the house did not have all the charm the holidays needed. When the captain was away for the holidays, as he would be this year, Mrs. Greevy grew almost inconsolably sad and was more than tiresome until the New Year came in, when she seemed to perk up and look forward to the spring, when the captain would surely touch port near home and come to see her.

"She's a good sort most of the time," Cumbers said of Mrs. Greevy, "and she bears up with his absence remarkably well. But the holidays are rather special to her, even if she is Church of State, and it sort of hits her hard when the captain's not with her. Just looking at her sitting at the dinner table is enough to make a man lose his appetite for Christmas dinner."

"Well," Hughes said, "perhaps we can help her to cheer up this Christmas."

"It'd take some doing," Cumbers said.

"Well, why not? After all, I have so much to share with others. It seems a shame if we don't help Mrs. Greevy."

When Cumbers left, Hughes felt that he had to bustle about and do things. But there was nothing to do and he began to fret over his idleness. Because he wanted the time to pass quickly he took a nap during the afternoon, lingered over his evening meal, and played patience until it was time for lights out. When he finally eased his body between the sheets and watched the cold moonlight on the floor he was aware of a deep contentment overlying a slight sense of thrill. It was his last night in the hospital. In the morning he would be up early, tidy his own room to surprise and please his nurse, and be ready the instant Cumbers called for him.

22

The morning Hughes was to be released was cold and clear, with the cruel purity that only December mornings can have. Hughes, who had arisen early, found the morning endlessly long. His impatience mounted with the minutes and he was in and out of his room a dozen times to find out what the time was. The supervising nurse finally grew tired of seeing him and told him to stay in his room or in the reading room until it should be time to leave. Hughes, with all the excitement and impatience of a small boy, could not stay in either, and hurried back and forth between the two rooms so often that finally he gave up all pretenses and lingered in the hall, watching the elevators.

His release papers came through before Cumbers arrived and the supervising nurse said he could leave at any time. The moment Hughes actually had the papers in his hand his impatience disappeared and he returned to his room to comb his hair, to brush his shoes, and to fix his necktie. He tried on the overcoat the social welfare office had sent up for him, since he had entered the hospital without one. It was well-made, of some heavy, coarse fiber, but Hughes felt that it did not fit too well and lacked style and distinction. Even Cumbers, who was not an overfussy dresser, seemed to have a smarter-looking coat. Well, he decided, it was quite sufficient for his purposes and there was a lot of wear in it. When he had money of his own he would buy a different coat but now this coat was perfectly fine. It represented the surest evidence that he was allowed to leave. He put the coat on with the idea that he would be ready on the instant to leave with Cumbers, but it soon developed that the coat was too heavy to be worn indoors so he took it off.

"What? Not ready yet?"

Hughes whirled at the voice and saw Cumbers' grinning face staring through the partially opened door.

"I've been ready for hours!" Hughes cried, struggling to get into the coat. "Where have you been?"

"I was a little late, I know," Cumbers said with a smile as he came in, "but there was a reason for it. I explained to Mr. Hampshire that you were coming home today and guess what he did?"

"Gave you the rest of the day off," Hughes cried, delighted with the good news.

"Right," Cumbers said, grinning from ear to ear. He came forward and clapped Hughes on the back but the coat was so thick that Hughes hardly felt it. "Now, *that's* a coat!" Cumbers said admiringly.

"Beggars can't be choosers," Hughes said with a shy grin, "but it ought to be warm enough."

"No, no," Cumbers insisted, "there's nothing wrong with the coat at all. It's fine, fine."

"Well, let's try it out on the weather," Hughes said, throwing open the door.

Once outdoors, Hughes drank in great draughts of cold, thin air that burned his nostrils and bit into his lungs. He was grateful for the coat's warmth, but he felt so fine, so glowing that he felt that he could have walked coatless and hatless through the streets and not been chilled at all. Cumbers, who had been watching his friend out of the corners of his eyes, smiled.

"It makes that much of a difference, does it?"

"It's—it's marvelous," Hughes said with a terrible sense of happiness and inadequacy to communicate that happiness. They fell into silence then during their long tramp through the winding streets to the station. Hughes looked everywhere—at the trees, the brown winter grass, the naked ugliness of privet hedges stripped of their leaves, the houses snuggled close to the earth showing chilled windowpanes reflecting the afternoon winter sun, at the thin streams of smoke that curled uncertainly from the chimneys, to drift over the roofs and then be sucked into the path of a sharp wind. The walk proved to be an exhilarating tonic for Hughes so that when they came up to the small, busy restaurant near the station he felt ravenously hungry.

There was a cheerful clatter in the restaurant of dishes, voices, and silverware. The long, curving oak dining bar was crowded while many of the tables were empty. It was only after Hughes and Cumbers had taken one of the tables with the prettier view of the herb garden behind the restaurant that they saw why the tables were neglected. Almost all of the help in the restaurant was concentrated behind the dining bar to take care of the luncheon crowds that had no time to dawdle over its meals.

"Well, we're in no hurry," Hughes said, enjoying the surroundings immensely, drinking in the sounds of voices, the sights of people eating, talking, gesturing. He sighed a deep, ecstatic sigh that brought a responsive smile of pleased sympathy from Cumbers. "I know I'm acting like a fool," Hughes apologized, "but to be out of that room, out of that building. The feeling can't be described."

"I know, I know," Cumbers assured him.

After awhile a waitress came and took their order and they would have been put out by the number of times she said she did not have this dish or that had they both not been in such good spirits. They both settled for plates of beef stew which, when it arrived, showed all the earmarks of having been made from leftovers reheated and covered with a thin gravy. The carrots were undercooked and spongy-hard and the peas and potatoes were out of cans, but neither Cumbers nor Hughes minded very much. The rice pudding proved a pleasant surprise—light, fluffy, and not too sweet, and the coffee was good.

Hughes sighed as he sipped his coffee. "Miraculous," he said with a small wave of his arm.

"Not the food, you can't mean the food," Cumbers said.

"The food, the restaurant, the people, the air, the sunlight, the world—all miraculous."

Cumbers shook his head admiringly. "To feel that way is almost compensation for the time you spent in the hospital."

"Yes, you understand that, do you?" Hughes asked in surprise.

"Well, yes, I suppose I do. It's like being reborn, isn't it?"

"Exactly," Hughes nodded his head soberly, "that's exactly what it is like, being reborn. Everything takes on a new color, a new feeling—as if my eyes were seeing for the first time, my ears hearing for the first time, my tongue tasting, my skin feeling. Just as if I had been born all over again. I enter the world as innocent as a child—as wondering, as delighted—"

"Well, from the amount of crying babies do I don't suppose there's much delight in it for them."

Hughes laughed appreciatively. Cumbers smiled, his cheeks coloring with pleasure. "Now, that was a feeble enough thing to make you laugh," Cumbers said.

"I am in the mood to laugh. I suppose if someone, any-one, were to walk up to me and begin to count to ten I would laugh."

"Well, now's the chance for me to get off all the weak jokes I know," Cumbers laughed, and Hughes joined him.

The two men were still laughing softly when they got on the train for the short ride to New Buxton where Cumbers worked and lived and where Hughes would now do the same.

To Hughes, leaning against the window and watching the approach of the town, it seemed both shimmering and miraculous. When he stepped off the train he was at once struck by the smartness, the alertness, the neatness of the train terminal. There was none of the usual confusion that one associates with train terminals. The floors were well clear of litter and the usual dirt. Metal was polished, windows cleaned, uniforms pressed, and shoes brushed. The haircuts on all the clerks, porters, conductors, and station officials were short and fresh.

The queues waiting for the buses outside of the station stood in straight lines waiting their turn, and buses arrived with a clockwork regularity, filling quickly, closing their doors, and surging off with blue exhausts.

"It's marvelously efficient," Hughes whispered to Cumbers as they stood on the line in front of a painted sign that read "Rizal Square."

"What is?" Cumbers asked.

"The buses—the way they arrive and fill up and leave," Hughes said. Cumbers shrugged his shoulders, evidently seeing nothing unusual in this.

When they finally boarded the bus and found seats, Hughes found it quite comfortable and he had selfishly taken the seat nearest the window so he could look out at the town. The first thing that surprised him was the speed with which the bus drove out of the terminal and then he was struck with the extraordinary width of the avenues and even the cross streets they passed. They were fully a hundred or more feet wide from curb to curb and the bus tore along at a very fast pace, roaring as its motor raced. Houses were neat and low, with well-barbered hedges and standing in astonishingly straight rows and files. The regularity of the streets both pleased and surprised Hughes, who mentioned it to Cumbers.

"Oh, I think I once heard something about the original design of the streets being planned for the passage of hundred-ton tanks. In the old days they were great believers in heavy firepower and great mobility."

"Well, whatever the reason, it gives a wonderful sense of spaciousness to the city," Hughes said.

"Maybe it does, but it takes a devil of a long time to cross the street. Of course, they've painted those safety islands in the middle of them but you can't get across the street while the light is in your favor unless you're young and willing to sprint for it."

Hughes smiled. "Well, evidently it was a city built for young people."

"Yes," Cumbers said with a suddenly saddened look. "I suppose that's it."

Hughes, who had turned back to the window, did not see his friend's unexpectedly sad look and was again devouring the shapes of the buildings, the way the winter light made them look clean and neat and solid.

They dismounted from the bus before its final stop and walked a long block filled with identical homes. Here and there a house stood out with some small detail, false shutters destined to remain open, some scrollwork around the entrance to a door, a cluster of evergreen bushes planted to flank the walk to an entrance. The numbers differed, and occasionally the condition of the paint or the age of the brick told one house from the other, but substantially the homes were identical. Hughes did not find the fact in the least disconcerting but rather felt that it lent a sort of unity that made for a sense of peace.

Cumbers' boardinghouse, like the houses that flanked it, was just three stories high. The door entrance was marked by two small iron dogs, cocker spaniels, to judge by the droopiness of their ears and their size. They had once been painted green, for it showed up under the coat of black where the top layer was chipped. Hughes thought it was rather pathetic to see the two dogs frozen in iron. Just what made it pathetic he could not tell. The glass in the door was clean but the coarse lace curtain that masked the hall from passers-by was faded and dingy.

The hall itself was neat if a little dark and Hughes could see where the rug had a worn spot, shining with a thin yellow pallor against the dark hall. There was an ancient umbrella rack with black painted iron hooks. Under the rack was a chipped, dirty dish to catch the drain from dripping umbrellas. The water had long since evaporated, leaving a gritty deposit in the dish. For Hughes this smacked of a homely touch and he thought no less of Mrs. Doughton as a housekeeper for its condition.

The entry was uncomfortably warm with that peculiar

sort of gassy heat that arose from the burning of synthetic fuel. Over the smell of the heat Hughes could detect the more delicate odors of lemon-oil polish and tobacco.

"My room's on the second floor. You're right above me on the third," Cumbers said, leading the way up the stairs. The staircase was narrow and dark and the banister had an oily feel that Hughes preferred to believe came from the polish that was used on it.

His room was near the end of the hall. By the time he got there Cumbers had already opened the door and entered.

"Well, this is your place," Cumbers said, extending his arm as Hughes walked in. He took off his coat and looked about for a place to hang it. Cumbers, who was evidently familiar with the room, sprang to one side and opened a door to a closet. The closet looked deep and wide and dark and Hughes could see a row of dirty wooden hangers arranged on the bar for him. He selected one and hung up his coat, looking over the rest of the room as he did.

It was not a small room, but it appeared so because of the low ceiling. Actually it was a square of fifteen feet. There were two windows in the room and they let in a flat, north light. The bed, an old sunken oblong with a pneumatic mattress, was a model once considered *avant-garde,* with its amputated feet and irregular footboard. Evidently it had been obtained secondhand since the finish did not match the somber walnut of the dresser, the dresser mirror frame, or the oak finish of the two spindly-legged night tables. A foot locker, painted to simulate grained oak, stood at the foot of the bed and smacked of a good buy from the Army quartermaster. A small desk with a chair and a reading lamp with an old pneumatic lounge chair completed the furnishings of the room. All of it stood on a rug that looked pathetically ancient and subdued from thousands of beatings and scrubbings.

"It's quite nice," Hughes finally said.

"It's all you need," Cumbers agreed. "It has its drawbacks, of course. You've noticed the low ceiling. Well, that's true of all the apartments on the top floor. There's a regular maze of ventilating pipes and heat ducts up there and of course the storage rooms, too. So they had to reduce the height of the room. I'm afraid you won't ever get direct sunlight in these windows—it's a northern exposure which would be fine if you were a painter. And it always gets damned cold up here—near the roof and facing north this way—so Mrs. Doughton's going to give you two extra blankets." When Hughes made a deprecatory gesture, Cumbers hurried on to say, "Oh, you'll need them. She isn't doing you any favors, you know. If you're wise you'll buy yourself a small electric heater and sneak it in. Mrs. Doughton doesn't approve of them on the grounds that they're liable to get overheated and set fire to something. That's her story. Actually she knows they use a lot of current and they can run up your bills something fierce. But since the price of the room includes your electric and breakfasts and dinners—well, who cares? It's her lookout, not yours. You've got to keep from freezing."

Hughes nodded but thought the observation a little sharp, a little unfeeling. It surprised him somewhat to hear it coming from Cumbers, whom he had always supposed to be such a gentle and generous soul. Apparently Mrs. Doughton was more a tigress than he had been led to expect, or there was more to Cumbers than he thought.

Mrs. Doughton came in unannounced while Hughes was alone, testing the bed by gently bouncing on it.

The bed was so low that he had difficulty in rising fast enough.

"Oh, the bed's good and springy," Mrs. Doughton said as she entered the room with a quick, proprietary look. "You're Mr. Hughes, aren't you?"

"Why, yes," Hughes said, "and you're Mrs. Doughton?"

"Yes. Welcome to your new home. I'm glad to see you came right in and made yourself comfortable."

"Oh, Mr. Cumbers opened the door for me," Hughes said, worried lest she think he was forward in having entered the room by himself.

"I know. I spoke to him before I came up. Well, we're glad to have you here after hearing all about you from Mr. Cumbers. I'm sure that being a friend of his you'll be every bit as nice as he is."

"I hope I shall be," Hughes said politely, looking at Mrs. Doughton and trying to decide what she resembled. She was a doughy-looking woman with plump arms which were, at the moment, encased in a heavy, knitted man's sweater. Her hair was thin on her head and heavy on her face, principally her chin, her upper lip, and down the line of her jaws. At a hurried glance she might have been mistaken for a short, fat man in need of a shave. For a reason he could not say, Hughes had the impression that she was an athletic woman in spite of her bulk and her advanced age, the sort who dominates weak-chinned men and who would be indefatigable at the tubs in a hand laundry.

"The room's plain but clean and large enough for you. I don't know whether Mr. Cumbers told you where the bathroom is—"

"Oh, yes," Hughes replied hastily, although Cumbers had not mentioned it at all.

"I'm sure you'll be happy here, Mr. Hughes, and tonight you'll get a chance to meet the rest of my people."

"Yes, I'm looking forward to it," Hughes said brightly. "Cumbers has told me so much about them all."

"You'll meet them tonight. Well, I suppose you'll want to get settled, so I'll leave you now."

"Thank you for stopping in, Mrs. Doughton," Hughes said. She left finally, looking at the room as she went as if she were inspecting quarters she had never seen before. Hughes hesitated about closing the door until he heard her footsteps creaking on the landing of the floor below.

His "things," brought up by Cumbers the evening before, were neatly put way. They were mainly extra clothes, shirts, socks, handkerchiefs, and the like. For Hughes, examining them, it gave him the slight sense of shock, discovery, and curiosity one might experience upon looking over the belongings of a corpse. Nothing looked familiar, not even the ties, which a man living alone might expect to know best of all his clothes. There were a few photos of people he did not know taken with him in their company at various places—a beach, an outdoor picnic park, and in front of something that resembled an amusement pavilion. One was taken into the sun so there were light flares obscuring people's faces, another was taken late in the day when shadows were so deep that his own face stared out at him like a death's head. Hughes decided they were unusually bad photographs even for an amateur, but he put them back into the drawer of the dresser where he had found them.

23

The welcoming dinner for Hughes was a minor-key success. Mrs. Greevy proved to be the main prop of the merriment and sustained a steady fire of chatter and small talk to keep Hughes the center of attention. The flute player and his family looked uncomfortable, ate quickly, and were the first to leave the table for the sitting room where the flute player, as if it had been planned, opened a small leather case and took out his flute. The others lingered over their coffee so long that finally the flute player's father came in and looked at all of them severely.

"Paul is ready," he said, and at that everyone began to rise. Hughes and Cumbers walked in flanking Mrs. Greevy, who had not ceased talking from the moment she had been introduced.

Hughes listened attentively to the flute solo which was executed without a mistake that he could detect and he joined in the applause of the others at the conclusion.

A second round of coffee and sweet cakes was served after the last musical selection but the artist and his family did not stay to enjoy them. Hughes came up to thank them but they were all busy disassembling and packing, like a traveling show in a hurry to get to its next scheduled stop.

"It was a nice party," Mrs. Greevy said, "wasn't it, Mr. Hughes?"

"It certainly was, Mrs. Greevy."

"Too bad *he* had to spoil it," Mrs. Greevy said bitterly, referring to Ralph Doughton's sudden and rude departure shortly after the flutist had begun. "But then, he's always spoiling things for poor Mrs. Doughton. Let Mrs. Greevy tell you that what that boy needs is a father. If he had a father like the captain—ho ho, it'd be a different story. Did Mr. Cumbers ever tell you how the captain handled a mutiny at sea?"

Hughes started to say no but caught Cumbers' distressed signaling at the last moment. "Why, as a matter of fact, he did. The captain sounds like a real man, Mrs. Greevy."

"Ah, he is—a *real* man. Not a very big fellow, you know. Just a little man, but he's filled to the eyes with courage. Absolutely raw courage. You'd never think it to look at him that he handles men twice his size as if they were children. Absolute children. When the captain speaks it's with the voice of the Lord and his wrath has iron in it. Oooh, what the captain could do for *him!* Ahhhhr," Mrs. Greevy ground her teeth in pleasurable anticipation of that circumstance occurring. "There's a *man*," she said again, more softly now, lost in a reverie, and then she stopped talking altogether and when she left Cumbers and Hughes in the sitting room she did not even say good night.

"Poor woman," Cumbers said, "she's going to miss him during these holidays. I can see the signs. Especially when she talks about him that way."

"He must be quite a figure," Hughes admitted. "Have you ever met him?"

"Ummm," Cumbers nodded. "A toy bulldog. Has orders for everyone. He shouts at you as if you were both caught in the teeth of a gale. Well, time for bed. You don't want to overtire yourself your first day out of the hospital."

"Nonsense," Hughes said, "I'm not tired at all. And I could have been let out of the hospital weeks ago as far as that goes."

"Come on, up to bed."

"Cumbers," Hughes said as his friend arose.

"Yes?"

"May I tell you again how happy I am that I'm here? That I have friends and that you're one of them?"

Cumbers made a face. "You're disappointed in them, aren't you?"

"No, no, not at all," Hughes reassured him. "They're good people, all of them."

"No, they're not," Cumbers said somberly. "Mrs. Doughton's not a bad sort—a little too sharp, perhaps. And Mrs. Greevy's apt to talk too much. But the rest of them—that Ralph Doughton and the Hennings and that flute player and his family!" Cumbers made a distasteful face.

"Well, they all mean well," Hughes said mildly.

"No, they don't mean well. None of them, not really. Those poisonous Hennings, waiting like a pair of vultures for an old man to die—they disgust me. And that flute player and his family—they're absolute lunatics about their son. You only saw a little part of it tonight. Did you see the look they gave Ralph Doughton when he left? I can't stand Ralph Doughton but, by God, you have no right to wish a man unspeakable things just because he won't stand still for an evening devoted to an earache.

That's all his playing is—a damned earache, and everyone but that doting family of his knows it. We're not people to them. We're things he plays to—like a net in tennis. Without the net and the court you can't play tennis—can't show off how damned clever you are, how bright, how promising." Cumbers was uncommonly bitter and resentful and Hughes looked at him with surprised and pitying eyes. "No one really gives a damn for anyone else in this place. Ralph Doughton sponges off his aunt and don't think she doesn't get something for it, too. The chance to mother him, to baby him, to pretend he's her child. That's important to her. And even Mrs. Greevy— she doesn't know we're alive. We exist just for her to play out her dreams about the captain, to get someone to listen to what's always running around in that head of hers. What about us, Hughes? Are we to be just the audience? Some damned conveniences for other people? I'm sick and tired of being a convenience. I—" Cumbers suddenly stopped as if he realized something. A queer, frightened look of shame crossed his face. "I'm sorry, Hughes. You've had so much trouble in your life it's damned inconsiderate of me to sound off about my feelings. I mean, it isn't fair, is it?" Cumbers ducked his head, barely said good night, and hurried out of the sitting room.

Hughes sat for a few moments, listening thoughtfully to Cumbers' footsteps on the stairs. When he arose and looked for the light switch the lights went out as if the switch had divined his purpose. When Hughes got out into the hall he saw that all but the entry light was off and decided that Mrs. Doughton somehow controlled the lights from another part of the house.

In his own room Hughes rested on the bed in the dark, unable to fall asleep. Cumbers puzzled him. He was not at all the little, gentle, colorless man he thought he was.

Cumbers had fears and longings and needs as deep and dark as anyone Hughes had known. But then, Hughes thought, he had not known so many people. As far as he was concerned, these people were the first. He felt as a man might feel coming from another world to earth. He neither liked nor disliked these people. All he felt about them was a curiosity, an interest, a little pity. Actually, the only person he felt any affection for was Cumbers and he was not certain now that he knew Cumbers at all. The thought did not distress him. Instead, it occurred to him that much of the life about him was only visible in fragmentary form. Much of it was subterranean, and it would not be fair to decide upon any of it until he had seen more—much more.

II

Hughes and Cumbers spent much of their time outside the house although the December week end was cold and blustery. The town's regularity began to pall on Hughes during the long walks and he began to understand Cumbers' lack of interest in New Buxton. Apparently there were three stages of awareness to the town. The first was wonder and excitement of the variety he felt upon first viewing it, and that was followed by a sense of despair over its sameness and regularity. Evidently the third stage was the one shared by all the regular dwellers—a sort of anesthetized eye, a glazed indifference, and a sure instinct for choosing one's own block and one's own house without reference to street or avenue signs.

From Cumbers he learned that he would be working for the Quartermaster section of the Defense Arm. Cumbers said he had tried to find out all he could about Hughes' job so he should be able to help him a bit with it before he began. He had brought home manuals on the organization of the Defense Arm and Hughes began to read them carefully, underlining words he did not understand. Cumbers was most patient and thorough in explaining each of the words that tripped up his friend but by Sunday evening Hughes felt that he would never completely understand the tables of organization and the administrative schematics.

Monday came and Hughes went off to work. Evidently Cumbers had prepared everything in advance so he was sent directly to his supervisor. It was an enormous room in which he was finally put to work and all the walls were lined with charts from ceiling to floor. For each section of chart a clerk was assigned with a lightweight rolling aluminum ladder, a box of chalk, dusters, and inventory reports from all the units in the Defense Arm. The sight of all those busy clerks marching up and down the ladders, erasing a figure here, chalking in another figure, and rolling their ladders back and forth bewildered Hughes. His own chart was devoted to small arms and there seemed to be a bewildering array of such types. There were, for instance, six classes of pistols, from atomic hand weapons to antique gunpowder revolvers in various calibers. Hughes had to take all the figures from all the units, add them up for each class of weapon on an adding machine, and then enter the figures in the appropriate spaces on the chalk boards. It was important to sort out weapons according to type, caliber, year of manufacture, condition, and availability. Hughes discovered that three to four hours had to be spent on reports before a figure could be changed on the chalk board. Each clerk seemed to have his own method. The more athletic and energetic men were constantly changing figures as new unit reports came in. More cautious men waited until the end of the day before entering all the new figures or allowing the old figures to stand. It was most important, Hughes learned, to have absolutely accurate figures at the end of the day. To change them as one went along in the reports meant a great deal of climbing and dismounting during the day, but to change them all at once an hour before the end of the day meant that there was a great responsibility involved, since some two hundred different figures had to be changed or checked and once it was done there was no time left for counterchecking what one had put up on the boards.

During the day a steady parade of officers and enlisted men came into the chart room to study the figures or to copy them. The job, Hughes learned, was one of great and exacting responsibility.

Within a few days Hughes caught the hang of it and because it broke the monotony of numbers and sitting at the desk with the computer he became one of the clerks who was constantly scurrying up and down the ladder. The bewildering maze of pistols, rifles, machine pistols, machine guns, the eighteen calibers of light mortars, anti-tank rifles, rocket and field bomb launchers, and all the other varieties of light weapons began to become routine to him and in a short time he was officially congratulated upon his speed and accuracy.

The work, however, proved to be exhausting to Hughes, who found that once he returned to the rooming house he didn't feel much like doing anything but eating his meals and retiring. Cumbers was highly pleased over his friend's rapid adjustment and assured Hughes that soon he would be able to do his work with less fatigue and would not need to go to bed so early every evening.

Christmas Day fell on a Friday so the various sections

of the Defense Arm worked a half day on Thursday and then dismissed its people.

Cumbers dropped by to pick up Hughes and on the way back to the rooming house the two men decided that they would accompany Mrs. Greevy to Christmas Eve services at the Church of State meetinghouse.

During the pre-Christmas dinner, Hughes watched Ralph Doughton behave disagreeably at the table. Hughes suspected that the landlady's nephew acted deliberately perverse for the attention it would net him. Perhaps, Hughes mused, the boy did not quite know how to be pleasant and be noticed and so had chosen the opposite tack. Cumbers, strangely enough, had taken just the reverse approach. He was all obliging, all sweetness, all light and gentleness and concern. Why couldn't they just be themselves? What was wrong with that? Why did they have to play these roles? Ralph Doughton was surly but Hughes felt that, basically, Ralph was not a surly person. And Cumbers—Cumbers was kind but was he basically a kind person? The thoughts remained in Hughes' mind throughout the dinner and afterward, while they walked with Mrs. Greevy through the chilled, deserted streets to the Church of State meetinghouse, Hughes expressed part of his thoughts aloud.

"Ralph Doughton isn't nearly as bad as he pretends," Hughes said.

"Oh, Mr. Hughes," Mrs. Greevy said with a heavy sigh, "if you only knew what that poor woman had to put up with in that boy you wouldn't say a thing like that. Mrs. Greevy's known Mrs. Doughton a long, long time and all during that time there's been no moment when the poor woman was free of worry or unhappiness over that boy."

"Still, I suppose he's been the source of some comfort

to the woman," Cumbers said thoughtfully. Hughes glanced at him out of the corner of his eye. The role again, the pose.

"Comfort is something she'll get only when she's gone from mortal desire," Mrs. Greevy sighed. "The trouble with the boy is that he thinks only of himself—himself, himself, himself all the time. Oh, the Church of State would be such a comfort to the boy. It would open up his narrow heart. It would let in the world around him. You know, we of the Church of State are never really alone, Mr. Hughes."

"Yes, so I understand," Hughes said. "But then, you do miss the captain so much, don't you?"

Mrs. Greevy's eyes turned sidewise to look at Hughes and for a moment he felt he had said the wrong thing. "Mrs. Greevy knows what you're thinking, Mr. Hughes. But the truth of it is that Mrs. Greevy has not been as true a believer as she might have been and it's the source of all her grief. Don't judge the Church of State by Mrs. Greevy, Mr. Hughes. She's a poor, foolish woman afflicted with mortal desire."

Hughes nodded, pleased and interested by the curious third-person manner of speech. He had heard that this was the mark of a Church of State worshiper and, of course, he had noticed it before in Mrs. Greevy's speech but she had generally, in the past, managed a tricky, elusive sort of speaking so that she never referred to herself.

The meetinghouse of the Church of State which Mrs. Greevy attended was a low, long shed, as unpainted outside as it was inside. It had no symbolic cruciform shape such as the Catholic churches, nor any marks on its outside to designate its special character. Hughes entered not quite certain what the interior would resemble but vaguely expecting an altar, or a pulpit of some sort. There was none. Nor was there any decoration of any sort—not even ordinary covering paint over the wooden walls and the ceiling. There were light brackets lining the walls with ordinary, unfrosted electric light bulbs that gave off a harsh, dazzling light. The room was filled with low benches in the form of a filled square and people sat in them facing toward the center of the square. There was an empty space in the center of the square no larger than a yard by a yard; otherwise the square was solidly filled with benches which were long in the rear, diminishing in size until they came to the short benches in the center, benches on which only three people could sit. Evidently they were late for services for a man was standing at his bench, all eyes turned toward him, and he was speaking.

"And a teacher was born," the man said, "and the teacher named Jesus Christ was ignored by the many and heeded by the few." Hughes hesitated to work his way down the narrow aisles between the benches while the man spoke but Mrs. Greevy urged him ahead with her hand at his elbow.

"And the many, hating the teacher, beseeched the governor of the province to have Him destroyed." Hughes, Cumbers, and Mrs. Greevy eventually found places for themselves on a bench near the front.

"The governor was from a foreign power," a man said, springing up without ceremony. The man who had been speaking sat down and listened. "A foreign power that had seized the land of the Jews and held it against their wishes. The Jews had fought wars with the Romans for many years but at last the Jews were conquered and the conqueror set a governor over them."

"They set also a king," a woman said, rising. The man,

in turn, sat down. "And the king's name was Herod. And it was to Herod that the three wise men came and said there is born today in the city of Bethlehem a great teacher. And to the Jews the teacher was the leader, the king, and Herod feared that the teacher might usurp his throne."

"Was He the Son of God?" a voice shouted and then Hughes was astonished to hear the group chorus, "No!"

"God had no son!" Mrs. Greevy shouted, springing up. The woman who had spoken of Herod sat down. "As God is a ghost and a ghost may have no issue. God favored no one man. God favored us all and God said you are all equal, you are all my children. God said that God has no son—He has many sons. And He said He has no daughters—He has many daughters."

"We are all part of the design!" a young man cried, rising, and Mrs. Greevy sat down, folding her hands in her lap to listen. "No one man can suffer without all suffering. No one woman may rejoice without all rejoicing. That is the only mystery and the mystery is made clear."

"All is one and one is all," the entire congregation boomed like an organ suddenly struck in the shed. Hughes glanced about him. They all listened so carefully, so intently that it puzzled him. There was none of the fidgeting he thought there might be in a place where no one led.

"There are neither angels, nor devils, nor ghosts, nor spirits, nor seraphs, nor cherubs, nor saints, nor sinners," the young man said heatedly, and applause came from the listeners, the sort of applause that might be expected in a theater. The young man hurried on over the applause, "nor is there heaven or hell, damnation or salvation, redemption or fall! We are all part of the human family, the

family of mankind, the family of God. Good, bad, or indifferent, we are all filled with grace!"

"Amen!" the congregation thundered and then, as an
outburst of the affirmation, came music. No sooner did
one begin to sing than another picked it up. Hughes listened to the words:

> "Oh sing and proclaim us all,
> Of blood one another,
> Of bone one another,
> Of birth, of death, of all.
> Oh sing and proclaim us all,
> In like one another,
> In life one another,
> In birth and death of all."

There were other choruses but Hughes did not understand them, for the sheer weight of the singing pounded
against the roof, the walls, hammered down on his ears.
Then when the song ended another began and it
was taken up. Song followed song until someone cried,
"Merry Christmas! The teacher is born!" The singing collapsed and the voices, like waves on a shore, murmured
and muttered, "Merry Christmas! The teacher is born!"
Benches began to scrape as people rose, smiling, chatting
to one another, shaking hands.

"Wasn't it lovely?" Mrs. Greevy asked as they made
their way through the crowds to the door.

"Yes, it certainly was," Cumbers said, and there was a
look in his eye, a note in his voice that led Hughes to
think that his friend meant precisely that. Mrs. Greevy
squeezed both their hands and smiled over her shoulder at
Hughes. "Oh, if you would only join us, Mr. Hughes!"

"Well, I don't know, Mrs. Greevy," Hughes said, knowing that he never would.

"The simplicity of it," Mrs. Greevy said with a sigh,

"each of us part of the other. No leaders, no followers, all men brothers, all women sisters, the great human family." Mrs. Greevy shook her head with a sigh and under her breath began to sing, "Oh sing and proclaim us all, Of blood one another, Of bone one another, Of birth, Of death, Of all!"

"Look, it's snowing," Cumbers said as they got to the door. A silent, heavy snowfall, filled the night. The people walking down the street away from the meeting place of the Church of State were already heavily coated with snow. Mrs. Greevy gave a delighted cry, let go of their hands, and skipped ahead happily, turning as she did to look up. Fat, heavy snowflakes struck her smiling face and the lashes of her eyes.

"Wasn't that thoughtful of the Lord?" Mrs. Greevy cried to them as they came up. "Mrs. Greevy loves snow. It's a mortal desire, we all know, but isn't it lovely?"

"We'd better get moving," Cumbers said, "otherwise we'll be buried under it before we can get back to the rooming house." They started off then into the night with the softly falling flakes, huge in size and falling heavy and straight. Mrs. Greevy loved it and held up her hands to catch flakes and she began to hum "Oh sing and proclaim us all."

For Hughes it was the first snowfall he could remember and it stirred and warmed him. It had such an enormous feeling of peace and it began to transform the regularity of the streets. Shapes that weren't square began to spring up, houses lost their corners in soft, flowing lines of drifted snow, the severe lines that marked the pavement from the gutter softened as flakes rested one against another—billions of them taking away the straight lines of New Buxton, giving it a new spirit that flowed and made gentle curves and rounds.

They were heavily laden with snow by the time they reached the rooming house and Mrs. Greevy playfully struck them to see the explosive shower of snow fly from their coats and hats. She ran ahead into the house laughing coquettishly, as if she fully expected to be chased and was deliciously afraid that she'd be caught. Cumbers and Hughes, however, had no such intentions. They clumped their boots prosaically on the top step in front of the entry to rid themselves of their snow and stepped into the entry. They hung up their dripping coats and hats. As they went toward the stairs they both stopped at the same sight.

There was a gorgeous flood of color from the sitting room and as Hughes followed Cumbers toward it he realized what it was—the boardinghouse's Christmas tree ablaze with glowing colored lights in the darkness of the room.

"Imagine that woman willing to let her electric bill run up for this," Cumbers whispered, looking at the tree.

"I think she left it on for us to see," Hughes whispered, deciding that Mrs. Doughton was probably a wonderful woman to have had such an impulse.

"I don't believe it," Cumbers said when something on the table near the sofa caught Hughes' eye. The two men advanced and Hughes saw it was a tray covered with sugar cakes and ginger cookies. There was a note lying in the middle of the tray. "Dear Mrs. Greevy, Mr. Hughes, and Mr. Cumbers," it read, "I expect you will be coming home late—too late for a snack with us. There's coffee and cocoa left in the kitchen for you. Just heat it and enjoy yourselves. Please turn off the tree lights before you go up to bed. Merry Christmas to you all."

"Well?" Hughes asked softly. The only reply from

Cumbers was the tiny crunch of his teeth biting into a ginger cookie.

"Let's go and get the coffee warm," Cumbers said.

"Shall I go upstairs and call Mrs. Greevy?" Hughes asked.

"Don't bother. I've got something to talk over with you that I'd rather she didn't hear." With that Cumbers went off to the kitchen.

Because Hughes wanted to have the coffee and cakes in front of the tree, they took their cups back into the sitting room and sat down on the sofa. From where they sat they could both see the tree glowing with colored lights and catch a glimpse of the heavy snow falling in the street.

"What was it you didn't want Mrs. Greevy to hear?" Hughes asked as he sipped his coffee.

"Well," Cumbers bit off a bit of sugar cake, regarded the piece left for a moment, and then talked, chewing the brittle cake as he spoke, "it's about this Church of State. To tell you the truth, this wasn't the first time I've been to one of their meetings. I've been a couple of times before. Just hopped in, stayed awhile, and hopped out. Didn't impress me much, to tell you the whole truth. I couldn't make much sense of it. But tonight—well, tonight was very different. I had the feeling that I wanted to belong. I had the feeling that these people were my brothers and sisters and that they wanted me. I don't pretend I understood it all. I don't. But then, I've never understood religion very much. As a kid, you know, your folks make you go to Sunday school and church and all that. It's the thing to do. But it didn't make much sense to me. Too many things wrong with the world that God couldn't seem to handle. And there were lots of things that weren't explained. And then I didn't particularly get the feeling that I was very important in the scheme of things."

"And does this Church of State thing make you feel that important?"

"Well, yes, in a way. I mean, it makes me feel as if I would be important with all the others. Mrs. Greevy's got a devil of a lot of friends. She doesn't see them because she's mainly too lazy to stir out of the house without company and then, there's the captain. She's afraid if she's left the house he'll drop in and she won't see him for an hour or more. Of course it's not likely that he will or if he does he'd mind waiting another hour or so to meet her—but Mrs. Greevy's queer in lots of ways and she was right when she warned you not to judge the Church of State people by her. But the point is she's got a world full of friends and all of them from the meeting place. Real friends, good friends. They'd do anything for her. Why, I remember last winter she was sick and there were people running in and out of the house taking care of her twenty-four hours a day. Different people almost every hour on the hour, but all of them worried about Mrs. Greevy. That's what I mean by friends."

"I see," Hughes said softly, looking at Cumbers and pitying the man more and more.

"Of course, I've never had much of a family. No brothers or sisters and my mother and father died before I was eighteen and it's cruel for a boy that age to be thrown on the world. In a way I know what Ralph Doughton's gone through. We're of different stripes, though, and I didn't turn out to be the sort of stinker he is. And he's better off even than me. He's got his aunt and she cares about him. No aunt for me—no one to give a damn, in fact. I was never much to attract a girl's eye. At least you've been married. I never was. No girl would have me and those that would—well, there was always something wrong with them, you know," Cumbers said and crooked a shoulder, grimaced grotesquely, and stuck out his tongue to display imbecility by way of illustration of the women who would have him. Hughes laughed softly out of politeness. "Well," Cumbers went on, biting into the sugar cake, "that was the situation. Not good. A lonely sort of life for me. Until you came along I didn't have a friend in the world. I could have had a furnished room somewhere else and made up my own meals. It would have been lots cheaper. But, my God, I'd die in a room like that. *No one* would know about me. The people here aren't anything to cheer about but in God's name at least they know I'm alive—they care a bit. They put up a show of being friends and I can sometimes get the feeling that I belong here. But I don't really belong. I don't really feel as if I belong." Cumbers stopped, sipped his coffee, and then, in a very small voice, asked, "Well, what do you think? Ought I to take the plunge?"

"Cumbers," Hughes said softly, "why did you ask me about it? I mean, after all, if you're thinking of joining this church—well, wouldn't Mrs. Greevy be a better person to talk to?"

"No, no," Cumbers disagreed, shaking his head, "she's prejudiced in the matter. She'd see nothing wrong in it. She'd be all for it. She'd pray me right out of my mind until I joined. No, I want to keep it quiet from her awhile. I mean, I feel I ought to collect my thoughts on the subject and talk it over with someone who knows me. I've decided lots of things for myself in my life but I don't feel many of them were very important. In a sense I've never had to decide anything important—it's been taken out of my hands and decided for me. Either by my parents, or the money I've had, or the jobs I've held, the places I've lived. I mean, I never decided *not* to marry. I just kept putting it off and the first thing I knew there wasn't anyone to marry me—at least that I could stand two days in a row. So that big decision was taken right out of my hands. It's been that way with all the big problems of my life—either put off or solved for me one way or the other. But this is something else. This is a big decision and it's the first I've had to face. What do you think, Hughes?"

Hughes thought about it for a long moment. He felt it was obvious that Cumbers would come to this. And it was probably the best road for Cumbers. But could he advise him without hurting his feelings? "Cumbers, you've put a great problem in my lap. I don't know exactly how to go about answering you." He hesitated for a moment, licked his lips, and decided the truth was what Cumbers needed and he would put it as tactfully as he could. "The fact of the matter is that you're asking me to call upon experience I don't have. I don't remember a great deal of my past life—not even now. Not much, that is. In a way, I've been seeing everything for the first time. It may sound strange to you, but that snowfall outside is the first I've seen. Oh, of course I know there are such things and I know more or less what they should look like, but I don't have any snowfalls in my memory to compare this one with. To me it's like the first snowfall primitive man must have seen his first winter on earth—magical, mysterious, beautiful—the first in memory. So I don't know if I can give you sensible advice. But here's what I've thought: You're a man who's miserable by himself. You don't really want to be Cumbers—Mr. Cumbers—*the* Mr.

Cumbers—the only one of your sort in the world. You want to be like all the others. You want to belong to something larger than yourself. Perhaps, as you say, it's because you've never had much of a family, or a wife, or good close friends or any of these things. But my feeling is that it goes deeper—my feeling is that there's a hole inside of you that gives you a hollow, scared feeling, and that hole demands filling. We're all born with the same hollow feeling and it gets worse when we find out how lonely we can be, how cruel the world can appear, how liable to death and hurt and misery we are. Some people always feel naked unless they're part of a crowd and that's what this church is—a crowd. It cares about all the parts of the crowd the way an animal with a thousand feet might care about the toes on one of his feet. He's got nine hundred and ninety-nine other feet, each with five toes on them, but this one toe on the thousandth foot hurts and he hurts all over because of it. Now, being a toe like that might make you happy. You know that there's something much huger than yourself to take care of you if you're in trouble. But you give up a lot becoming a toe. For one thing, you give up the chance to walk by yourself. You give up being yourself. In this church they never say 'me' or 'I' or 'mine.' It's always 'us,' 'we,' 'ours.'"

"Is that so bad?" Cumbers asked.

Hughes saw then that nothing he would say could dissuade Cumbers. It was bad but if Cumbers did not see it there was no point going on. "If you want to give up your individuality then I'd say this is the best way to do it. Life will be simpler, warmer, more comfortable for you once you've given up being just Mr. Cumbers."

"You wouldn't do it, would you?" Cumbers asked, looking at him closely in the gloriously mingled colored lights from the tree.

"No," Hughes said, "I have a great deal to find out about myself. I'm really only a bit of myself but I add to the bit every day. One day I'll be Hughes—the one Mr. Hughes of which there is no other on earth. It may not be the happiest thing in the world for me—but it's what I want."

24

New Year's came and went and on the first business day of the new year, which was Monday, the fourth of January, Cumbers received a letter from the Department of Internal Examination requesting that he present himself for an interview with the Deputy Commissioner, Mr. Lark. Cumbers went to work, informed his superior of the letter, and was given the morning off.

At eleven o'clock that morning Cumbers presented himself to the receptionist and was sent up in the elevator, down long corridors, and then finally to the anteroom of Lark's office. There he was told by the male secretary to wait—that the Deputy Commissioner was occupied. Cumbers sat down and waited, his pale blue eyes patient, his manner relaxed. This was undoubtedly the first report on Hughes and there was nothing to report on Hughes that was not favorable. His antisocial behavior was nonexistent. He was warm and friendly, willing to mix with others, did his work well at the quartermaster section, and was, in every way, a credit to himself and to the State. Cumbers was pleased to report this and this pleasure made him patient.

Lark was occupied in his office with the heretical political analyst, Doctor Wright. And the subject of the conversation which had been going on for over an hour before Cumbers arrived was Hughes.

"There's one thing I don't understand," Wright said, pulling unhappily at his mustache.

"Yes, Doctor?"

"Why should you care whether I know if you've succeeded or not? I wasn't directly connected with the project."

"But you were," Lark said, smiling. "You were the person I had to convince. Not the Commissioner, not my associates like Conger or Julian Richard or Doctor Emmerich or any of the others, not even myself. You," Lark pointed a bony forefinger, "were the one. None other."

"But why?"

"Because you wanted us to fail. You wanted it more than anything else."

Wright shrugged his narrow shoulders as if it were a matter of indifference to him. "Why should I care either way?" he asked in the face of Lark's knowing smile.

"Don't you remember your own analysis of the situation? That Burden represented the beginning of the heresies and the heretics with which we would have to deal in enormous numbers twenty, thirty, forty years from now?"

Wright hesitated. It had been a rash thing to say but true—wonderfully, splendidly true. If they failed with Burden it meant the end of a hideously benevolent state. If they succeeded, the future would be smothered for untold generations. Wright had prayed for their failure as he had never prayed for anything in his life, but prayer

301

was all he could ever manage to help Burden. He shrank from any action and these devils knew it—none better than Lark. "Yes," Wright finally said, "I know what my analysis was—and still is."

"That's why I wanted you here. I wanted you to hear a progress report on Burden, now Hughes," Lark said, coldly confident.

Then they had not failed, Wright thought unhappily. Lark would not have called him in to hear a progress report if he did not already know what the report would contain. Lark lifted the telephone receiver on his desk.

"Has Mr. Cumbers arrived yet?" Lark nodded with a smile to Wright. "Send him right in, please."

Wright could not help but stare at Cumbers when he came into the room. Cumbers did not resemble one of their agents. But then, they were particularly astute in their choices. They used thousands of agents of varying abilities and responsibilities and told them only so much of the truth as they felt necessary for an agent to function.

"Mr. Cumbers," Lark said, indicating a chair with his hand. Cumbers thanked Lark with his eyes and looked vaguely respectful in his glance at Doctor Wright.

"Mr. Cumbers has been a good friend of Mr. Hughes ever since he left the hospital, Doctor," Lark said to Wright by way of explanation.

"I've tried to be, sir," Cumbers said soberly, wondering whether the doctor was one who had helped treat his friend.

"Tell us about Hughes, Mr. Cumbers," Lark said gently. "Has he made a good adjustment, do you think?"

"Oh, yes, sir," Cumbers said vigorously. "Why, he's just fine."

"Made friends?"

"Lots of them, sir. Everyone in the rooming house has a kind word for him and he for them. And at work the other clerks think he's a grand fellow. No complaint on that."

"Well, I know a great deal about Mr. Hughes and his work, Mr. Cumbers," Lark said patiently. "There have been other reports on his progress in those directions. I want to get a little deeper into the things he's talked over with you—his attitudes, his feelings. Has he any moods? Depression? Unhappiness? Anything out of the ordinary?"

"Absolutely none," Cumbers said, shaking his head. "He's been in good humor, takes things calmly, doesn't keep to himself. We've gotten to be real friends, sir."

"Discussed a great deal, you two?"

"Almost everything and anything you can name. Talked about his wife and about his loss of memory, all those things, you know. He hasn't held back a bit."

"Was there anything about those things that disturbed him?"

"No, sir," Cumbers replied with certainty.

"Has Hughes raised any questions about the State that might cause you to doubt his loyalty to it?"

"Absolutely not," Cumbers appeared so shocked that both Lark and Wright smiled faintly. "He's a good citizen, a fine man, an honorable man. He would never think or say such a thing."

"Yes, yes," Lark said by way of soothing the obviously upset Mr. Cumbers, "but we have to know everything about Mr. Hughes. You understand that he was once guilty of antisocial behavior, of disloyalty to the State. That's why I asked the question." Lark did not use the word heresy to Cumbers because it was more than likely that Cumbers would not understand it and in order to explain its official meaning Lark would have had to upset

Cumbers' thinking, a situation one avoided with such minor agents as Mr. Cumbers.

"You need have no fear on that score, sir," Cumbers persisted. "Hughes is loyal and no man can say a word against him. I don't know what he was before. I can't speak too much about that. But the man who's become my friend is a man who wouldn't lie, who would tell the truth—even if it hurt himself or others. He's hiding nothing."

Lark sensed something in the remark and glanced at Wright. But the political analyst sat in his chair, his hands patiently in his lap, watching Cumbers. "Tell me, Mr. Cumbers," Lark said softly, "what makes you think Hughes would tell the truth about something if it would hurt him?"

"Well, I've got reason for that, sir," Cumbers said seriously, "because I've seen it happen."

"What was it and when did it happen?"

"Christmas Eve. I'll never forget it as long as I live, sir. It showed me what a true friend Hughes was."

"Well, tell us about Christmas Eve, Mr. Cumbers."

"Hughes and I and Mrs. Greevy, she's one of the boarders in the house, all went to a Church of State meetinghouse for the services, I guess you'd call them. Mrs. Greevy's Church of State and she was lonely and I forgot whose idea it was, but Hughes agreed right away, although he's not Church of State and he doesn't think much of it."

Lark felt a muscle jump in his throat. "Mr. Cumbers—how do you know Hughes doesn't think much of the Church of State?"

"Well, I was coming to that, sir. It's all part of what happened. I mean, proving to you how good a friend

Hughes is and how he'd tell the truth even if it hurt himself or someone he liked."

"I'm sorry, Mr. Cumbers," Lark said, forcing his voice to remain controlled and even, "please go on. I won't interrupt again."

"Well, as I said. We all went to the services and I'll tell you the truth, I was impressed by them. I came home with Hughes and Mrs. Greevy and after Mrs. Greevy went upstairs I had a long talk with Hughes. I talked about something that had been weighing on my mind for a long time. I told Hughes that I was thinking of joining the Church of State." Cumbers paused, thinking back.

"Was that when Mr. Hughes said he did not think much of the Church of State?" Lark asked, feeling a terrible sense of impatience growing inside him.

"No, sir," Cumbers said, knitting his brows, "that isn't what he said at all. Come to think of it, he never did say that—not in so many words. He said—the Church of State was like a crowd, and if I felt happier in a crowd I ought to join. He said—" Cumbers nodded then as if he had finally collected his memory on the conversation, "he said that I'd be like a toe on the foot of an animal with a thousand feet. That I would get all the attention of the animal when I was in trouble. He said if that was what I wanted then I should join the Church of State. Now, you see, right there he was telling me a truth about myself—a painful truth. He was saying that I wasn't much of anything—which, God knows, is the truth, though you always go on believing that it isn't so, that you do amount to a hill of beans when you don't. He wasn't saying it out of meanness. There isn't a mean bone in that man's body. But this problem was weighing on

305

my mind and I didn't know how to solve it and I had asked Hughes for help. Now, to solve a problem as big and tough as the one I had means that you need help—honest help. You need someone to take you by the hand and say, look here, here's the truth about yourself whether you like it or not. Here's the truth about you, Cumbers, not what you'd like to hear me say but what I ought to say because you want the truth and you need it. Hughes could have lied to me, made me feel good—he's a friend of mine and he wants me to like him just the way he likes me. I can see that. You lie to people sometimes to get on their good side. God knows I've done it and I suppose you, too, sir—meaning no disrespect. That's the way people are made. It makes life easier, makes feelings better all around—those little lies, I mean."

"You think Hughes was risking your friendship by telling you the truth about yourself?" Lark asked, feeling that at any moment Cumbers would say it, name the heresy. For it was heresy. He knew it in his bones. Hughes had uttered his first heresy and it would be his last. Wright, who was now leaning forward in his chair, his hands clutching its arms, his face tense and drawn, knew it, too.

"Well, sure he was," Cumbers said. "After all, people are always asking us for advice and for the truth but you and I know damn well that's not what they want. They want to be told that they're right and a set of pretty lies that'll make them feel right. But Hughes wasn't going to do that because he knew that if he lied to me he'd be betraying our friendship." Cumbers stopped and colored faintly, as if he had inadvertently admitted something shameful or embarrassing.

"Go on, Mr. Cumbers," Lark said softly, feeling numb now. Nothing would stop Cumbers now. The avalanche was still out of sight and out of hearing. But there was an uneasiness in the air, a certain terrible silence, and the smell of loose rock dust hanging about him.

"Well, he went on to say that I was the sort of person who had to join things, to feel that I belonged even if I had to give up being Cumbers—*the* Cumbers I've always been. It hasn't been a happy thing being Cumbers, sir. I told Hughes that. He said he understood. He said it isn't happy being a hollow person because when you're just yourself, outside of everything else, it's lonely and frightening. He gave me the feeling that he wouldn't blame me if I joined the Church of State. But I couldn't decide. I asked him if he would and he said no, he wouldn't. He said he was Hughes, an individual, and he wouldn't give up being an individual."

Lark's eyes grew bleak with an awful sense of loss. Cumbers talked on but it was meaningless talk. He had heard Hughes' heresy. It was the vanity, the ego, the drive to be and to retain the individual. It had been a short-lived experiment. Not twenty or thirty or forty years but just eighteen days. Less than that since the heresy had been spoken on Christmas Eve. Just seven days since Hughes had left the hospital and heresy had recurred. Lark looked at Wright, who now sat back in his chair, impassive, no longer listening. What was going on in that mind? Lark no longer cared. The world would go back to Wright and Burden and their sort in twenty years, thirty years. Lark no longer cared.

"That's all," he said to Cumbers brutally. Cumbers stopped in midsentence, looking uncertainly from Lark to Wright, wondering what he had said out of place.

"Don't you want any more of a report, sir?" Cumbers asked.

"No. Your report's quite complete, thank you," Lark

said, recovering. "We'll call you again when we need you, Mr. Cumbers." Cumbers rose then with a hesitant smile, nodded both to Lark and to Doctor Wright, and half sidled, half bowed his way out of Lark's office. When the door had closed Lark looked at Wright. The political analyst kept his eyes down.

"Don't take too much comfort out of this, Doctor," Lark said, his heart shrinking with rage. "Hughes was just an experiment. We'll run hundreds of such experiments in the next twenty years. We'll have the answer when we need it." Lark was almost hissing now. "You see if we don't have the answer in time."

Wright looked up at Lark now, the weak eyes intent on him. "You'll never have the answer," Wright said softly, "not if you have two hundred years. And you don't have that much time at all."

"You'll be alive when we have the answer, Doctor Wright. I'll personally see to that."

"God grant me that much life," Wright said, rising from his chair.

"That's the first time you've mentioned God in a conversation, Doctor," Lark said softly, puzzled.

"Is it?" Wright said calmly. "Well, imagine me turning to God at this stage of my life. You know, Lark, I used to be a churchgoer—long, long ago. I left because I thought science was the answer."

"And you're going back to religion now for the answer?" Lark asked with a sneer that he could not keep out of his voice.

"Oh, no. I'm not a hypocrite, Lark. I'm going back to church just for one visit. To thank God for whatever it was He gave us that can't be bullied out of us—not by torture, not by lies, not by threats, no, not even by kindness." Wright walked out then without glancing at Lark.

Lark looked at the door for a long moment before he turned to his phone, pressed a button, and asked for the Commissioner's office.

"This is Lark," he said softly into the mouthpiece. "We're going to have to implement the order of execution against Hughes, sir. I have evidence of recurred heresy. Yes, sir." Lark checked the calendar on his desk. "Thursday, the seventh of January, sir. If that meets with your approval. Thank you, sir. No, I don't feel too badly. I only feel that we have to be more resourceful in the future. We'll find the right combination of techniques eventually. Yes, sir." Lark depressed the disconnect pin and waited a moment for his line to clear and then pressed for the operator. "Medical Division, please. Doctor Emmerich." Lark waited until Doctor Emmerich answered. "This is Lark. The order of execution against Hughes will be effective at 4:00 A.M., January 7. Will you kindly arrange for death by embolism? Yes, the order of execution will be read to him in my office on Wednesday at noon, which gives us the required sixteen hours. Yes, Doctor, this will be confirmed by written order today. What? No, I don't feel too badly about him. We'll have to keep on trying, that's all. Thank you for your cooperation in the case."

Lark hung up, pulled the dictation machine over, and dictated the memoranda necessary to implement the order of execution of a heretic named Hughes. His final bit of work for the day was the dictation of a letter to Hughes directing him to appear at the Deputy Commissioner's office at noon, January 6. When he had done that he sat in his chair for a long time listening to the even thud of his heart.

II

At a few moments before noon on Wednesday, the sixth of January, Hughes presented himself to the male secretary in the anteroom of the Deputy Commissioner's office and offered the letter to the secretary. The secretary told him to sit down and wait a few moments and the Deputy Commissioner would see him.

Hughes sat down, crossing his legs at the ankles, looking at the room with a curious and lively eye. The letter had given no reason for his summons but Hughes had his own ideas. He did not want to discuss those ideas with Cumbers or any of the other clerks in the quartermaster section because it would have seemed vain on his part. He had done his work well, caught on to the hang of things quickly. The supervisor of the chalk board room had openly congratulated him and his very first rating had been "excellent"—something that newcomers to the section rarely got. The work was really simple and Hughes found lots of time in which to daydream as he worked. He did not yet know the procedures for applying for advancement in his job, but he would go about seeing to that in due time. Meanwhile this letter from the Deputy Commissioner had impressed his supervisor. A Deputy Commissioner was nothing to be sneezed at and his supervisor knew it. Hughes had always felt that he had made an impression on people in the hospital while he was there. He had been a good patient—an intelligent patient—not one of the general run as, say, Cumbers, decent as he was, might have been. He knew that there was keen competition in all the departments of the State for the best brains in government and the Department of Internal Examination was always on the lookout for a man of ability. He had heard from the clerks that they actually scouted other branches of the State for good men. Well, he thought with a smile, he was a good man. Perhaps they'd start him in a minor position with the Department. He did not much mind that. One had to start somewhere. Of course, all the scrambling the various governmental departments went through for the best brains and talent was justified. They knew how imperative it was to have thoughtful men, men with independent minds, men who were not mere rubber stamps but true individuals.

Hughes smiled at his own vanity and resolved to keep it more to himself. He noticed that vanity offended some people and the last thing he wanted to do was to offend anyone.

"The Deputy Commissioner will see you now, Mr. Hughes," the secretary said, putting down the phone.

Just noon, Hughes noted, looking at the clock on the secretary's desk. Well, that was one good thing—they were punctual.